DIVINE MISCHIEF

*The Chronicles of Seraphina
and the Gods*

PART I

ECHO EVERGREEN

Table of Contents

1

Burton Coast in the summer was like a bustling carnival, with throngs of people jostling for a spot in the sun. Ladies twirled lace umbrellas as if wielding delicate shields against the sun, while children constructed sandcastles that rivaled any medieval fortress, their shovels their noble swords. Gentlemen puffed on pipes, their eyes darting like bees in search of nectar, until they landed on a slender silhouette that seemed to capture their very souls.

Ah, but this was no ordinary figure.

She stood there, a young woman with hair cascading like golden seaweed down her back, brushing her waist. Her dress was a masterpiece of light blue silk, with a skirt puffed out like a decadent tiered cake, layered with gauze that whispered of wealth and privilege. Yet, curiously, she was alone—no servants doting on her every whim, which was as rare as finding a mermaid lounging on the beach.

Nearby, a gaggle of young men, their intentions as transparent as the gauze under her skirt, mustered the courage to approach her.

But our heroine, Seraphina, was oblivious to their antics. Her gaze was glued to the azure expanse, as if it were a mirage that might vanish if she dared to blink. Her breath came in uneven gasps, her cheeks as pale as the foam kissing the shore. The sea breeze, salty and mischievous, played with her senses, but she remained statuesque, lost in the endless blue.

"Is this... the sea?" she whispered, though the words barely made it past her lips. Her eyes remained fixed on the cool, shimmering line where water met the sky, each wave a gentle slap of disbelief against her understanding of reality.

In her world, the sea was a murky, brooding entity, the sky above it perpetually cloaked in a shroud of fog.

Such picturesque vistas were the stuff of fairy tales, the kind that made you question if the authors had perhaps indulged in a tad too much creative liberty.

"This is the Middle Ages, darling, where everything is as it should be. The sea is, naturally, blue," chimed a voice in her mind—cheerful, obnoxiously so. Seraphina frowned. The incessantly chipper voice belonged to none other than the System Little N , the meddlesome hitchhiker in her mind.

She had landed here, in this bewildering time and place, all thanks to System Little N, who seemed to find endless amusement in her predicament.

But as Seraphina stared out at the impossibly blue ocean, she couldn't shake the feeling that this might just be the chapter where her own story took an unexpected twist.

In a realm where time and space are but mere playthings, she hailed from an era three thousand years ahead. Though technology was dazzlingly advanced, humanity still basked—or perhaps squirmed—under the stern gaze of divine beings.

Indeed, the pantheon of gods in this world was a curious tapestry of contradictions and eccentricities. Each deity, a vibrant thread woven into the fabric of existence, brought their unique blend of quirks and powers. It was a realm where the gods' whims and caprices painted the sky with endless colors and shaped the fate of mortals in the most unpredictable of ways. To worship them was to embrace the chaos and beauty of a universe ever in flux, a dance of divinity that defied understanding yet demanded reverence.

The God of Light was characterized by his abstinent and aloof nature, ruling his domain with an uncompromising set of principles that emphasize discipline and order. His realm was governed by stringent regulations, the most notable being the prohibition of romantic entanglements for those under the age of 30. This decree was intended to cultivate focus and maturity, ensuring that the younger generation prioritizes personal and societal development over fleeting emotions.

As a result, the people of his continent lived cautiously, much like quails under constant prudence. The societal pressure to adhere to these rigid standards had fostered an atmosphere of restraint and conservatism, where individuals treaded carefully around matters of the heart. The fear of transgressing these divine laws loomed large, influencing every aspect of daily life.

Despite the restrictive environment, the God of Light's intentions were not entirely without merit. He sought to create a society that valued wisdom and stability, free from the distractions of youthful passion. However, the implementation of such severe measures had left many feeling stifled, yearning for the freedom to explore their emotions and relationships naturally.

Within this framework, the population had developed a quiet resilience, finding subtle ways to express their individuality and forge connections within the confines of the rules. While the God of Light's vision was one of order and enlightenment, the reality for his followers was a delicate balance between adhering to divine expectations and nurturing their human desires.

The Dark God was a figure shrouded in both fear and awe, ruling his domain with an iron fist and a heart seemingly devoid of compassion. His bloodthirsty nature and cruel disposition had shaped a realm where survival often hinged on strength and resilience. Inhabitants of his territory had grown accustomed to harsh realities, becoming fierce and unyielding in the face of adversity.

This deity's indifference to the plight of his followers only served to harden them further. His apathy was exemplified in the chilling way he observed his followers being torn apart by monsters, never lifting a finger to aid them. Instead, he watched with a detached curiosity, as if testing their mettle and endurance.

Under his rule, the people had adapted to this brutal environment, developing a toughness that mirrored their god's own cold demeanor. They had learned to rely on their wits and strength, becoming formidable in their own right. The harshness of their lives had fostered a community where only the strong survived, but also where bonds forged in hardship were unbreakable.

Despite the Dark God's lack of visible divinity or compassion, his presence was an ever-looming shadow that demanded respect through fear. His realm was one where the weak perished and the strong thrived, reflecting the dark and merciless nature of their deity. Yet, within this darkness, a fierce sense of pride and resilience burned brightly among his followers, testament to their ability to endure and overcome.

The Sea God was indeed an intriguing figure among the pantheon, known for his generally benevolent and humane laws that governed the ocean's vast expanse. His approach to rule was more lenient compared to his divine counterparts, fostering an environment where the sea's inhabitants thrived under his watchful care. However, his affection for the ocean's creatures was so profound that it bordered on the whimsical.

His unrestrained behavior had led to a unique relationship with the sea and all its life forms. From the majestic whales to the tiniest plankton, he cherished each creature as a beloved companion. This deep connection, while beautiful in its sentiment, had inadvertently created a dilemma for humans who relied on the sea for sustenance. The notion that every fish or crustacean might be a cherished lover of the Sea God instilled a sense of reverence and apprehension, making them hesitant to partake in seafood.

This dynamic had spawned a culture of respect and caution among coastal communities, where fishing practices were approached with a blend of gratitude and trepidation. The Sea God's love for his domain ensured that the ocean remained a sanctuary of life, vibrant and teeming with diversity. Yet, his whimsical nature also served as a reminder of the delicate balance between divine affection and the practical needs of human survival.

The gods, with their distinct personalities and often contradictory actions, had created societies that mirrored their own complexities.

Over time, this had led to a growing unrest among their followers, who found themselves yearning for change.

It was within this climate of dissatisfaction that a system emerged, one with the radical ambition of reshaping the divine order.

These folks had a rather bold agenda: they wanted to dethrone the gods.

"Well, it's not exactly about dethrone them," System Little N explained with a hint of caution. "but to help them evolve. The goal was simple yet profound: to dethrone the God of Light, thereby granting people more freedom and emotional expression; to guide the God of Darkness towards a path of empathy and balance; and to transform the Sea God into a figure of chastity and discipline..."

Seraphina gave a derisive snort. "Sounds like blasphemy to me, no matter how you spin it."

"As long as it solves our problems, who cares?" Little N chuckled. "Theologians have found that these divine flaws are because the gods have been stuck in their own ways for millennia. If we could just shake up their eternal personalities a bit, the frosty god wouldn't have to be an ice sculpture forever, the ruthless one might take a day off from being a tyrant, and the playful deity might finally graduate from being the eternal jester. Imagine a world where the gods could loosen up a bit—just like us mere mortals."

"Just look at the sea before you. Doesn't it seem so inviting and serene? Now, think of the sea where you live. Thanks to the Sea God's indulgence, the fish have morphed into monsters, and the waters are tainted with dark magic. Wouldn't you prefer a sea that's as blue as this?"

"You've got a point," Seraphina conceded, nodding. "So, you picked me for this mission?" Her spirits lifted. Sure, being suddenly zapped back thousands of years might rattle the average person, but not Seraphina. After all, when you're trusted by all of humanity, a little time travel is just another day in the life of a celebrity goddess-in-training. As a top-tier star in the entertainment industry, renowned for her beauty and business acumen, these three divine tasks felt like they were made just for her.

Seraphina felt a wave of confidence wash over her. The weight of the task was immense, yet invigorating. She could envision a world transformed, where the gods were allies rather than distant rulers, and where people lived with the freedom and harmony they deserved.

With humanity's hopes resting on her shoulders, Seraphina felt ready to embrace the challenge, determined to make a difference in the fabric of time itself.

"There is one more thing," Seraphina asked, her brow furrowing slightly. "After I complete the mission and return to my original world, will the gods come after me for causing all this divine drama?"

"Not a chance," Little N replied confidently. "Look, Host, you've got a whole new look now. Plus, everything you're about to do is in the Middle Ages—literally. The gods of your time won't even connect the dots."

With a slight flicker, the air in front of Seraphina shimmered, and a mirror appeared, visible only to her. She blinked, her pupils dilating as she took in her reflection. Her features were now elegantly westernized, every imperfection smoothed into perfection.

Her skin was a porcelain white, her cheeks a lively rose, and the subtle lift at the corners of her eyes added an intriguing blend of innocence and allure. She had always been beautiful, but now she radiated an ethereal, almost otherworldly charm.

Seraphina tilted her head, a hint of amusement playing at her lips. "Well, this isn't bad at all. I barely recognize myself."

Little N puffed up with pride, practically glowing with satisfaction. "Naturally! You can always trust my sense of aesthetics."

"Miss Doyle—"

A slick, middle-aged voice oozed from behind Seraphina, like honey with just a hint of vinegar.

"Miss Robus is wondering just how much longer you'd like to gaze at the sea? Not that I'd want to interrupt your delightful experience, of course. I understand you've been living in the southern countryside with hardly a glimpse of the ocean. But, you see, the Duke and the Lady are awaiting your return. Best not to keep them waiting too long..."

Seraphina spun around abruptly, her gaze locking onto the speaker. There stood a middle-aged man with slicked-back hair, dressed in a well-tailored suit that screamed sophistication. His face bore an expression of pride, as if he owned the very air he breathed. As Seraphina's eyes met his, a fleeting glimmer of admiration flickered in his eyes, only to be swiftly replaced by his usual air of arrogance.

"Doyle, that's you—Seraphina Doyle," Little N piped up. "We've arranged this identity for you to ease your settling in. This man is your uncle's butler. Your uncle happens to be an earl, and you've come to Burton from the countryside to study.

Your two cousins are here to pick you up, but they're a tad snooty and are still sitting in the carriage, refusing to greet you."

Ah, so that's the lay of the land. Seraphina's eyes flickered with understanding.

"I had to give you a background that allows you to blend in, yet not stand out too conspicuously," Little N explained. "Hence, the country girl narrative. But fret not, your family's far from destitute. With an earl for an uncle, your father's no pauper either. It's just that your city relatives have developed a misplaced sense of superiority because you've been managing the ancestral estate in the countryside."

Got it. As long as she wasn't penniless. She had missions to accomplish, not a financial crisis to manage.

"It really is quite stunning here," Seraphina said to the butler with a charming smile. "Apologies for lingering. Let's head back now." No need to ruffle feathers with the butler; his attitude was merely a reflection of his master's. To ensure future comfort, she'd need to win over the earl.

Without waiting for a response, Seraphina gathered her skirts and strode purposefully toward the carriage, her resolve as unyielding as the waves she'd just been admiring.

Seraphina walked along the straight road outside the beach, where ornate carriages lined up like jewels on display. Guided by Little N, she soon spotted the carriage sent by her uncle's family—a pumpkin-shaped vehicle adorned with a rose-colored family emblem. There were two of them: one with its doors firmly shut, orange curtains drawn tight, and the other open, unoccupied, with several suitcases strapped to its roof.

It didn't take a genius to guess where her two cousins were hiding—in the closed carriage, clearly not keen on sharing it with her. Seraphina shrugged off their snub with a wry smile and climbed into the carriage with the luggage, finding it the perfect opportunity to continue her conversation with Little N.

"By the way, why are you called Little N?" Seraphina asked as the carriage lurched forward, swaying gently with the motion.

"Well..." Little N sounded suddenly sheepish. "You've played games before, right? You know how cards are ranked—like N, R, SR? Our system works similarly."

"So you're saying you're an N-level system, the most basic one?" Seraphina's expression darkened.

"Hehehe," Little N chuckled nervously. "Don't think of it like that. My level is determined by you. You can upgrade me with the heartbeat points you earn from winning over the gods. The higher my level, the more I can help you."

Seraphina pondered for a moment, a frown creasing her brow. "It's a bit odd, don't you think? Why would they give such an important task to me but bind me with such a crap system? Shouldn't it have been an SSR level?" Suspicion tickled her instincts. "Are you hiding something from me? If you don't spill, I won't do the task. Let's go back and find someone else."

"No, no, no," Little N panicked, the pressure making it crack. "Actually, you weren't supposed to be the one. To ensure nothing went wrong, there were two systems made. The SSR system was meant to activate once the right person was teleported by me first. But I was too nervous and accidentally bound to you. That's why I'm just a N at the moment."

Seraphina was a little speechless. "You managed to bind it wrong? Am I close to you? How could that happen?"

"You're not close to me, but you are close to the person who's actually supposed to be teleported. You live in the same community," Little N said, scratching his head. "I think, after discovering the binding error, another system must have been activated over there to teleport the real candidate."

Seraphina's heart skipped a beat as she racked her brains to remember if there was any notable figure in her community.

"Do you know who it is?" she asked, her voice tinged with urgency.

"I don't. For confidentiality reasons, I could only see coordinates, not identities."

"Does this mean I don't have to complete the mission?" Seraphina took a deep breath, the sense of trust and purpose she had felt earlier evaporating. Now, her only desire was to return quickly, unsure of the state of her body after the hasty teleportation.

"We can't go back," Little N explained. "We're now privy to the secret of dethroning gods. To ensure we stay on task, I consume a point of divine favor every three days to maintain my N level. If there's no point to consume, I'll self-destruct. And I reside in your brain..."

"Okay, okay, I get it," Seraphina interrupted, not wanting to hear more about potential cerebral explosions. The twists of the day had her head spinning. What started as a playful challenge had spiraled into a perilous adventure.

"Do you think the other person will join us?" Seraphina asked, grasping for any potential allies.

"No," Little N replied with certainty. "The SSR system consumes a lot of divine favor points daily, making their risk of self-destruction much higher. They'll likely compete with us for resources. Just like now... you know what I mean?"

Seraphina shook her head, feeling lost.

"Oh, that's it. According to the ancient lore, in the first year of the Middle Age, the gods waged a colossal war. Now, the gods are at their weakest. The God of Light plummeted to the mortal world, the God of Darkness retreated to mend his wounds, and as for the God of Sea... well, the records are mysteriously silent on his fate."

Puffing up with a hint of pride, Little N continued, "Even though I'm just an N, I know the current whereabouts of the God of Light and the God of Darkness. Let's become their benefactors and earn some favor points."

Seraphina took a deep breath, trying to steady herself. This was no ordinary escapade—it was a chance to change the fate of gods, and perhaps, her own.

"If that's the case," Seraphina mused, her thoughts tangling like yarn in a particularly mischievous kitten's paws, "Do I have to pick between the God of Light and the God of Darkness? I mean, I've only got two legs, and they can only carry me to one divine shindig at a time."

Little N chimed in with all the subtlety of a brass band, "To make sure you ace this quest, we've timed our jaunt through dimensions to perfection. The broody fallen angels of dark god are taking their sweet time escorting their God across the continent. So, let's pay a visit to the God of Light first. Oh, and I totally have his coordinates. SSR's got them too."

Seraphina's eyes went wide as saucers. "Why didn't you spill the beans earlier?" she exclaimed, almost catapulting herself out of her seat.

Outside, a carriage clattered past, and Seraphina's scalp prickled as if someone had spilled cold water down her back. A sense of urgency wrapped around her chest like a corset two sizes too small.

The lucky duck who finds the God of Light first gets their hands on the all-important starter artifact. The poor God of Light has crash-landed in the human realm, knocked out cold and shedding his divine glow like a disco ball with a dimmer switch. But soon enough, he'll be conscious again. This fleeting moment is Seraphina's golden ticket to make a lasting impression on the divine amnesiac.

That's why the system chose this very moment to zap the task executor into action. Once the God of Light regains his memory and swans back to his temple, getting close to him will be as tricky as trying to hug a porcupine.

"By the way, you've got a newbie gift pack you haven't unwrapped yet," Little N added. "Plus, I have a teleportation trial feature. But if you want to use it next time, you'll have to level me up to R first."

"Fine, fine," Seraphina said with a wave of her hand. "I'll upgrade you after we win the favor of the Light God. Now, teleport us there pronto, and we'll deal with the gift pack later."

The race was on. Find the God of Light before another task executor.

A whisper of light flitted through the pumpkin carriage, and—poof!—its passengers vanished into thin air. The driver, blissfully oblivious to the magical vanishing act occurring right under his nose, simply adjusted the reins, steering the carriage onward as if nothing more unusual than a gentle breeze had passed by.

2

In the bustling metropolis of Burton, the richest city in the southern continent, where the sea kisses the largest port in the world, life's a tale of two cities. The affluent bask in their southern splendor, while the northern district is a packed sardine can of the less fortunate.

Seraphina found herself zapped into Bessen Road, the southern district's crown jewel—a bustling avenue lined with shops that could make even a pauper feel like royalty.

Peering through the expansive glass windows, the treasures on display shimmered with an allure that could tempt even the most steadfast saint. The streets, with their medieval charm, felt plucked straight from the pages of an exquisite oil painting album.

But Seraphina had no time for wistful gazes or leisurely strolls. Clutching her skirt to keep it from tripping her, she sprinted down the street, her sights set on the Church of Light nestled at the corner. Rumor had it that the human form of the God of Light was destined to make an appearance there.

She could only wonder how he'd landed on Earth — hopefully, not with the fanfare of a comet blazing through the sky, leaving a fiery tail in its wake. Such a celestial spectacle would undoubtedly have every member of the Church flocking there faster than moths to a flame.

The Church of Light, with its high, pointed roof adorned in seashells, sparkled like a crown of pearls under the sun's gentle caress. Though not Burton's grandest church, this quaint branch on Bessen Road, tucked behind the chaotic commerce, was a serene oasis encircled by oak trees. Typically, it was a tranquil spot, but today it was buzzing with spectators, the small clearing in front packed tighter than a festival crowd.

Seraphina's heart plummeted as she halted at the edge of the throng. She peered through the mass of bodies, anxiety creeping in. Had the God of Light made his descent in an overly theatrical fashion once again? If so, it seemed every soul in Burton had come to witness the spectacle.

She tapped a bystander, "What's going on over there?"

"Someone took a nosedive in front of the church," the bystander replied, craning for a better look. "Even the resident priest's on alert. Must be someone important."

"Bet it's the Grand Duke's son," another guessed.

"Nah, it's a prince!" The crowd buzzed with speculation.

Then came the unmistakable clatter of hooves, and like the Red Sea, the crowd parted to make way for a carriage as ornate as a Fabergé egg. Seraphina caught sight of an old man in a red robe, his expression graver than a funeral director's.

"The cardinal!" The crowd erupted in awe, eyes twinkling with the kind of excitement usually reserved for royalty or rock stars.

"Talk about a lucky day! Nobles are the only ones who get a peek at him." "When did the bishop arrive? I missed him entirely." "Whoever fainted must be quite the VIP to warrant a cardinal's personal escort."

Seraphina's gaze fixated on the carriage, her heart sinking faster than a stone in a pond. If the God of Light had been ID'd by his faithful, her chances of getting close could be slimmer than a catwalk model. But then again, if she couldn't approach him, maybe neither could her rival with the SSR system.

"Did you see that young man? Handsome as a marble statue! He made the snow on the holy mountain of Crabgal look like a dirty snowman. As he fell in front of the church, frowning in pain, it was like watching a fallen angel struggle to adjust to gravity. My heart felt like it was about to shatter into a million snowflakes."

"Oh, My God of Light, please let that handsome lad be safe. He's just too handsome to suffer." Seraphina could hear the hushed whispers of admiration from the crowd behind her.

"How many cardinals are there in Burton?" she wondered aloud, scanning the crowd for any sign of another task executor.

"The southern continent boasts seven cardinals and one archbishop," Little N chimed in. "Burton's capital hosts the archbishop and three cardinals. That was Bishop Saen, steward of the southern district. His home's a stone's throw from your uncle's place."

"Interesting," Seraphina mused, her mind racing. She might not be fond of her system-gifted persona—a country girl crashing with wealthy kin—but perhaps destiny had a trick or two up its sleeve.

"What's the plan now, host?" Little N asked, anxiety creeping into its voice. "I've only got two days before I need a drop of divine favor to recharge. Without it, I'll self-destruct."

Seraphina sighed at the thought of lugging around a system that demanded more maintenance than a vintage car. "Didn't you mention a newbie gift pack?" she recalled, a glimmer of hope sparking.

"Indeed, I did. Ready to open it?"

"Yes," she nodded. Who knows, maybe it held the key to flipping her fortunes.

A metallic chime echoed in her mind as a faint light materialized on her wrist, transforming into a simple, yet intriguing handbag. Little N explained, "Open it, and magical items will emerge randomly. Their quantity and rarity are at the mercy of your luck."

People with unlucky streaks tend to dread moments like this. Seraphina, clutching her mysterious bag, made her way to the fountain at the heart of the street, planning a quick hand rinse before opening her newfound treasure.

The summer breeze waltzed through the street corner, playfully brushing against the statues in the fountain. This was a gathering of sculptures—men, women, young, old, and even some small animals, each frozen in a unique pose. Yet, all shared the same expression and gaze, eyes lifted toward the heavens with devout reverence. Up in the sky, the radiant sun shone brightly, symbolizing the god of light who cast his glow upon everyone.

Seraphina perched beside the statue of a girl, her alabaster form shimmering like a pearl. Water cascaded from the statue's waist, resembling a delicate, flowing skirt. As Seraphina submerged her hands into the cooling stream, she murmured, "Wash away the bad luck, and maybe fortune will finally turn my way."

The coolness swept over her hands, whisking away the oppressive summer heat and settling her nerves. With steady fingers, she pried open the cloth bag's mouth, revealing four faintly glowing treasures nestled within.

Her heart skipped a beat. Four—a bounty beyond her wildest dreams.

"Congratulations, host, on drawing four magical items!" Little N's voice chirped with excitement. "You've got the 'Fish in the Desert,' 'little Lisa's discarded playdough,' 'The Wind at Night,' and 'You Can Only See Me.' All are single-use items."

Seraphina blinked in bewilderment.

"Sounds like the luck of the unlucky kind," she muttered dryly.

"Let me explain," Little N interjected eagerly. "The 'Fish in the Desert' induces extreme thirst. Use it on yourself or others, but beware—it causes temporary face blindness for an hour."

"The 'little Lisa's discarded playdough' mimics actions or effects, whether it's a snippet of someone else's actions or a divine spell. Feel free to experiment, but it makes you afraid of the dark for three days."

"'The Wind at Night' can transform you into a breeze for one minute, whisking you off to any destination your heart desires. The catch? You'll feel a brief heaviness in your body once the magic wears off. You can only see me, and pick a familiar person to develop an interest in you for 24 hours—no side effects included!"

"Wait, why does the last one have no side effects?" Seraphina asked, intrigued.

"The rarity of an item dictates its value. The more potent and harmless it is, the higher its rarity. After all, who wants a magical boomerang boinking them in the face?"

"So, I've snagged a top-tier item?"

"Indeed, you have!"

"Not too shabby," Seraphina grinned, contemplating how best to deploy her newfound arsenal.

But first things first—returning to her relatives' home. Being neighbors with the cardinal might just grant her some insider scoop, thanks to dear Uncle Duke. Perhaps having this particular identity wasn't all that bad.

The teleportation function of Little N was a one-time wonder, now expired like yesterday's magic. She had no choice but to flag down a public carriage.

In this era, carriages were the luxury limousines of the nobility and upper middle class. After all, horses, stables, coachmen, and feed cost a king;s ransom. Families without their own carriages had to rely on public ones—extended carriages pulled by two stately horses.

Inside, long wooden benches lined the carriage on both sides, with passengers sitting face-to-face, their knees practically mingling. It was stuffy and cramped, the perfect setting for a hot afternoon. Half an hour later, Seraphina handed over ten copper coins and disembarked at the fork of Oak Street, relieved to escape the human sardine can.

Oak Street was the prestigious neighborhood where her uncle, Earl George Doyle, resided. It boasted six grand houses, each with manicured gardens, home to the crème de la crème of society.

Outside one of the grand homes, Seraphina spotted a stunning carriage parked at the garden gate, unmistakably the one that had transported the God of Light. Its two chestnut horses munched on the grass, oblivious to their role in a divine drama, while the coachman leaned against the door, lost in thought.

From this vantage point, it seemed the cardinal hadn't fully recognized the God of Light's true identity or was perhaps grappling with suspicions and had decided to bring him home first. If that was the case, Seraphina might still have a shot.

***

As the evening descended, George Doyle's family gathered around an opulent table, dressed to the nines for a feast that would make even the sun jealous. Candlelight flickered over sumptuous dishes of smoked roast goose, herb-crusted lamb chops, seed cakes paired with pickled cheese, and cold roast meats mingled with creamed asparagus and peas. The heady scent of champagne, red wine, and Bailey's floated through the air, setting the scene for a dinner in Seraphina's honor.

Seraphina had concocted a plausible tale to cover her mysterious vanishing act from the carriage earlier. Claiming she'd been practicing divine magic and had accidentally transported herself to an unfamiliar street, she spun a web of believable details about Bessen Road, the Church of Light, and her eventual return via public carriage.

"So, my dear niece can perform divine arts successfully?" Earl George inquired with interest. Training a family member to enter the temple would significantly elevate the Doyle family's status.

He'd initially thought Seraphina, being from the countryside, wouldn't have a knack for theology. Agreeing to host her was merely a favor to his brother. But perhaps he'd underestimated her potential.

"It was just a fluke," Seraphina replied cautiously, ensuring she didn't invite requests for an impromptu demonstration.

"That's still impressive," Earl George beamed. "Your sisters haven't even brushed the surface of divine arts. You should teach them when you have time."

The Countess's eyes flashed with disapproval as she turned to her daughters. "You who grew up in Burton can't let your sister outshine you. I'd rather not hear that at the dinner table again."

Ah, the classic city slicker versus country bumpkin debate! The Countess is clearly hinting that folks from Burton, a bustling city, can't hold a candle to their countryside counterparts.

But really, it's all about perspective. Cities can foster a certain savvy and resourcefulness, while the countryside might cultivate a deeper connection to nature and community. Both have their unique charms and challenges, shaping people in different ways.

So, in the end, it's not where you come from, but what you make of it. The Countess can have her opinions, but I'd say both city and country folks have their own special magic.

Her cousins' glares could have bored holes through steel, but Seraphina met them without flinching. They'd never warmed to her before, so what did it matter now?

For Seraphina, the real intrigue lay next door with the cardinal. She had no idea if the God of Light had regained consciousness but hoped his memory remained dormant a while longer.

"I heard something interesting happened at the church on Bessen Road today," the Countess said, her voice a mixture of curiosity and superiority.

"Bishop Saen brought back a young man of striking appearance. There's speculation about his relationship to the bishop—perhaps a nephew? If so, our daughters might make a charming acquaintance."

Seraphina's cousins lit up like fireworks. As eligible young women, they were eager to impress and enchant a man of high standing.

"Keep your composure, girls," the Countess chided, casting a wary glance at Seraphina.

"When can we see him?" Robus, Seraphina's cousin, asked eagerly.

"Bishop Saen is hosting a dinner on Saturday, isn't he?" Rose, another cousin, turned to their mother. With so many social events in Burton, it was hard to keep track.

"Yes, I hope he doesn't leave before then," the Countess replied nonchalantly.

Oh, the banquet at the Cardinal's house is two days away, isn't it? Seraphina's heart skipped a beat. The day after tomorrow was Little N's self-destruct deadline. If she couldn't gain even a smidgen of favor from the God of Light, it would also mark her own self-destruction.

"Host, come on. We only have two days left to live," Little N said weakly, sounding like an overly dramatic sidekick in a bad play.

"Host, hang in there. We've got two days left," Little N's voice wavered, tinged with urgency.

***

Come Saturday night, Seraphina donned a simple yet elegant lilac silk dress, devoid of excessive embellishment, and positioned herself in the foyer. When the Doyle family descended the stairs, she seamlessly joined them.

Earl George remained silent, but the Countess's expression was as rigid as a porcelain doll. She'd intentionally left Seraphina out of the loop, hoping to prevent her pretty niece from overshadowing her daughters. Who knew what kind of miraculous skincare existed in the countryside? Seraphina might even outshine the capital's famed rose, Princess Anna.

But with Seraphina already present, there was little choice but to proceed.

"Your dress is rather plain," Robus remarked critically, "yet the quality is exquisite. It makes you appear even more radiant."

Seraphina curled her lips but kept silent. If the God of Light hadn't awakened, she might just have to sneak into his room. Naturally, the simpler the clothes, the better. After all, less fabric means less chance of getting caught, right?

"Aren't you wearing a bustle?" Rose inquired, eyes wide with surprise.

"No," Seraphina replied, prioritizing ease of movement. She hesitated before adding, "I felt it was cumbersome, so I opted for extra petticoats."

"That's so much more natural and comfortable," Rose lamented. "Why didn't I think of that?"

"Enough, girls," the Countess intervened, anxious that her daughters' outfits were now outshone. Compared to Seraphina, they were like peacocks mid-display, lacking the natural elegance and grace.

Meanwhile, the cardinal's house brimmed with guests. The dinner hadn't yet commenced, and aside from a few gentlemen enjoying billiards, most guests mingled in the reception room, sipping tea or juice as they chatted.

Their conversation inevitably revolved around the enigmatic young man the bishop had brought home.

"I heard he hasn't regained consciousness."

"Oh, that's dreadful. May God of Light bless him. Any idea who he is? Bishop Saen has three nephews not residing in the capital."

"No clue; the bishop remains tight-lipped. But he seems rather significant."

Seraphina pretended to admire the floral arrangements while inching closer to a group dressed as priests. Unfortunately, she couldn't quite catch their hushed discussion.

"I can amplify their voices," Little N offered, suddenly remembering its capabilities. The priests' conversation then reached Seraphina as if they were speaking directly to her.

"Does the bishop suspect the young man is the God of Light incarnate?"

"That's the word. They're not certain, though. But the temple doors remain shut, confirming He hasn't returned."

"Did he just appear at the church doorstep? No miracles?"

"None at all. If he had, we wouldn't be sneaking around like this. Miracles have a way of making things crystal clear, don't they?"

So, the God of Light hadn't made a grand entrance. Seraphina exhaled in relief.

"Lord Saen is keeping a close watch. He's stationed clergy to guard the small white building in the back garden round the clock. If it truly is the God of Light, Lord Saen's fortunes will soar."

"And surely, we'll rise with him. We're his closest aides."

The priests' excitement grew palpable. Seraphina navigated through the crowd, exiting via the billiard room's side door.

The small white building stood in the garden, a modest two-story structure. Seraphina had scoped it out beforehand. The unknown variable was the number of clergy keeping watch.

Seraphina moved like a shadow through the garden path, surrounded by guests who were savoring the moonlit blooms.

But the back garden lay behind the main building, and from afar, she spotted two priests standing guard at the arched flower gate, turning away any curious souls.

She halted beneath the shelter of an oak tree, reaching into her pocket to retrieve something almost intangible—a breeze, so light it seemed unreal. With "The Wind at Night," she could transform into a gust for a minute, whisking her wherever she wished. The catch? Her body would feel like lead for ten minutes afterward. She could only hope it wouldn't anchor her to the spot.

With a mental smirk, she crushed the breeze.

Suddenly, a swirling wind lifted her, and she felt weightless, swept up by the very air she'd summoned.

As her feet left the ground, panic flared—she looked down to find nothing beneath her. Her body was now part of the breeze, invisible and ethereal.

"Host, fifty-six seconds left," Little N's voice echoed urgently.

So fast?

Seraphina broke away, riding the wind toward the gatekeepers.

The breeze caressed the priests' hair, and they tilted their heads in bliss, hoping for more relief from the lingering heat.

Seraphina slipped through the archway and circled the small white building.

"Thirty-two seconds remaining," Little N's voice tinged with concern.

There! A second-floor corner room, its candlelight revealing Bishop Saen and his men.

No time to waste, Seraphina realized, darting into the building rather than entering the room—if discovered, she'd be trapped with nowhere to hide.

She landed in the corridor, quickly seeking refuge.

"Fifteen seconds," Little N now a frantic whisper.

A low cabinet caught her eye, topped with a round fish tank. It looked just large enough to conceal her, provided it was empty.

"Eight seconds. Seven, six, five···" Little N's countdown was frantic.

At the same moment, a door creaked open, and Bishop Saen stepped into the corridor.

Seraphina dove into the cabinet without hesitation.

"Three, two, one."

Seraphina felt her body sink, and her skirt exploded in a flurry of fabric. No longer a graceful breeze, she reverted to her human form.

Luckily, the low cabinet nearby was empty and just the right size for hiding. She squeezed into the cramped space, her heart pounding as the footsteps drew closer and closer. They even paused right beside her.

"Keep this place secure," Bishop Saen's voice drifted down. "I'll return after the banquet."

"Rest assured, my lord. I won't budge," his subordinate vowed.

No, you really should leave, Seraphina thought desperately.

Bishop Saen's footsteps receded, leaving only the subordinate behind. Through the keyhole, Seraphina spied him lounging in a window-side chair. She moved with painstaking slowness.

The promised heaviness set in, her limbs dragging as if she'd just climbed from a swimming pool. Still, she managed to inch toward her pocket, retrieving a slender item with two fingers.

The "Fish in the Desert" promised to paralyze with thirst. Its side effect was temporary face blindness an hour later.

Seraphina crushed the fish, its powder escaping through the keyhole with a seeming will of its own.

The subordinate leapt up, clutching his throat, face twisted in agony. He glanced at the door, indecision warring within him.

A few agonizing seconds later, he surrendered, abandoning his post in search of water.

Seraphina waited, breath held, until his footsteps faded. She emerged from the cabinet, relieved the powder hadn't done him in. The "Fish in the Desert" was potent indeed. If it could affect someone through a wall, surely the God of Light would feel its touch too?

She slowly approached the door and gently pushed it open a crack. A man's hoarse panting sound suddenly spilled through the gap. The suppressed and seductive sound didn't seem like thirst, but more like he'd been injected with some kind of charming little potion.

Amidst the panting, Seraphina faintly heard a low, hoarse voice, as if asking for water.

She pushed the door open wider, and her pupils reflected a face she would never forget. Divine features were never described, for gods weren't meant to be seen.

The God of Light, in mortal guise, had dimmed his celestial glow, revealing a visage that could only be described as breathtaking. He was beauty incarnate, like the purest snow on the Holy Mountain, a cloud in the azure sky, the sun's most dazzling ray.

"Water⋯" came a hoarse plea from his slightly parted lips.

He lay in a plush bed, hair a pale gold, almost platinum, tousled as if by discomfort.

His eyes were shut, brows knit, golden lashes trembling. He tugged at his collar, the candlelight casting his smooth collarbone in exquisite relief.

Seraphina, entranced, traced a finger along his cheek. But before she could withdraw, he captured her hand, pressing it to his neck as if seeking solace. Jolted back to reality, she gently pulled away.

Having mingled with godlike men in the entertainment industry, Seraphina had never been so captivated. Yet, amidst the glittering allure and heady charm, she felt the pressing weight of the moment. Time was of the essence, and with a steely resolve, she refocused, grounding herself in the urgency of the now.

She retreated to the adjacent bathroom, filling a cup with cold water. Within her limited arsenal, this was her chosen path—offering water to the fish in the desert was a small yet significant act of benevolence.

"Water⋯" The urgency in his voice spurred her on.

"Here it is," Seraphina said softly, approaching with the cup.

<h1 style="text-align:center">3</h1>

"The water is coming," Seraphina murmured softly, but the figure on the bed remained motionless, seemingly caught in the throes of a restless dream.

Seraphina pondered for a moment, then stretched out her hand and pressed the mouth of the cup against his lips. The overflowing water instantly soaked his parched lips. In the next second, she pressed her lips against his, ready to seize the advantage.

She had thought a light press would wake him up, but she hadn't anticipated the instinctual response of someone parched. As her lips met his, he reacted with a thirst-driven urgency. Before she could pull away, a strong hand cupped the back of her head, drawing her into a fervent embrace. His lips, hot and demanding, sought relief, intensifying with each elusive promise of water.

The unexpected kiss sent Seraphina's heart into overdrive. Whoever claimed the God of Light to be distant and austere had never experienced this side of him.

Yet, this was beyond what she intended.

As her mind raced, trying to regain control, she realized she needed to extricate herself without escalating the situation. In the heat of the moment, she focused on calming her racing heart and gently withdrew, hoping to diffuse the intensity of the encounter.

"Host, hang in there! The heartbeat value is soaring!" Little N exclaimed with palpable excitement.

"What?" Seraphina's voice was a whisper, but it was enough to stir the young man from his slumber. His eyes snapped open, revealing a piercing gaze that seemed to see through her. The coldness in his narrow eyes, along with the striking azure of his pupils, made Seraphina's heart skip a beat.

Startled, she sat up abruptly, feeling a mix of fear and awe. In her original world, the divine had always been a distant concept, embodied in grand rituals and the reverent words of the archbishop. Even the cardinal, a figure of authority, served merely as a conduit for the divine voice channeled through the archbishop. Direct encounters with deities were unheard of for the common folk, making this moment both extraordinary and intimidating.

Here she was, face-to-face with the embodiment of divine power, a being whose very presence challenged the boundaries of her understanding. Yet, amidst the fear, there was a burgeoning sense of purpose. Perhaps this encounter was a sign—a reminder of the monumental task she had taken on, and the divine forces she would need to navigate and, ultimately, transform.

In Seraphina's original world, the presence of the divine was a reality that most could only experience through indirect means. While a select few were gifted with the ability to access the realm of divine arts, for the vast majority of mortals, the divine light was something they could only perceive through technology. This technology served as a bridge, allowing people to sense the divine presence in their everyday lives, whether through the flicker of a sacred device or the hum of consecrated machinery.

For most, this technological connection to the divine was a source of comfort and reassurance, a reminder of the gods' watchful gaze over their world. However, it also created a sense of distance, as the true essence of divinity remained out of reach, shrouded in mystery and mediated through human invention.

In this context, Seraphina's mission to reshape the gods was all the more daunting. She was stepping into a realm that few mortals had ever ventured, confronting the very beings who had shaped the world through their distant yet potent influence. It was an unprecedented challenge, one that required not only courage but also an understanding of the delicate balance between the divine and the mortal, a balance she was now tasked with redefining.

Thus, when Seraphina first laid eyes on the human form of the God of Light, she was captivated by his beauty, not overwhelmed by his divinity. But now, with his eyes upon her, she felt the weight of his celestial presence.

After a tense silence, his voice broke through, low and questioning. "What are you doing?"

"I didn't do anything," Seraphina replied, feigning innocence as she gestured to the fallen cup. "I heard someone asking for water, so I brought some. But then you pulled me down and kissed me."

"Kiss?" His brow furrowed in confusion.

"Yes, a kiss."

"A kiss?" His puzzlement deepened.

Does he truly not know what a kiss is? It seems fitting for the God of Light, who decreed no one under thirty should fall in love prematurely. Well, at least this encounter earned me some points of favorability.

"What is a kiss?" he inquired.

"Just a normal way people interact," Seraphina quickly deflected, wary of prying eyes.

"Do you still want water?" She gestured to the cup as she attempted to steer the conversation away.

"No, I have my own." His voice was frosty, and with a flicker of light, a golden, intricately carved cup materialized in his hand, brimming with clear water.

A display of divine magic, Seraphina noted, her eyelashes fluttering. Though mortal, he hadn't lost his touch with magic. Did he remember more than he let on?

"May I have your name?" Seraphina ventured.

He hesitated for a fraction before replying, "Milos," the name slipping coolly from his lips.

Seraphina's heart sank. Milos Xenodek—none other than the God of Light himself. His ready response was unsettling.

"Strange," Milos murmured.

"What is?" Seraphina asked, her curiosity piqued.

"This name is all I recall," Milos admitted, his gaze lingering thoughtfully on the cup in his hand.

Seraphina followed his gaze, noticing the tiny figure etched into the cup's rim. The ancient script formed a triangle, a symbol historically tied to the God of Light.

The triangle glimmered subtly, reminiscent of a watchful eye, scrutinizing her actions. Seraphina felt a prickle of unease and an urgency to leave before the guard returned.

Placing the cup on the bedside table, she announced, "I'm leaving now."

Milos's eyes flickered with a trace of confusion. "Where are you going?"

"To dance," Seraphina replied with a playful smile. "I was exploring the garden before the party. Please keep this little adventure a secret, won't you? It's quite impolite to wander into the host's home uninvited."

Her playful, innocent demeanor softened Milos's guardedness.

"Farewell then," Seraphina said, lifting her skirt in a graceful curtsy before exiting the room, making the encounter seem like nothing more than a chance meeting.

When seeking favor, patience was key. Too much enthusiasm could easily betray her intentions.

The corridor remained silent in the aftermath of Seraphina's departure, with the thirsty guard still absent. Seraphina had made her escape carefully, slipping down the stairs and along the wall, recalling the layout she'd seen while transformed into the wind. With only two clergymen in the lobby, she quickly made her way to the outermost room, opening a window and stepping out into the night without raising any alarm. Navigating through the cover of flowers, she left the premises unnoticed.

Back inside, Bishop Saen returned to find an empty corridor. His face was stern as he pushed open the door to find Milos standing by the window, seemingly lost in thought.

"Are you awake?" Saen asked, surprised. When Milos didn't respond, Saen's mind raced, considering the possibility of Milos's true identity. Panic flared as he realized he hadn't informed the archbishop—what if Milos was indeed a god? Would the archbishop suspect him of ulterior motives?

Saen's gaze darted around the room, landing on a mouthwash cup that shouldn't have been there. His expression shifted. "Has anyone disturbed you?"

"No," Milos replied, his voice calm as he turned his gaze from the garden to the bishop. During his slumber, Milos had been aware enough to know he was brought here by Bishop Saen.

Meanwhile, Seraphina was making her way back to the hall, brushing grass leaves off her shoulders. "When will he recover his memory?" she asked.

"It could be today, or maybe later," Little N replied.

"Then I need to be cautious," Seraphina mused. "I can't reveal that I know who he is. I'll need to take things slowly, like boiling a frog in warm water. By the time he gets used to me, I'll have achieved what I came for."

"Exactly. And by the way, you earned one point of favorability tonight. That point will sustain us for another three days," Little N added, pleased.

"Only one point?" Seraphina was a bit taken aback.

"Yes, he is, after all, the God of Light, unfamiliar with love," Little N explained. "By the way, why did you change your strategy at the last minute? I thought you'd give him water."

Seraphina chuckled. "Even without his memory, the God of Light isn't foolish enough to accept something from a stranger. I realized that and adapted on the fly."

"Impressive, host! If we can continue to increase his favorability, not only can we survive, but we can also exchange for more magical props," Little N praised.

"Like those in the gift package?" Seraphina asked.

"Yes."

More props would certainly be useful, Seraphina thought, especially when she had no magic of her own to rely on. Returning to the banquet hall, she noticed no one seemed aware she'd been gone. However, she was troubled by the side effects of the desert fish; face blindness had set in, rendering everyone in the hall identical.

Seraphina didn't want to encounter Milos again so soon, yet time pressed on her. With only two days left to live, she spent the previous day poring over old newspapers to grasp the current state of affairs, resisting the urge to rush to Bishop Saen's house.

"Shouldn't we wait a bit longer?" Little N suggested cautiously. "After all, meeting him again so soon seems hasty."

Seraphina leaned against the window, watching the sun-scorched earth below. "Has he recovered his memory and returned to the temple?"

Little N hesitated. "If he has, we're in trouble. We can't just pursue him to the temple to improve his favorability now."

"What about the other two gods?"

"When the Dark God's archangel escorts him back to the underworld, he'll pass by the Misty Forest. That's the closest place to us. But the capital of Burton is still some distance from the Misty Forest. To reach it, you'd either need to upgrade me to the R system for teleportation or gain the God of Light's favor to exchange for teleportation props."

"The same goes for the Sea God. He's never left Atlantis. To reach him, you'd need to upgrade me or exchange for props."

Seraphina sighed, realizing she had to focus on Milos.

Seraphina took a moment to appraise herself in the mirror, ensuring her appearance was just right for the task ahead. She wore a pure white skirt that accentuated her figure with subtle elegance; the half-petticoat gave just enough volume to add a graceful movement to her steps, resembling the gentle sway of a fishtail. The overall effect was one of understated allure, a natural charm that she hoped would appeal to Milos in his current, more human state.

She exchanged her diamond necklace for a simpler one made of tiny beads, a choice that highlighted the gracefulness of her neck and lent a sense of purity to her look. The low neckline of her dress revealed a considerable expanse of skin, a calculated decision to blend innocence with a hint of allure. While such an approach might not sway the God of Light in his divine form, it could very well catch the attention of Milos, who was now human and potentially more susceptible to earthly charms.

Satisfied with her reflection, Seraphina gathered her resolve and descended to the hall, requesting a basket and flower-cutting tools from a servant. Equipped and ready, she ventured into the garden. Her plan was simple yet strategic: to be present, to create an opportunity for a chance encounter.

The heat was oppressive, nearly driving Seraphina back indoors the moment she stepped outside. The sun blazed fiercely, casting a relentless glare over everything it touched. Despite this, she persevered, making her way to the small garden at the back of the property. Once there, she sought refuge under the shade of a tree, fanning herself with a handkerchief to ward off the sweltering heat.

Her eyes drifted across the iron fence separating her from Bishop Saen's home, noting the small white building nestled within the garden. It was a point of interest, a place where she hoped Milos might eventually wander during the course of the day.

With that thought in mind, Seraphina turned her attention to the task at hand, slowly picking flowers from around her. Each bloom she gathered was a part of her subtle strategy to make her presence known, to become a fixture in the garden that Milos might notice during his own contemplative walks.

However, as the sun began its descent, painting the sky with hues of orange and pink, she had yet to see any sign of him. The garden remained quiet, undisturbed by the presence she hoped to encounter.

It became clear that serendipity would not be enough. To orchestrate the kind of meeting she desired would require more than mere chance—it would need careful planning and perhaps a bit of daring.

With her basket full of flowers and her heart holding a touch of disappointment, Seraphina returned indoors. She maintained her composure, hiding her feelings behind a calm exterior. Though today had not gone as she had hoped, she remained resolute. Tomorrow would bring new opportunities, and with them, another chance to engage with the enigmatic god who now walked among mortals.

***

The morning began with an insistent knocking that pulled Seraphina from her dreams.

Today was the day for the enrollment at Inoway Seminary—a significant event that Count George viewed with utmost importance. The count had made sure to wake Seraphina and her two cousins early, emphasizing the gap between ordinary mortals and those who could wield divine arts.

In this world, as in Seraphina's original one, diviners held a status far above the rest. A single diviner in a family could elevate their entire status, transforming them from mere nobility into something much more revered. For Seraphina, who was used to the societal divides dictated by divine favor, the situation felt all too familiar.

Once downstairs, Seraphina and her cousins were ushered into the morning living room, where they spent hours being primped and dressed. However, Seraphina was left mostly to her own devices, as the Countess focused her attention on her daughters, Robus and Rose. The Countess seemed intent on turning them into peacocks, piling their hair with gems, feathers, and even miniature sailboats.

"It's decent to wear it this way," the Countess declared, directing maids to lace corsets tightly. "Today is crucial. All eligible children in Burton will be at the selection. You must distinguish yourselves unless you want to mingle with commoners."

Robus and Rose recoiled at the thought, shaking their heads with exaggerated horror, as if the Countess had suggested they befriend baboons.

As the countess continued directing the maids to pile on more gems and wigs, Seraphina couldn't help but shake her head internally. She knew that such ostentatious displays would be more of a hindrance than a help. The extra weight would only add to the embarrassment should her cousins fail the assessment.

Opting for simplicity and elegance, Seraphina had chosen a light blue polka dot silk dress. The delicate ruffles at the neckline gave it a touch of charm, and her hair was tied up casually, adorned only with a beautiful sapphire side clip. It was a look that emphasized grace and authenticity over flamboyance.

Robus and Rose seemed convinced of their impending success, their eyes sparkling with a smug sense of superiority. They fully believed their mother's assurances that their extravagant attire would endear them to the seminary professors, completely unaware of how misguided this belief was.

"Add more blush! It's still not enough!" the Countess called out, determined to enhance her daughters' artificial appearances.

Robus, covering her mouth with a smile, added, "Oh, what will she do? Poor little girl, dressing so plainly will surely lead to rejection."

Seraphina, unfazed by their taunts, chose not to engage with their condescending remarks. She turned her attention to the window, her thoughts far removed from the trivialities of their competition. Her mind was occupied with more pressing matters—specifically, the looming depletion of Little N's energy. After today, Little N would be at risk of shutting down.

Stuck in this situation, Seraphina felt the weight of her predicament. She needed to find a way to encounter Milos, the God of Light, as his favor was key to her mission and survival. But trapped here with her cousins, the opportunity seemed distant and elusive.

"Host, what should we do?" Little N's voice trembled with anxiety, mirroring Seraphina's own concerns.

Seraphina took a deep breath, trying to maintain her composure. She knew she couldn't afford to let panic take over. Somehow, she had to find a way to navigate the obstacles in her path and reach Milos. Her determination was unwavering, even as they prepared to leave for the Inoway Seminary. She resolved to stay alert for any chance to advance her mission, knowing that her success depended on her resourcefulness and perseverance.

Before she could devise an escape plan, the countess ushered them into the carriage, and they set off toward Inoway Seminary.

The ride was filled with the chatter of her cousins, but Seraphina's mind was elsewhere, strategizing her next move.

The Inoway Seminary, with its grand architecture, stood imposingly by a tranquil lake. Its tall towers and stained glass windows gave it an air of solemnity and reverence, befitting a place where the divine arts were studied.

Upon arrival, Seraphina quickly seized the opportunity to slip away under the guise of needing to find a bathroom.

Once under the shade of a tree, she took a moment to breathe deeply, the quiet surroundings offering a brief reprieve from the chaos of the day. As she scanned the area, her gaze landed on a figure sitting by the lake. His hair shone like spun gold in the sunlight, and his eyes mirrored the clear expanse of the sky. His very presence seemed to radiate a light that was impossible to ignore.

It was Milos, the God of Light.

Seraphina's heart pounded in her chest, her pulse quickening at the sight of him. Here was her chance—a critical opportunity to gain the favor she so desperately needed. In her mind, Milos appeared not only as a god but as a beacon of hope. Securing his favor would grant her the vitality and time required to continue her mission.

Seraphina took a moment to gather herself, ensuring she looked her best before approaching Milos. Her sky-blue skirt fluttered around her like petals in the breeze, and she adjusted her collar just enough to enhance her appearance without seeming too deliberate. She wanted to strike the right balance between innocence and allure, knowing that her charm might help bridge the gap between them.

With a slight spring in her step, she made her way over to the bench where Milos sat. As she approached, she called out softly, her voice tinged with genuine surprise, "Lord Milos, I didn't expect to see you here."

Her expression was crafted to convey a mix of relief and pleasant surprise—like someone finding a friendly face in an unfamiliar setting. It was a calculated move, designed to make her presence feel natural and welcome, rather than forced or intrusive.

Milos looked up, his eyes meeting hers with a calm, steady gaze, which was unsurprising to Seraphina. His light, detached gaze suggested that the events of their previous encounter had slipped from his memory. She had anticipated this reaction from the God of Light, whose nature was as aloof and serene as the elements he was born from—mountains, rivers, and seas. His inherent reserve and restraint meant that he was unlikely to display obvious emotions or surprise.

Seraphina understood that forging a connection with Milos required patience and subtlety. She knew that any attempts to elicit familiarity from him would need to be gentle and respectful of his natural disposition. Unlike the God of the Sea, who was more personable and open to interaction,

Milos's temperament was such that any warmth would have to be carefully nurtured over time.

Still, Seraphina was not discouraged. She took his reserved nature as a challenge, an opportunity to engage with him thoughtfully and sincerely. Her strategy was to create an environment where he felt comfortable and unpressured, allowing any rapport to develop organically.

"Are you also here to take the seminary assessment?" Seraphina asked, maintaining a casual and friendly tone.

"No," Milos replied, his voice calm and composed. "I simply find the atmosphere here quite pleasing." His gaze shifted momentarily to the serene surroundings, as if drawing strength from the tranquil environment.She followed his gaze as it lingered on the academy's main tower, where a grand statue of the God of Light stood—a focal point for prayer and reflection. It was clear that this place held a certain significance for him, even if he didn't consciously remember why.

It seemed her memory hadn't recovered yet, and Seraphina felt a wave of relief. She smiled sweetly, "I'll be taking the test soon. To be honest, I'm a bit nervous. It's my first time here, my first time in the capital. I'm worried I'll make a fool of myself if I fail." The girl's slight frown was enough to make anyone want to soothe her worries.

Her slight frown and candid admission were designed to evoke empathy, to present herself as vulnerable and relatable.

It was a subtle invitation for Milos to offer reassurance or guidance, a chance to deepen the connection between them.

Milos's response was gentle yet firm, his eyes meeting hers with a quiet intensity. "No," he said, his voice carrying a reassuring certainty. "I can sense the spiritual power within you. There's no doubt you will pass the test."

Seraphina was genuinely taken aback by his words. In her original world, she had no affinity for divine arts, yet here Milos spoke of a spiritual potential she hadn't been aware of. Could the journey through time and space have awakened something new within her?

"If what Lord Milos says is true, that would be positively splendid!" The girl beamed, her smile as bright as the sun that bathed her. She seemed to shimmer with amber honey, so sweet and radiant. "You can't imagine how much I long to step into the seminary and the temple of the God of Light. It's like a dream."

Milos found himself catching a bit of her cheerful contagion, the corners of his lips curling up in response.

"A sprinkle of favorability," Little N's voice echoed in her mind, barely containing its excitement.

Fantastic, that's another three days of survival in the bag!

Seraphina felt a flicker of triumph. Each small victory, each moment of connection with Milos, brought her closer to her overarching goal. Though the path ahead was still fraught with challenges, she was determined to navigate it with courage and ingenuity, forging a future where she could reshape the world and its divine entities for the better.

~51~

<u>4</u>

Seraphina sat down next to Milos as naturally as if they were old friends. As she adjusted the hem of her skirt, she keenly observed the differences in him from when they first met.

Milos was dressed in a white shirt with gold buttons, dark brown trousers, and matching riding boots. His attire was simple yet elegant, indicative of someone who was well cared for. The slight opening at his collar revealed the smooth line of his collarbone, adding a touch of casual elegance to his appearance.

Clearly, those around him were attentive, likely recognizing the potential significance of his identity even if they weren't entirely certain of it. They seemed to be waiting, perhaps hoping for some sign or miracle that would confirm his divine nature.

As the midsummer wind swept across the lake, it carried with it the scent of flowers and a refreshing coolness that softened the atmosphere. Milos seemed more at ease, his gaze less distant and perhaps even tinged with curiosity.

"Ah, how cozy this is," Seraphina mused, stretching her arms with a contented sigh. "For some reason, being in Lord Milos' presence puts me at ease. It's as if the anxiety about the approaching exam has simply evaporated."

Seraphina's arms, glowing softly in the dappled sunlight, exuded a certain elegance and charm. She had carefully chosen her perfume, Polar Night, knowing it was a scent steeped in allure and mystery. It was a fragrance from the northern lands, known for its seductive and captivating aroma—quite unlike the pure, sunlit scents of the southern continent overseen by the God of Light.

As she stretched, Seraphina allowed her fingertips to lightly graze Milos's chest, a seemingly accidental touch that was anything but. The subtle gesture, combined with the intoxicating scent, was designed to capture his attention without overtly demanding it.

Milos, accustomed to the natural fragrances of his domain, was momentarily taken aback by the exotic allure of the perfume. The scent was rich and inviting, carrying a hint of the unknown, a tantalizing contrast to the familiar purity he was used to. It was an aroma that evoked imagery of the God of Darkness's realm, where danger and temptation wove through the very air.

Though the touch was brief, it left an impression. For Milos, who had experienced little of human interaction in such a personal way, the combination of the scent and the fleeting contact was a new experience. It stirred something within him, a curiosity perhaps, that made him more aware of Seraphina's presence beside him.

Before Milos could fully process the first touch, Seraphina's fingertips brushed against his chest once more, this time with a bit more pressure. She could feel the warmth beneath his white shirt, a subtle reminder of his humanity in this moment.

"Ah, sorry," she repeated, her voice carrying a playful undertone, devoid of genuine apology.

Milos's reaction was subtle, but there was a definite flicker in his eyes—a response that betrayed his inexperience with such interactions. As the God of Light, and even now in his human guise, he had little exposure to the intricacies of human contact and the nuances it carried. What might have been a negligible gesture to others was, to him, a novel and intriguing sensation.

The brief contact was like a spark flaring briefly on a frozen lake—a momentary burst of warmth and color against a backdrop of cool detachment. Though it was transient, it left an impression on Milos, a lingering trace of something unfamiliar yet not unwelcome.

For Seraphina, it was a calculated move, one that required careful balance. She knew that each small interaction could be crucial in building rapport and trust with Milos. His reaction, though understated, suggested that her approach was having an effect, slowly chipping away at his aloof exterior.

In the recesses of her mind, Little N's voice echoed with enthusiasm, "Host, that move earned you two more points of favorability!"

Seraphina felt a quiet satisfaction, knowing that these small gains were important steps toward her ultimate goal.

As the melodious chime from the bell tower signaled the start of the assessment, candidates began to make their way toward the auditorium. Seraphina stood up, preparing to join them, but paused to extend a friendly invitation to Milos.

"Lord Milos, would you care to accompany me to the auditorium?" she asked, her smile warm and inviting.

Milos stood, his expression unwavering. "I regret that I have prior commitments and must decline," he responded, preparing to depart.

Seraphina wasn't fazed by his response. Her invitation had been more of a formality, knowing she'd already gained valuable three favor points from their encounter. With nine days of extended life secured, she felt reassured and ready to continue her journey. She nodded, maintaining her cheerful demeanor. "Lord Milos's magic is so advanced, it's no wonder a low-level assessment might seem a bit dull."

Milos, however, surprised her with his next words. "I don't find the low-level magic assessment boring," he said. "But I'm going to leave Burton."

The unexpected news hit Seraphina, and her expression wavered momentarily. "Where are you going?" she asked, her voice tinged with urgency.

Milos's reply was calm and contemplative. "To a place. I suddenly remembered the name of this place yesterday and wanted to go see it. Maybe it will remind me of something."

Seraphina's mind raced. The thought of Milos leaving worried her; he was her lifeline, the key to her survival and plans. "Will you come back?" she asked, trying to hide her anxiety.

Milos gave a small, enigmatic smile. "You're asking the same question as the bishop."

Of course, Seraphina thought. Bishop Saen likely suspected Milos's divine origins and wanted to maintain his connection to him, just as she did. For Seraphina, Milos was more than a potential ally; he was a critical part of her strategy, the source of her continued existence in this unfamiliar world.

Seraphina had a pretty good idea of what was gnawing at Milos. Especially since Bishop Saen, despite not knowing who Milos really was, treated him with the kind of respect usually reserved for someone with a very impressive resume—real or imagined. For Milos, whose memory was as blank as a fresh canvas, everyone around him probably looked like they were wearing masks, and not the fun masquerade ball kind.

"I heard about Lord Milos at the banquet..." Seraphina began, her brow furrowing just so, while her fingers twisted the ribbon on her skirt like a cat playing with yarn. Her voice was a careful mix of hesitation and guilt, the sort that might make you think she was admitting to something far more scandalous.

"While I might have been casually wandering past your room, I wasn't exactly performing acts of goodwill. But when I heard someone groaning about being thirsty, the little mischief-maker in me couldn't resist. So, I dashed to the washroom and fetched the iciest water I could find. Later, when I learned about your amnesia, I felt a twinge of guilt. Thank goodness you didn't actually drink that water!"

"Ah, so that's the story," Milos chuckled softly. He'd already suspected that the timing of this young lady's appearance was just a bit too perfect. But considering the antics of a cheeky girl, it all made sense. "No harm done. But even if I had drunk the bathroom water, it wouldn't have been the end of the world."

Seraphina grinned, her relief genuine. "Glad to hear it! I do hope we cross paths again in Burton."

Please say you'll be back soon!

Milos paused, a slight nod accompanying his words. "I think I will. There's something about this place that feels... familiar. Perhaps more memories are waiting for me here."

"That's fantastic," Seraphina said, her smile sincere and wide. "Strictly speaking, you're the first friend I've made in Burton, Lord Milos. I'd hate to see you leave."

"Friend?" Milos echoed, the word rolling off his tongue like a foreign delicacy.

"Yes, the kind who hang out and have fun. The ones who never want to part are the best friends," Seraphina explained with a grin, all the while a tiny inner voice was doing a victory dance and plotting grander schemes.

"Is that so." Milos gave a faint smile, casting a glance toward the auditorium. "You should get to your test."

"Alright, Lord Milos, time to skedaddle out of the city," Seraphina chirped with a grin. "I hope next time we cross paths, you'll have a bag full of tales from your journey, and I'll have wrangled my way into the seminary as a student. Oh, and it just dawned on me—you don't even know my name yet."

"My name's Seraphina, Seraphina Doyle. Commit it to memory," she declared with a playful flutter of her lashes, each blink as delicate as a butterfly landing softly.

Milos gave a gentle nod, his gaze softening like a warm breeze over still waters. But as he turned to depart, that fleeting warmth vanished, swallowed by the vast, indifferent sea of his usual stoicism.

"Host, two points again," Little N murmured.

"How touching," Nan remarked, gazing at the spot where Milos had disappeared, her smile tucked away like a secret.

Breaking new ground is no walk in the park, that's for sure.

***

Seraphina perched on the edge of her seat in the auditorium, clutching her exam number like it was a lifeline.

Inoway College threw open its doors to new students only once every three years. Her cousin, a mere two years her senior, was stuck taking the exam alongside her. Needless to say, this opportunity was as precious as dragon scales. Everyone in the room hung on to their hopes like moths to a flame.

The assessment method is delightfully straightforward. Step into the magic circle at the hall's center, and it will reveal whether you possess the spark for theology. For those blessed with talent, beams of light will dance forth.

There are five beams in total, with more beams signifying greater talent. If the circle remains dark, well, better luck next time. Those who manage to light up all five beams earn themselves a weekly sojourn to the temple—a golden ticket, if you will.

Seraphina isn't particularly interested in unraveling the mysteries of mysticism. Her sights are set solely on getting closer to the God of Light. She's unsure if she can max out her favorability score before Milos's memory makes a grand return. Hence, she absolutely must light up all five beams. It's her ticket to approach the God of Light through a cleverly indirect route.

One by one, hopefuls step up, then descend from the circle, either on cloud nine or with spirits deflated.

Seraphina was taken aback when both Robus and Rose managed to conjure a beam of light. This sparked a flicker of concern. With the formidable Doyle family genes coursing through her veins, she feared she might also be destined for a mere single beam. To outwit fate, she pulled out "little Lisa's discarded playdough". With its uncanny ability to mimic behaviors and effects, she crafted a sneaky replica of a five-beam wonder, It was a crafty little insurance policy, ready to save the day if her talent fell short.

"My, what a surprise," the Countess murmured hoarsely, "Both of my darlings did splendidly."

Robus flushed with excitement, hissing in a whisper, "It must be the hairstyles Mother crafted for us. Pure magic, I say. Hiss."

Rose chimed in with a giggle, "Poor Seraphina. I should've told her to bring some bling and wigs. But could she even afford such luxury? Oh, the horror if she's the only one to fail!"

Seraphina felt like she was surrounded by a trio of serpents, their hisses echoing in her mind.

"Seraphina Doyle," the professor's voice called out, snapping her back to reality.

She stood, feeling the weight of countless eyes on her, like being under a spotlight on a red carpet. For Seraphina, who thrived in the limelight, this was child's play.

The magic circle, a grand concave stone pit etched with interlocking seven-pointed stars, lay at the center of the hall. Stepped seats surrounded it in a theater-like fashion, giving everyone a front-row seat to the spectacle.

Seraphina was determined to avoid any mishaps. If she only managed one beam, crushing the playdough would be futile, as the overlapping light would betray her. She had to be swift, activating the playdough's magic the moment she stepped in.

Seraphina pursed her lips and strode confidently toward the circle, her hands tightly clenched in resolve.

But the magic circle had other plans.

Before she could even process the moment, the light responded with breathtaking speed. Five pure, dazzling beams shot up like colossal pillars, piercing the void from the magic circle.

Stunned, Seraphina quickly relaxed her grip to spare the plasticine from an untimely squish.

The room erupted in a cacophony of astonished gasps and exclamations, the sound echoing off the walls like a symphony of disbelief.

"Five beams? She's the second today! We usually see only one in years past. And two in one day?"

"This is the pinnacle of talent. The archbishop and cardinals hit five beams in their time."

"Who is she?"

"Seraphina Doyle."

"Seraphina Doyle."

"Excellent, your score is noted," the professor beamed with newfound warmth.

Seraphina, still reeling, steadied her steps and returned to her seat with a grace that belied her inner turmoil.

The three serpents fell silent, their expressions a mix of disbelief and curiosity, lips twitching as if to ask how she managed five beams without looking like a Christmas tree.

Seraphina settled back into her seat, watching as the magic circle began its next test. Her heart, once a storm of confusion and shock, gradually found its rhythm again.

Five beams of light, and they came from me, she mused, a hint of amazement coloring her thoughts. It was a revelation that both startled and thrilled her, a testament to her own hidden potential.

5

The night at Earl George's residence was a whirlwind of clinking glasses and effusive toasts, the air thick with celebration.

The grand chandelier overhead cast a warm, orange glow, a nod to tradition despite the advent of gas lamps. The nobles, ever the connoisseurs of elegance, favored the twinkling crystal chandeliers, like ethereal blossoms suspended mid-air.

Maids paraded through the crowd with steaming platters held aloft, offering Burton-style boiled lamb, roasted partridge, cauliflower with coriander sauce, chocolate shortbread, stewed fruits, lobster, and even the peculiar steamed quail with hair.

It was a feast fit for those now touched by divine magic in the Doyle family. With Seraphina's unexpected five beams of light, the Doyle name was now aglow with divine favor, elevating them to new heights among the nobility.

Earl George, proud as a peacock, basked in the glory of his nieces' accomplishments, even if Seraphina's triumph had overshadowed his daughters' dual beams. The Countess, however, wore a mask of joy, her true feelings hidden beneath layers of social grace as she accepted congratulations with feigned delight.

Seraphina herself felt like a prized trophy all evening, her every move met with praise and admiration. While it was a night of triumph for Earl George, Seraphina found it all rather monotonous. Her thoughts drifted to the night beyond the window, wondering where Milos might be amidst the evening's festivities.

After the banquet, Seraphina dismissed her maid and sank into the solitude of a hot bath. The milky water embraced her, dotted with pink and white petals, a luxury afforded by her five beams. The candles overhead, nestled in gold chains, cast gentle light through the crystal, painting the bathroom in ethereal hues.

Bathing, a laborious affair, required servants to haul hot water from a copper stove in the kitchen, a privilege not often indulged. Tonight, however, the five beams had afforded Seraphina this rare treat.

"Once you master divine arts, you can bathe at your leisure," Little N chimed in, ever the opportunist. "Or consider exchanging for bathing props—they come with perks!" It was a not-so-subtle nudge towards more exchanges, which would, in turn, upgrade Little N.

"Only three points left, right?" Seraphina mused, catching her reflection in the misty bathroom mirror.

"This time, the God of Light granted us four points," Little N replied cheerfully. "We used one, and if we spend another by midnight, we'll have three more days."

The relentless countdown of three days was a constant reminder of her precarious situation. With a splash, Seraphina dipped her arm into the water, rippling the surface.

"In three days, the God of Darkness will pass through the Misty Forest," Little N warned. "Miss this chance, and you'll only see Him again in the underworld, where only the dead and monsters roam."

"How many points do I need to redeem the teleportation props?" Seraphina asked, though in her mind, she was really calculating the cost in lifelines. Each point was three more precious days of life.

"Three points," Little N replied, treading carefully.

Seraphina was taken aback, her eyes widening in disbelief. "So, I'd teleport and then promptly go kaboom? Talk about a one-way ticket!"

"Host, we have other options," Little N interjected hastily. "Remember your history lessons? Back in the Middle Ages, there was a rather adventurous profession known as gold hunting."

"Of course I know," Seraphina replied with a nod. Not only was she familiar with it, but she'd also dabbled in the art of gold hunting herself.

In a world governed by gods, there are always shadowy corners beyond the reach of divine light. These places are havens for monsters and malevolent spirits, yet they also harbor rare plants and minerals—prime ingredients for alchemy.

Despite the perils of such adventures, these treasures, akin to gold, lured gold hunters like moths to a flame, promising fortune and glory.

While perusing old newspapers recently, Seraphina had noticed numerous ads seeking gold hunters. The risks in this line of work were notoriously high.

"Do you want me to join the gold hunters?" Seraphina pondered aloud.

"Host, you could use their teleportation magic to reach the Misty Forest," Little N suggested. "It's the most economical and swift option we have."

"Would they even hire me?" Seraphina asked, a tinge of skepticism in her voice.

"Your college admission letter, adorned with five stars, is your golden ticket. Fear not, host—no one else knows you're a divine magician still learning the ropes. However, to increase your chances of survival, I recommend exchanging something with me."

"Can I afford it?" Seraphina raised an eyebrow.

"I have a blind box available for just one point of favorability. You could give it a shot if you're feeling desperate," Little N offered quickly.

Seraphina was skeptical. "Is it guaranteed to yield a useful prop?"

"Well, there's a 1% chance you'll hit the jackpot and get something amazing," Little N explained, "and a 99% chance you'll end up with, well, something more... quirky, with amusing side effects. But who knows, those can be useful too! Remember, you get what you pay for," Little N sighed, as if imparting ancient wisdom.

Seraphina: "..."

Even a single point represented her hard-earned effort—a means to live for three more days.

"There's one more thing," Little N added. "The Misty Forest is up North, where the God of Darkness holds sway. Unlike the South, where blondes and redheads reign, the North favors dark hair. To avoid the God of Darkness wanting to strangle you on sight, I'd suggest changing your hair and eye color."

Seraphina shrugged. "I won't waste a point on this. If he want to strangle me, let him try."

"Host, you don't need to spend a point. Don't dismiss this! It's a feature of my n-level system," Little N boasted, puffing out its metaphorical chest.

"Not bad, Little N. You do have your uses."

"Of course, so keep working to upgrade me and unlock even more features," Little N replied. As soon as it finished speaking, a soft light enveloped Seraphina's head like a brisk splash of ice water, sending shivers down her spine.

The chill cleared away the mist, revealing a clear reflection in the mirror. Seraphina stepped out of the bathtub and approached the mirror, curious to see her transformation.

The girl staring back from the mirror had long, black hair that cascaded like seaweed, slightly curled and dripping wet, adding a mysterious allure. Her eyebrows and pupils matched the inky hue, making her skin seem even more porcelain and radiant.

Seraphina blinked, and her reflection did the same. Gone was the angelic blonde girl. In her place stood a nymph out of water, dangerous yet enchanting, with an air of coquettish charm.

"Wow, Little N, you've outdone yourself!" Seraphina admired her new look from every angle, feeling like she could pass for a true northern belle.

"Hehe," Little N beamed with pride. "Host, allow me to change you back."

"Ah, no, that's not necessary..." Seraphina protested, not eager for another icy splash. But before she could finish, a gentle warmth enveloped her, as comforting as sunlight on a crisp morning.

Turns out, the temperature depended on the hair color.

Wrapping herself in a plush bath towel, Seraphina stepped out, leaving the maids to tidy up.

She settled into a cozy armchair, flipping through newspapers for any mention of mercenary groups. After a fruitless search, her eyes landed on a tiny ad tucked in the corner of the Burton Evening News:

"Misty Forest Mercenary Team seeks divine magicians. Departing soon. Meet at Oak Street Tavern."

Seraphina folded the paper with a snap and reached for her outing dress.

"Where are you off to at this hour?" Little N inquired as Seraphina dressed with haste.

"I'm going to take full advantage of the teleportation magic to reach the Misty Forest and find the Dark God," Seraphina replied, deftly braiding her hair.

"So soon?" Little N was taken aback.

"Time waits for no one, little comrade," Seraphina said with a sage nod. "We must prepare for the possibility that the God of Light won't return. If we don't act on these three points, they'll vanish in nine days. Plus, there's an SSR we've yet to meet! Who knows what stage he's at?"

Little N flushed, feeling chastised by Seraphina's determination. Here she was, hustling between gods, while he, a mere crap system, lounged passively without a hint of ambition.

Seraphina flicked open her fan, exuding an air of casual elegance as she glided past the maids. Once in the garden, she donned a cloak, pulled up the hood, and slipped out the back door, vanishing into the night.

As she gazed up at the starry sky, Seraphina couldn't help but marvel at her own industriousness. Here she was, a veritable juggler in the cosmic circus, balancing the whims of multiple deities like a seasoned acrobat. Burning the midnight oil for the sake of divine performance, she mused that perhaps she should add "celestial multitasker" to her ever-growing list of titles. After all, it wasn't every day you found yourself moonlighting as both a diplomat and a divine magician, all while keeping one step ahead of the gods' cosmic game of chess.

<u>6</u>

The Oak Street Tavern, aptly named and situated on Oak Street, was easy enough to find, especially since it was just a stone's throw from Earl George's residence. Its rustic exterior, adorned with logs, bore the bold sign "Oak Tavern."

Seraphina pushed open the creaky wooden door and stepped inside, greeted by a haze of smoke. Several burly men sat by the entrance, puffing on pipes. Their heads turned in unison at the sound of the door, eyes lingering on her with less-than-chivalrous intent.

Quickly covering her mouth to block the smoky assault, Seraphina made her way to the bar. Those eyes, she noted, followed her all the way, dripping with mischief.

"Good evening," Seraphina greeted the bartender from her perch on a log stool.

The bartender, engrossed in wiping the counter with a rag that looked like it had seen better days, barely acknowledged her presence.

Seraphina, unfazed, tapped the table with a finger, her voice light. "A glass of cold malt liquor, please."

She'd seen the advertisement for that liquor in the newspaper—surely, they had it here.

"Fifteen coppers," the bartender grumbled, finally looking up and shaking out his rag with more drama than necessary.

"The rest is for you," Seraphina said with a smile, handing over twenty coppers. The bartender's scowl softened into something resembling a smile as he took down a greasy glass, gave it a perfunctory wipe, and filled it with amber liquid.

"You shouldn't be here," he advised, dropping ice cubes into the malt liquor with rusty tongs. For the sake of the tip, he added, "It's a bit rough around these parts."

Seraphina accepted the drink, though she had no intention of tasting it. "Actually, I'm here because of this ad." She unfolded the newspaper and showed it to the bartender. "I'm a divine magician."

The bartender blinked, then called out to the burly men by the door, "Hey, she's a divine magician. No problem. Follow me, you're in luck; the recruiter's here." He tossed his rag aside and led the way to the stairs.

Seraphina followed, feeling the weight of unwanted attention lift as she ascended.

The second floor served as a makeshift office, cluttered with items that obscured the single window. A young man sat at a worn table, counting coins under the dim glow of a candle. Gold coins glinted enticingly on the tabletop.

Next to him, a bearded middle-aged man lounged in an armchair, watching Seraphina with an inscrutable expression.

Seraphina's gaze flitted between them before settling on the bearded man. She waved her college admission letter, "I'd like to join your team."

The man glanced at the letter, then dismissed it with a wave. "We're full."

Seraphina smiled, unfazed. "I'll halve my commission. The rest is yours."

The man straightened, interest piqued. "Not many offer such terms. Usually, it means they have a bigger agenda. I don't want trouble for my team."

Seraphina chuckled softly. "No trouble here. Just a divine magician eager to learn. My first foray into mercenary work, and I'm willing to trade half the commission for experience."

"And," she added, "I'm after Jiji grass from the Misty Forest. It's a rare alchemical ingredient, hard to find on the market. If I locate it, I'll trade the rest of my commission for it."

The bearded man nodded, skepticism dwindling. "An alchemy-focused divine magician, I see. You value your materials. Fine, I'll keep an eye out for Jiji grass."

He tossed her a small pouch. "Take this. We leave tomorrow at noon. Sound good?"

"Perfect," Seraphina said with a smile, as she opened the pouch to reveal a handful of gold coins and a round, intriguing badge. The gold coins were an advance payment—a sort of hazardous duty pay, given the nature of the job. After all, not everyone who set out on these missions returned, and the coins served as a financial cushion for one's family should the worst happen.

Ignoring the coins, Seraphina picked up the badge. It flashed briefly at her touch, a testament to the magic woven into it. This enchantment ensured that no one could take the gold and run; the captain would track everyone, badge discarded or not.

Seraphina traced her fingers over the words engraved on the badge.

"Hunting Darkness?" she mused. "Sounds promising—a good omen."

"I also need someone who can change their appearance to pose as me." After securing her plane ticket, Seraphina lingered, making her request to the bearded man.

"You know, my family can't know about this—they'd never agree. If you have someone in mind, I'm willing to pay an introduction fee."

Seraphina was confident the man had connections; seasoned gold hunters like him always knew the right people.

"One gold coin for the introduction fee, and I'll find someone for you," the bearded man replied without a second thought.

"Deal," Seraphina agreed.

"Be sure to come early tomorrow. We depart at noon, and the teleportation array waits for no one," the bearded man advised. "Nine o'clock in the morning, behind the tavern, I'll have someone for you. Bring twenty-one gold coins—one for the introduction fee."

"No problem," Seraphina said, pocketing the pouch with a smile. Yet, as she left the room, her smile faded into a look of exasperation.

All this hassle just for a free flight? She sighed inwardly.

***

"The sky's a nice, uniform pearly white today, which means good visibility and no glaring sun," the bearded man announced to the group gathered at the edge of the room.

They were back in the tavern's second-floor office, now transformed from its former cluttered state. The worn-out furniture had vanished, leaving behind a space so clean it seemed like a different room altogether. Seraphina had to blink twice upon entering, half convinced she'd stumbled into the wrong place. Five men and one woman stood assembled, and if it wasn't for the bearded man's presence, she'd have thought she'd walked into a wrong place.

Earlier that morning, Seraphina finalized her plans for her departure. She secured a divine magician, recommended by the bearded man, to take her place in the capital. They signed a binding agreement outlining exactly what her stand-in could and couldn't do, with their signatures witnessed by the world's will itself. This way, Seraphina could leave without the nagging fear of returning to chaos.

Sure, the cost was steep—five gold coins per day. But when weighed against the favor of the gods, gold coins seemed like mere pocket change.

"Let me introduce myself," the bearded man began. "I'm Lusahu, a sixth-level divine magician, and your captain." He nodded toward the tall, thin man beside him.

"Tony, seventh-level archer," said the tall, thin man, his expression as flat as his delivery. The short, stout man next to him chimed in, "Kevin, seventh-level divine magician." Another man, neither tall nor thin, added, "Stephen, seventh-level divine magician."

Seraphina hid a smile, amused by the bizarre familiarity of their names—just like the barbershop team back home. Stephen, in particular, had always been her go-to stylist.

"Your turn," the bearded man gestured to Seraphina.

Here, seventh-level was the base, with first-level being top-tier—archbishops and bishops, for instance. A seminary professor might rank at fourth level. Seraphina, however, wasn't even half a level yet. She was merely a student, fresh off receiving her admission letter and eager to exploit the teleportation array.

Without missing a beat, Seraphina declared, "Robus, seventh-level divine magician."

"Looks good," Lusahu remarked with an approving nod.

"Bullshit," Little N snarked, "a bunch of subpar players. Host, you're the exception, of course."

Are divine magicians not supposed to be rare? Seraphina mused at the gathering.

"This is the capital, the hub of talent," Little N explained. "Not everyone graduates from the seminary, and many never make it to Burton's capital. The southern continent is vast."

Lusahu placed a palm-sized black nameplate in the room's center. Instantly, it dissolved into black lines, weaving a dark seven-pointed star on the floor. "One minute, no dawdling. Once we're there, follow my lead," he instructed solemnly, stepping into the teleportation array first.

A swirl of black mist engulfed him. Mister Tony followed suit.

"Host, remember, once you arrive, ditch them quickly," Little N advised. "We still have work to do."

"Got it," Seraphina replied, stepping toward the teleportation array. As the tip of her shoe touched the black line, the world went dark, swallowing her whole.

Maybe this teleportation array is just a particularly dark one, Seraphina tried to reassure herself.

After what felt like an eternity—ten seconds, at least—she heard the unmistakable sound of chewing, as though someone were enjoying a rather crunchy meal. Yet her surroundings remained pitch black. Was teleportation supposed to take this long? It was certainly not what she had imagined.

"Host..." came Little N's nervous voice in her mind, "Take a few steps back slowly."

Without hesitation, Seraphina carefully stepped backward. Slowly, the darkness eased from her vision, turning blurry, then slightly clear. She blinked and rubbed her eyes, only to find a monstrous creature, bristling with spikes, looming in her line of sight.

Her scalp prickled and her legs threatened to give way. It wasn't a delayed teleport; she'd been sent right next to this beast and was now trapped in its cave. Fighting the tremor in her limbs, Seraphina gingerly backed away.

Yet even the faintest sound was enough to alert the creature. It pivoted its massive body, fixing her with eyes the size of basins. Beside it lay a half-eaten human body, clad in a red plaid shirt eerily similar to Tony's.

This time, Seraphina needed no prompting. Terror-stricken, she spun on her heel and bolted deeper inside, praying for an alternate exit.

"Don't worry, host," Little N reassured her. "This cave is deep, and the monster's too big to follow."

The reminder steadied her nerves. She paused and glanced back toward the cave entrance. The monster hadn't pursued her and seemed content to resume its meal on what was left of Mr. Tony.

"Should I... continue further into the cave?" Seraphina hesitated, staring into the cave's dark maw. If something else was lurking, it certainly wouldn't be a party.

Just as she wavered, a hoarse voice echoed from the depths.

"Water..."

Every hair on her body stood on end, goosebumps rising in a wave. Hearing a voice in such a place was never a good sign.

Perhaps it wasn't even human.

Abandoning the cave seemed wise, but the monster's growls outside complicated things.

"Water..." the voice grew louder, while the monster belched contentedly.

Seraphina shifted indecisively, caught between two equally unappealing options.

"Host..." Little N's tone was oddly hesitant, "That might be... the God of Darkness."

What?

Seraphina's eyes widened, lashes fluttering in disbelief. Could she really have stumbled upon her mission target here? "Which Dark God?"

"Let me check..." Little N recalibrated, its voice bubbling with excitement. "Yes, it's the God of Darkness. There's only one in the world. He must be injured and hiding in the cave. Host, this is your chance!"

What? Seraphina's mind reeled.

"Water..." the rasping voice pleaded again, sounding so parched it was almost painful.

Seraphina couldn't help but wonder—were these gods perpetually short on hydration in their elemental makeup?

It seemed a tad ironic that beings so powerful could have such a mundane weakness. Maybe they should consider adding a water cooler to their divine arsenal.

Z

Seraphina retrieved a white candle from her waist bag and lit it carefully.

The cave was a murky abyss, and she feared that any noise might alert the lurking monsters. Until now, she had been navigating by the faint glow of exposed ore embedded in the cave walls.

With the candle flickering to life, its flame offered a small but comforting beacon, bolstering her courage to venture further into the shadows.

"There won't be any fallen angels standing guard over the Dark God, will there?" Seraphina mused aloud.

"Probably not," Little N replied. "Otherwise, it seems odd that the master is parched while his minions stand idly by. Then again, maybe they're all dehydrated. I can just imagine a bunch of black-winged figures sprawled out like crows."

Seraphina chuckled at the mental image of a heap of thirsty angels. "But why aren't there any fallen angels guarding the Dark God?"

"Perhaps something unforeseen occurred that's absent from the history books," Little N speculated. "The annals only mention that the fallen angels discovered the wounded Dark God and escorted Him through the Misty Forest back to the underworld. The details are vague. But you're not eager to encounter fallen angels, right?"

"Nope, they sound quite unfriendly. Why are they called fallen angels, anyway?"

"Fallen angels," Little N began, "because the gods have always resisted the Dark God, Cecil Horace Horus Biserengeti Morellus. They consider any angel who aligns with the Dark God to be 'fallen.'"

"You actually remember the Dark God's full name?" Seraphina was surprised. "We just simplify it to Cecil."

"I'm the system," Little N quipped with a laugh.

"Why is the Dark God's name so long..." Seraphina's voice trailed off as she froze, eyes fixed on an indistinct form ahead. With each breath she took, the shape seemed to rise and fall gently.

Is that... Cecil, the Dark God?

A shiver ran through Seraphina, unnoticed wax dripping onto her fingers. The cave's cold seemed to seep into her bones, making her reluctant to approach. The weight of the Dark God's name alone was intimidating.

Unlike the God of Light, who had transformed into a human form and lost His memory, this one was a god through and through. The Dark God had ruled the North for millennia with an iron fist.

Seraphina recalled the history of gods: Cecil, creator of the underworld and embodiment of the abyss, abandoned at birth.

He was said to be extremely handsome, yet filled with hatred for all things, bloodthirsty and cruel. While other gods resided in the divine domain, this ancient deity forged the underworld and relocated His kingdom there. The frigid North became His domain.

Wouldn't humans who dared to confront a god meet a grim fate?

"Water..." The weak, hoarse plea echoed through the cave once more.

The sound shattered the eerie silence. Her candle was burning down to a stub, and once it extinguished, she'd be swallowed by darkness—a precarious position to be in.

Seraphina, holding the candle gingerly, advanced toward the Dark God. With each step, the figure became more distinct in the candle's warm glow.

There lay the Dark God Cecil, sprawled on the cold ground. His slightly curly, disheveled hair obscured his eyes.

As Seraphina leaned closer, trying to see more clearly, an overwhelming sense of dread emanated from him—like a powerful, unseen force clamping around her throat.

Seraphina gasped and stumbled backward, the candle slipping from her grasp. Little N was too terrified to utter a word. In the presence of a true god, everyone, even a system, trembled instinctively.

You cannot look directly at a god unless granted permission by Him.

Seraphina had one of those forehead-slapping moments as she recalled the ominous words etched on the cover of The History of Gods.

"Oh, brilliant, I've forgotten it," she muttered, fumbling about for the candle she'd dropped. Her cloak was pulled snug as the cave transformed into an icebox fit for the most discerning of penguins.

At last, her frozen fingers found the candle's cool surface. Despite her numbing digits, she recognized its unique texture and reached out, encountering fabric, skin, and—

"Where exactly do you think you're touching?" a gravelly voice rumbled from above. Seraphina felt a chill sharper than any winter wind as something far more menacing than the dark pinched her chin. Her complexion mimicked a ghost's in an instant. She was in the presence of the God of Darkness.

His frigid fingers twirled a strand of her hair, inspecting it as though it might reveal secrets of its own.

"What, are you from the North?" he inquired with a smirk.

"Yes, Kvina County," she stammered, her voice shaking like a leaf in a gale.

"Hmmm…" His chuckle was a rasp against her ear. "Well, congratulations, you're under expropriation." A frosty hand found her cloak's tie and snapped it with ease.

"What's the big idea?" Seraphina spat, her fear momentarily overshadowed by indignation as she shoved him. To her surprise, he toppled over with a rather undignified thud.

"Oof…" came a pained groan from the shadows.

With her eyes useless, Seraphina relied on sound, realizing she'd hit a sore spot. Guilt nipped at her conscience. "Well, who told you to be so… inappropriate?"

Cecil, regaining his composure, leaned against the wall, his breath ragged with pain and irritation. "Freezing to death here. If I wanted to assault a human girl, I'd wait until I wasn't on the verge of hypothermia. Right now, I just need your cloak."

"Oh, well, that's a relief!" Seraphina remembered her grand mission: reform the Dark God. She quickly brightened, thrusting the cloak at him. "Here you go, mysterious sir! If you need more, I've got layers to spare!"

Cecil: "…"

"Really, I'm practically a walking wardrobe!" She rolled up her sleeves to prove it, revealing the absurd number of garments she wore to fend off the northern chill.

Cecil wrapped himself in the cloak, unimpressed. "Your fashion choices don't suit me."

"I've got candles and matches," Seraphina offered, digging through her pockets. "If there's wood around, we could make a fire!" She paused, remembering the divine decree about not gawking at gods. Light would expose everything. But backing down now? Not an option. With a deep breath, she struck a match, her fingers blindly seeking the candle.

As she fumbled, a large hand gently cradled her head, and Cecil murmured something in an ancient tongue.

"Wow, Host, you've got permission to gaze upon His face," Little N translated, astonished.

Wait, what?

"Maybe the Dark God doesn't want you to know who he is."

The matchstick ignited a tiny flame, casting a soft, orange glow that carved a miniature world out of the surrounding darkness. Seraphina blinked slowly, her lashes fluttering as she dared to glance across. But one glimpse was all it took before she had to avert her gaze, utterly flustered.

The allure emanating from him was a force of nature, a captivating blend of power and peril that defied description. It was like standing on the precipice of a vast, dizzying canyon— terrifying, yet compelling enough to demand reverence. In that moment, she grasped why mere mortals were advised not to stare directly at a god.

Seraphina's thoughts spun in a chaotic whirlwind, though in reality, only a few heartbeats passed. The flame raced up the slender matchstick, its heat biting at her fingers. With a startled yelp of "Ah!" she let it drop, and once again, the cave was swallowed by the deep, enveloping dark.

Seraphina pursed her lips and struck another match. Once more, Cecil's strikingly handsome face was illuminated before her eyes, and she realized she'd vastly overestimated her ability to withstand such beauty. The flame fizzled out, leaving her momentarily dazed.

"Chtua—" Another match lit up the darkness.

In the renewed light, Seraphina saw not only that devastatingly handsome face but also a pair of narrow, dark eyes watching her with a mix of cold impatience and faint amusement.

In that moment, she felt a bit like the little match girl herself, each flickering flame a tiny portal to a beautiful dreamscape, offering brief escapes from the cold reality surrounding her.

"Are your hands shaking?" Cecil finally asked, unable to hide his exasperation. He took her hand, guiding it steadily to light the candle.

Seraphina lowered her gaze, biting her lip hard to shake herself awake. If she kept this up, she'd not only fail to fleece this little black sheep but might even end up willingly shackled to him. Was that why fallen angels served the Dark God? Simply bewitched by his looks?

Cecil struggled to his feet, leaning against the rocky wall. The cloak she'd given him was woefully undersized, failing to cover the dark blue robe beneath, now stained with black splotches.

"Let's go," he said, as if they were merely out for a stroll.

Seraphina blinked, "What?"

"You don't want to die here, do you?" Cecil asked, a hint of amusement curling his lips.

"No, of course not," Seraphina replied, an idea sparking in her mind.

"Neither do I," Cecil chuckled, extending his arm like a monarch to her, hinting for assistance.

As Seraphina slipped his arm over her shoulder, she heard him suck in a breath, as if the movement had aggravated a wound. He leaned heavily against her, all his weight pressing down. Her hand brushed his chest, finding it wet and sticky with blood. Only then did she realize the stains on his robe were not just dirt.

"Injured by an old friend," Cecil said, his eyes flashing with disdain. "But I didn't let him off easy. Nearly skewered him and tickled his heart. I'd guess he's dead now."

No, he's not, Seraphina thought. He must have turned human to maintain his divine power, while you're stuck with a god's form but no spells. Otherwise, how could you be bested by a mere mortal? There must be some crisis here that even he can't handle.

But what could she possibly do about a crisis that even a god couldn't solve?

8

Seraphina wiped the blood from her palm onto Cecil's robe, allowing him to lean on her as they made their way toward the cave's entrance. Each step seemed to drain him, his breath coming in labored puffs, but he was determined not to show weakness in front of a mere mortal, matching her pace with stubborn resolve.

She, too, was weary, burdened by the weight of his frame pressing down on her. The uneven terrain made every step a challenge.

"You didn't come here alone, did you?" Cecil asked between breaths.

"Of course not," Seraphina replied, shifting his arm that was slipping. "I got separated from my group. A monster trapped me in this cave, and that's when I found you." She squinted, trying to discern the path ahead. "If nothing unexpected happens, that beast is still blocking the exit. I can't handle it alone."

"Don't worry," Cecil said with practiced indifference, though a sharp hiss escaped him as he clutched his chest again, pain etched on his face.

Seraphina shot him a disbelieving glance, skeptical of his reassurance.

As they talked, they drew closer to the cave's exit, where a colossal beast lay snoring, its massive form rising and falling like a hill. Its thunderous snores shook loose stones from the walls. Surrounding it were dozens of bizarre creatures, scuttling about.

These creatures had elongated limbs and bloated bodies, resembling a grotesque mix of humans and spiders. Their eyes were devoid of pupils, replaced by eerie white bubbles. Clad in tattered linens, they crawled rapidly, their sharp claws raking the ground with a piercing sound.

"What are those?" Seraphina whispered, her eyes wide with fear.

"Gold hunters who ventured into the Misty Forest," Cecil explained, casting a glance at the creatures. "Transformed into zombies after being tainted."

"Zombies?" Seraphina echoed, horrified.

"Anyone who delves into divine magic risks mutation after death," Cecil said with a cynical smile. "The price of craving power—becoming a mindless monster, denied an afterlife."

Seraphina's face drained of color as she recalled reports from her world about a powerful magician's sudden death, which had led to a swift military and magical response. Was it to prevent the uncontrollable rise of such creatures?

She blinked, her lashes fluttering. If she failed her mission and perished, would she too become a monstrous fragment, denied reincarnation?

"Is there no way to avoid such a fate?"

"The only way is to live as an ordinary person, untouched by theology—or," Cecil added with a peculiar gleam, "become a partner recognized by the gods."

"A partner recognized by the gods?" Seraphina mused.

Cecil looked at her, a slight smile playing on his lips. "Do you really think you could marry a god?"

"Why not?" Seraphina shot back defiantly.

Cecil chuckled, an amused glint in his eyes. "Would a human marry an ant? I can't speak for other gods, but the God of Darkness certainly wouldn't."

Seraphina bristled, "You're not the Dark God, how would you know His thoughts? In my heart, the Dark God is kind and noble. People say He rules the North with cruelty, but He only punishes those who stray from the path."

"He established strict laws and elevated the status of women. In the North, women can do everything men can. It's only the men who despise Him. To me, He isn't an evil god; He's my favorite god," Seraphina declared with conviction.

"I must master the divine arts and enter the Dark Temple to become His most loyal believer. Even turning into a monster after death wouldn't matter."

"Even turning into a monster after death?" Cecil echoed softly, turning his gaze toward her.

Just moments ago, she had been pale with the fear of becoming a monster, but now, at the mention of the Dark God, her eyes shone with a pure, clear light, like the first glimmer of dawn breaking the long night.

"But so what?" Cecil murmured with a lazy smile, "Anyone can say nice things. His followers always do."

"Oh, really?" Seraphina's enthusiasm dimmed slightly. Maybe she had flattered the wrong person.

"Congratulations to the host for gaining one point of favorability," Little N chirped in triumph.

Huh?

Seraphina blinked, puzzled. She hadn't earned any favor by offering him the cloak or supporting his injured frame, yet a few heartfelt words had gained her a point.

Perhaps the Dark God truly did lack love, as the history books suggested. Was it because he was abandoned at birth, shunned for embodying death?

He had no shortage of fear from his subjects, loyalty from fallen angels, or the calculated devotion of his followers—but none of these came from a place of love. What he truly yearned for was genuine affection, a rare and unfeigned bond that transcended duty and fear.

But one point was hardly enough; the Dark God was proving more challenging to win over than she'd anticipated.

While Seraphina pondered this, a creature scuttling along the cave ceiling spotted them and shrieked in delight. The noise roused the sleeping beast, which immediately bristled and charged the cave entrance, its barbed body tearing through the rock and ore like paper.

Seraphina recoiled in terror, knowing they'd be overrun in moments.

Cecil abruptly tightened his grip, pulling her against his chest. She looked up in surprise, her eyes tracing his smooth jawline to meet his narrow, impassive gaze.

A terrifying, profound power emanated from Cecil, the same divine force she'd sensed when first confronting him. Yet now, under his protection, she felt entirely shielded from its overwhelming might.

The massive beast cowered, lowering its head, daring only to focus on his boots in the presence of a god. The grotesque zombies flattened themselves against the ground, faces pressed to the dirt in submission. Even the evil creatures within a hundred-mile radius cried out in supplication, and the entire Misty Forest trembled.

God had unleashed His majesty. All creation trembled before Him, compelled to bow.

The power lingered for over ten seconds before vanishing abruptly.

Seraphina felt Cecil's arm slacken, and he collapsed against her, his face pallid. She quickly steadied him as the creatures behind them scattered like a retreating tide.

"We have to get out of here quickly," Cecil gasped. Releasing his divine majesty had drained the last of his energy, and he could feel some of his wounds reopening, blood seeping out.

"Okay," Seraphina agreed, supporting him without hesitation.

"Forget it, it's too late," Cecil frowned, glancing toward the cave entrance. His handsome face was shadowed with deep frustration. The exposed ore on the cave walls glimmered with a cold, dangerous light, casting an eerie glow on his features. He sneered, "I've been found after hiding for so long."

Found by who?

Before Seraphina could voice her question, Cecil pressed her against the rocky wall, his grip firm yet unsteady as it pulled at his injury, causing his breath to hitch with pain.

"Listen to me," he said, his voice a soothing murmur as his dark eyes locked onto hers, both gentle and hypnotic. "Don't speak, don't resist. It will be over soon."

"What are you going to do...?" Seraphina began, but her words were cut off as Cecil leaned in, brushing his lips near hers but stopping just short, hovering mere millimeters away.

"Don't move," he whispered, his breath a soft caress against her skin.

Seraphina's heart raced wildly, her eyes wide and unblinking. They were so close that even the flutter of her eyelashes might bridge the gap between them.

Then came the hurried sound of footsteps approaching through the mist, drawing closer. Seraphina felt Cecil's muscles tense against her. She turned her head slightly, catching a glimpse of several figures under the moonlight—the archangels from the Temple of Light, their pure white wings unmistakable.

So that's what was happening, Seraphina realized with a slight curl of her lips. Cecil's predicament made sense now: he was being pursued by the Light Camp's enforcers.

But could she let it end like this?

No way.

With a boldness that surprised even herself, Seraphina wrapped her arms around him like the tendrils of a soft vine, threading her fingers through his hair. She pulled him close, kissing him with a passion that was both fierce and unyielding.

Cecil was momentarily taken aback, his muscles tensing at the unexpected contact. He was a god with a reputation that was far from pristine, and kisses weren't exactly part of his usual interactions. The only time he'd been kissed before was by a fallen angel, and even then, it had been a reverent touch to the tip of his shoe.

But this... this was different. And perhaps, not entirely unpleasant.

Under the gentle embrace of moonlight, they looked every bit like lovers caught in a moment of pure, unguarded affection.

Outside the cave, the archangels halted abruptly, shielding their eyes in unison. Their Lord God had always instructed them to avoid witnessing human intimacies. They were, after all, still young and unversed in such matters.

"Someone is doing something inappropriate," one muttered.

"Is it... mating?" another inquired hesitantly.

"Oh, God of Light, spare us from these indecent thoughts," a third groaned.

"But how do we confirm it's not the God of Darkness without looking?" yet another pointed out.

"I'll take a look," one brave archangel offered, peeking through his fingers with a blush. But one glance sent a fiery flush through his cheeks, and he quickly shut his eyes. "It can't be him," he declared, flustered. "Who would kiss the God of Darkness?"

God of Darkness: "..."

2

"Ten points! Oh my god—" Little N spiraled into a miniature frenzy, like a giddy, squawking chicken.

Seraphina felt her mind was about to burst from the chaos. "I can't believe the Dark God is such a pure little black sheep and so generous," Little N continued to squawk.

"Why only one point from the Light God for a similar kiss?" Seraphina asked, genuinely puzzled.

"Maybe the Dark God is just a bit more... shall we say, responsive?" Little N mused. "A little spark can ignite him. Do you think the Sea God would rack up more points? I heard he's quite the wild one."

"Wild means experienced," Seraphina said with a knowing nod. "The Sea God might present himself as passionate, but those types are often the most ruthless and tricky to deal with."

"Host, keep at it! Just 50 points will upgrade me to level R, and then I'll be able to teleport freely," Little N cheered.

"Fifty?" Seraphina echoed, incredulous. Her current total was a mere fourteen points.

"You'll stay an N for now."

Meanwhile, the Angels of Light had retreated, leaving behind only a scattering of feathers. Seraphina gently pushed Cecil away, breaking the fervent kiss. Her lips tingled, slightly sore—no doubt from Cecil's lack of kissing finesse and his inability to control himself.

After being released, Cecil sat back, utterly spent. His long lashes fluttered over his pale cheeks as he pressed a hand to his chest, looking fragile. Whether this was from his injuries or the unexpected kiss was unclear.

"Are you okay?" Seraphina asked, squatting beside him with concern. She didn't want her newfound source of points to perish suddenly. "They've gone."

"I know," Cecil replied, his deep eyes locked onto hers, a hint of irritation in his voice. "How dare you blaspheme..."

"What?" Seraphina blinked, confused.

Cecil clamped his mouth shut, swallowing the word "God." "Why did you do that to me? You could've just pretended."

"But that would have been too obvious," Seraphina said, resting her chin in her hand. "I'm no expert, but I knew a stiff pause would give us away. Honestly, I hesitated, but I realized this would help you, so I went for it."

Cecil was taken aback. "Why did you help me?" In his world, every face he encountered had an agenda. Even the most loyal followed him out of reverence for power. So why was this human girl different? He was now just a battered being teetering on the brink of death.

"Because you saved me," Seraphina answered earnestly. "You drove away the zombies and monsters. Without you, I'd be dead in that cave. I know you're gravely injured and probably hurt yourself further, but you didn't leave me behind. Helping you was the least I could do."

Cecil retorted coldly, "I didn't do it to save you. I did it for myself."

"I know," Seraphina said with a gentle smile. "But you saved me all the same."

Cecil's lips pressed into a thin line, the shadows in his eyes lifting slightly. He attempted to stand, using the mountain wall for support, but his strength waned from blood loss.

"Your injuries are serious. Let's get out of this cave first," Seraphina suggested, slipping his arm around her shoulder to help him up.

The girl was slight, and Cecil's weight bore heavily on her, making their progress slow. The moonlight cast a delicate glow on her face, highlighting the exhaustion that made her bitten lips appear even redder.

Cecil glanced at her and asked, "Have you kissed anyone else besides me?"

Seraphina focused intently on the path. "No, just you."

Cecil fell silent, the shadows in his eyes vanishing completely.

"Wow, host, you've got another point of favorability," Little N exclaimed, buzzing with excitement.

Seraphina felt reinvigorated, despite her exhaustion. With renewed determination, she supported Cecil as they staggered out of the cave and managed to walk more than ten meters.

"I can't go on," she confessed, feeling as though she might collapse under the weight.

"Help me to that tree," Cecil panted, every step a painful ordeal. "Feels like I'm walking on knives. That damn bald guy... he's merciless."

They stumbled to the tree, and Seraphina eased Cecil down onto its roots. "Too bad I don't have a teleportation array. Otherwise, we could head to a nearby city and find a doctor for you."

"It wouldn't help," Cecil muttered, pulling the cloak tighter around himself. His blood loss, combined with the North's chill, left him shivering. "I was hit by the highest level of divine magic. Only time can heal this."

"I saw those people earlier, with wings... are they real angels?"

"They are, angels under the command of Milos, the God of Light."

"No wonder," Seraphina mused. "No wonder you pretended to kiss me. I've heard the God of Light is strict, but I didn't realize it was this severe. What are angels doing here in the Northland?"

"I don't know," Cecil said, glancing at the angel feathers scattered on the ground. "You should collect those feathers. They're high-level materials. Very rare."

Really?

Seraphina, unfamiliar with theology, didn't initially appreciate the feathers' value. In the God Realm, angel feathers and god blood were prized materials. Enough god blood could even elevate a first-level divine magician to angel status.

She gathered the feathers from the cave entrance—five in total, large and white, gleaming in the moonlight. She couldn't help but think they'd make the perfect shuttlecock.

"Host, you were so fake earlier," Little N teased. "Wondering what the angels were doing? Of course, they were hunting the Dark God."

Seraphina gave it a playful tap. "I still have to act surprised. It's not every day ordinary people see angels."

Returning to the tree, she found Cecil with his eyes closed, seemingly asleep. She gently shook him, but he didn't stir— likely passed out from exhaustion and injury.

"Host, if you don't get him to warmth soon, he might not make it," Little N warned.

"Hmm..." Seraphina considered, "Let's use three points to get a teleportation item and head to Kvina County."

Classes at Inoway College were starting tomorrow, and she needed to report in—and perhaps find out if the God of Light had returned. But first, she had to ensure the Dark God was safe and leave a way for them to meet again.

Just like the plant, shrouded in gloom and devoid of love, lies deep beneath the earth, waiting. Yet, given the slightest glimmer of light, it will break through the soil, seeking and embracing the warmth it so desperately craves.

No one had ever dared to breach that tough exterior, hidden away in the darkness. But perhaps it was time for her to become that first ray of light, illuminating the shadows and offering hope where there had been none.

***

Cecil awoke to find warm sunlight spilling lazily through a window, casting playful patterns on the floor as the mint green curtains swayed. The room was modest, and he was alone.

A sweet, strong fragrance of mignonette lingered in the air, wrapping around him. He reached out, realizing his robe was gone.

Cecil sat up, startled, catching sight of his reflection in the dressing mirror across the room. His bare upper body displayed a messy yet captivating beauty, with broad shoulders tapering to a narrow waist. His once gruesome wounds were now carefully bandaged, exposing patches of pale skin and taut muscle beneath.

Relieved, he lifted the quilt to find his pants still in place. The bandages seeped a light green ointment, and when he touched a bit with his fingertips, he recognized the scent of mignonette.

On the bedside table lay a piece of paper weighed down by three white feathers. Picking it up, he saw a few lines of elegant cursive on pale yellow stationery bordered with painted irises:

"Feel free to stay here and rest. I've covered the rent for three months. Please don't feel burdened by this kindness. Thanks to you, I saved my life and gained angel feathers. Food, water, and keys are on the cabinet by the door. I found five feathers and left most for you. The ointment on your bandages is hemostatic; I bought two bottles to ensure your wounds don't worsen. Wishing you all the best."

There was no signature.

Cecil's eyes lowered, filled with a complex emotion he couldn't quite place. Never before had he encountered something so inexplicable.

In a single day, he'd lost his first kiss and been thoroughly cared for by someone who didn't even know his name—and whom he knew nothing about. Like a fleeting breeze, she'd passed through his life with no aim.

Returning the letter, he accidentally knocked over an empty glass jar. The leftover green paste bore the imprint of a delicate, slender fingerprint.

Expressionless, Cecil muttered to himself, "I told you ordinary medicine has no effect on me."

He rose from the bed, his feet meeting the cool floor, and walked to the door. There, he found a basket of buttered bread wrapped in paper and a pot of warm black tea, complete with washed mint leaves in a small dish, ready to be crushed and added.

Surveying the thoughtful setup, he turned an obsidian ring on his finger. It emitted a faint glow, dissipating into the air, signaling his intent to summon his subordinates.

Moments later, beams of black light descended from the void, materializing five fallen angels in the room. Their expressions were a mix of excitement and fear.

"Master, forgive us," they trembled, prostrating themselves at Cecil's feet. "We saw you collide with Milos, the God of Light, in a blaze of energy. When we arrived, there was no trace of either of you. We split up—some to find you, others to pursue Milos—but found nothing."

Cecil regarded them with indifference. "Gods have their ways of hiding. Check if the Temple of Light is closed. If it is, search among his followers. Any family with a remarkable young man could be harboring him in human form."

The fallen angels nodded, taking note as they prepared the teleportation array to the underworld. "Master, let's return to heal your wounds."

Cecil acknowledged them with a mild "hmm" but didn't step onto the array immediately. His hesitance froze the fallen angels in place.

Under their watchful eyes, Cecil retrieved the copper key from the cabinet, pocketing it before stepping onto the teleportation array with a detached demeanor.

***

At Earl George's residence, Seraphina stood on the balcony, watching the diviner who had helped her with her disguise, when Little N's excited voice echoed in her mind.

"Host, the favorability value just jumped by 5 points. How did it increase like that?"

Could it really be this easy?

Seraphina was bewildered but pleasantly surprised.

10

"This score shouldn't have increased out of thin air," Seraphina mused, calming down from her initial excitement. "I've only interacted with two gods so far. It can't be the God of Light, so it must be the God of Darkness. Maybe seeing the light I brought into his life made him feel a bit of favor."

"That makes sense," Little N agreed, scratching its head. "It seems that favorability can be gained both directly and indirectly, behind the scenes."

"It sounds like you're not entirely sure about the rules," Seraphina remarked.

"I'm a garbage system," Little N admitted shamelessly.

Seraphina, a bit speechless, opened a notebook, dipped a feather pen in ink, and wrote: "Total points: 20. Teleporting to Kvina County and Burton consumed 6 points. Remaining: 14 points, and two days of life.'

Little N peeked over, "Host, let's use these two days to work on boosting favorability."

"I get it," Seraphina sighed, closing the notebook. "But it also depends on the cooperation of the gods. Any news about the Sea God?"

"The Sea God is staying put in Atlantis. He doesn't engage in the war of gods nor leave the sea easily. To meet him, you'd need to go to the sea or lure him onto land, but that requires special items."

"With only fourteen points, I can't afford that," Seraphina frowned. "I should save these for your upgrade. Constantly spending points on teleportation is unsustainable. I need to acquire some teleportation arrays..." Her thoughts were interrupted by a knock on the door, followed by the maid's voice urging her to head to Inoway College.

"Got it," Seraphina called back, tossing down her pen. She moved to the dressing mirror, observing her reflection. The blonde girl in a white gauzy dress looked as radiant as clouds at sunrise, pure and lovely.

"Too plain," Seraphina critiqued, reaching for a straw hat from the rack. She placed it on her head, allowing a wisp of white gauze to drape over her eyes, making her red lips stand out.

"It's perfect," Little N exclaimed. "If you meet the God of Light now, you'd earn 100 points instantly."

***

Count George had only sent one carriage, hoping it would foster bonds among the cousins. But they remained uncooperative, each pair of eyes fixed in different directions during the ride.

Upon reaching the school, everyone went to collect their class schedules. While waiting, Seraphina noticed a particularly striking girl in the crowd.

The girl's hair was styled elegantly, adorned with an expensive jeweled comb. Her cheeks were rosy, her smile cheerful. Her attire was lavish, a noble dress with wide lace and gold-threaded floral patterns. Nearly everyone's gaze was drawn to her.

"That's Princess Margaret, the capital's rose," Robus murmured, half-hiding her face with a fan. "She has five beams of light, just like you."

Seraphina was taken aback. During the entrance exam, she had copied another candidate's results, though she didn't end up using them. She remembered sitting far away, not getting a clear look at the person.

A royal under the divine light—an intriguing situation. Divine law was the gods' domain, and while the king ruled the land, the gods could reclaim authority whenever they wished. People revered divine magicians more, leaving the royal family striving to enter the divine magic realm.

Seraphina shifted her focus back to her course schedule.

Inoway College used a flexible class system: choose a course and attend freely. You could take multiple classes or focus on one. Without hesitation, she chose magic arrays, hoping it might solve her teleportation dilemma.

Perhaps everyone was more interested in spell classes. When she reached the south tower's top floor, the classroom was empty, not even a professor present, leaving her feeling awkward.

As she stood there dazed, another person entered. The half-lit, half-dark room seemed to brighten with her presence.

It was Princess Margaret.

Seraphina's curiosity piqued. She was here to learn magic arrays for teleportation. Why wasn't Margaret pursuing more practical spells? Then again, as an SSR, Margaret should already have teleportation capabilities.

Maybe she was overthinking it.

The classroom was spacious, dominated by a two-meter circle in the center surrounded by black stones, each about a finger's height. It seemed purpose-built for demonstrating magical formations. The chairs were arranged around this circle, with Seraphina seated near the door.

Margaret entered, gave Seraphina a calm glance, and chose a seat three or four spots away. Their wait was short; soon, the professor arrived.

He was a middle-aged man, dressed in a well-tailored brown suit, with shoulder-length hair parted in the middle and a stylish beard. A gem flower adorned his collar. His demeanor suggested he was unfazed by the small class size. He casually placed the long wooden tray he carried on the ground and began his lecture.

Seraphina checked her course schedule, which read "Magic Formation Professor: Henry Hunet, Fourth-level Divine Magician". She was surprised to learn that one of the college's two fourth-level Divine Magicians taught magic formations. Was this what drew Margaret to the class?

"There are many types of magic arrays," Professor Henry began, "and their uses are broad. They can be employed for summoning, attacking, defending, and teleporting. But the most common use is prayer. While we often pray to the statue of the God of Light, the effectiveness is limited. Using materials to conduct a summoning ceremony yields the best results."

He gestured to the wooden tray. "These are some of the materials involved. White wax is a staple for all rituals. Sunflower essential oil, a ruler, and moonstone are used for prayers to the God of Light."

Seraphina smirked at the mention of sunflower essential oil—basically sunflower seed oil, which sounded more culinary than divine.

"To pray to the God of Darkness, you use black mandragora essential oil, obsidian, and graveyard soil."

"There are other gods, too," the professor continued, "like the God of Wisdom, the God of Seasons, and the God of Destiny. Each has unique preferences and materials. However, never mix materials haphazardly, or you might attract unknown evil spirits."

Seraphina listened intently. "Professor, what do we need to pray to the God of the Sea?"

"For the God of the Sea," Professor Henry replied, "you need sea crystal fragments, beds, and water."

Seraphina's mind went blank for a moment. Typical of the King of playboys—so flamboyant and extravagant in his ways. She couldn't help but chuckle inwardly and made a mental note to try the ritual later, curious about what might happen with such unique offerings.

"Now, let's attempt a prayer to the God of Darkness."

Seraphina and Margaret both raised their eyebrows in surprise. Seraphina's concern was deeper—if the summoning succeeded, she risked exposure. Her current persona was that of a northern girl with black hair and eyes.

"The Dark God is not an evil god," Professor Henry addressed their concerns earnestly. "While His name is taboo here in the southern continent, theology makes no distinction between faiths. Even the spell class covers black magic."

"Why not pray to the God of Light?" Seraphina asked.

"The God of Light is too conventional. I want to demonstrate something less common," Professor Henry replied, somewhat awkwardly.

Seraphina pursed her lips. Perhaps the professor had caught wind of the Holy See's internal matters and knew the God of Light was missing. But that wasn't the primary issue. The real danger lay in the potential success of the prayer, which would reveal her true identity.

She had just told the Dark God she hailed from the North, yet here she was in the southern continent's seminary with blonde hair.

Panic bubbled within her. The day was warm, yet she felt the chill of sweat.

She needed a plan, and quickly.

Professor Henry began to sprinkle essential oils around himself, forming a circle, and placed cemetery soil, white wax, a ruler, and moonstone at the circle's four corners.

"Professor," Seraphina interjected, feigning fear, "if you truly summon the Dark God, we might be in grave danger."

"No worries," Professor Henry assured as he continued his preparations. "This is merely a teaching demonstration, and the gods are unlikely to take notice. You shouldn't expect your prayers to actually succeed."

"You might really endanger us," Seraphina insisted, her tone urgent. "I've heard the Dark God can be particularly ruthless. And with it being dark in the North now, what if He gets angered by being disturbed and awakens..." Her voice trailed off as she covered her face with her hands, watching anxiously as Professor Henry began chanting prayers to the Dark God.

When he finished, the room remained unchanged. The curtains stayed still, sunlight streamed through the windows, and birds chirped merrily outside. Nothing happened.

Professor Henry chuckled. "See? I told you it wouldn't work. The gods are quite occupied; it would be unusual for them to respond. Since class isn't over, why don't you all give it a try? We shouldn't waste these materials."

Margaret rose gracefully, nodding. "I'll go first, then." With a slight rustle of her skirt, she approached the circle.

As she clasped her hands and murmured the prayer, Seraphina strained to listen. Margaret's voice was low, her words indistinct, but Seraphina had a nagging feeling that Margaret had deliberately altered the prayer.

Minutes passed, yet the room remained unchanged.

"This is normal," Professor Henry affirmed. "If the gods responded, that would be out of the ordinary." He turned to Seraphina with an encouraging smile. "Now it's your turn. We all failed, so there's no reason you should succeed."

Margaret smiled at Seraphina, her eyes glinting with a hint of challenge. "Don't worry, this ritual rarely succeeds."

Seraphina sensed an underlying message in Margaret's words, a subtle mockery: "I know why you're hesitant."

To Seraphina, her classmates seemed suspiciously like SSRs—someone of extraordinary capability. With Professor Henry being a fourth-level divine magician and Margaret possessing five beams of light, they fit the SSR profile. Avoiding the task might raise suspicions, so Seraphina decided to play along, just as Margaret had.

"What if I actually manage to summon something?" Seraphina asked, feigning uncertainty.

"If you're worried, just cover your face," Professor Henry advised lightly. "Even if you do summon something, it would likely be a mere wisp of consciousness. It won't remember your face."

Seeking a plausible excuse to conceal her identity, Seraphina donned her straw hat, pulling the brim low. She draped a shawl over her head, tying it securely around her neck, with a large sunflower embroidered on it obscuring her features. She resembled a beekeeper, and anyone who could identify her through this disguise would have to be incredibly perceptive.

Professor Henry and Margaret exchanged baffled glances.

With her disguise in place, Seraphina stepped into the circle. She was mentally prepared for nothing to happen. But as she uttered the first note of the chant, an unexpected gust of wind swept through the room, lifting the heavy velvet curtains as if they were banners.

The classroom dimmed abruptly. The atmosphere turned eerie and still, with white frost forming on the window frames. An unknown, awe-inspiring power filled the space.

Seraphina's eyes widened in disbelief as the unlit white wax at her feet flickered to life. Simultaneously, a narrow, beautiful eye materialized in the air, fixing its unblinking gaze on her.

Margaret's hands clenched into fists on her knees, shock flickering beneath her long lashes.

Professor Henry's face went pale, and he instinctively stepped back.

Such phenomena were unheard of; typically, the lighting of candles indicated a god had heard the prayer. But this eye... An eye signified the presence of a true deity.

Seraphina felt her heart race.

Stay calm, she told herself. It can't recognize me. Please......

"You summoned me?" The eyes floating above the classroom surveyed those below, their gaze cold and lazy—the unmistakable eyes of the Dark God, Cecil.

Under different circumstances, Seraphina might have been entranced by them, but now, she wished she could disappear entirely.

"Quick, make your wish," Professor Henry urged in a breathless whisper. He never imagined he would witness the appearance of a true god, but now was not the time to marvel.

As the girl foretold, it was indeed the witching hour in the North. Their relentless, perilous calls had roused the slumbering Dark God from his celestial nap.

And when you wake a deity with nothing but silence on your lips, well, you can only imagine the fate that awaits the summoner.

Professor Henry, caught between dread and disbelief, thought it prudent to hide his face. Was it too late for that? In his desperation, he ruffled his perfectly parted hair into a haphazard ghost style, hoping for some semblance of anonymity.

Margaret remained statuesque in her chair, eyes fixed downward, her hands clutching her skirt with such force her knuckles turned a ghostly white.

The trio stood there, in the eerie glow of that single, unblinking eye, like a scene straight out of a horror novel.

After a few agonizing seconds, Professor Henry, unable to bear the charged silence, whispered urgently, "Make your wish, quickly, or we might all meet our doom. Once you state your wish, He'll extinguish the candles, and this whole nightmare will be over."

In his haste, he forgot the precariousness of his ghost disguise. His hair slipped sideways, revealing his face.

"Blast this infernal smoothness," he muttered, ducking his head with a curse.

Seraphina, meanwhile, was a bundle of nerves, terrified that one wrong move might expose her true self. She had no grand desires, no elaborate requests. Her sole wish was for the Dark God to make a swift exit.

Lowering her gaze, she pinched her throat to alter her voice. "Great Dark God, I summoned you. My wish is for your good health and happiness. That's it—please, blow out the candles."

Cecil: "..."

What an odd bunch. He had heard a familiar voice and thought the little girl from the North might be in trouble, so he decided to investigate.

Tsk, it's not like he cared for that girl. She'd left without a name, nor had she checked on him afterward. Not that he wanted her to. His curiosity was piqued to see what she would summon him for.

Perhaps it was the Northern cold; people might act irrationally at night. Cecil glanced lazily at those below, deciding to vanish without further inquiry into the peculiar wish. He'd encountered many summoning attempts before, where shock left people speechless. He had no time to linger.

With a soft "crackling" sound, the white wax at Seraphina's feet extinguished.

As the god's presence faded, the warm air rushed back in. The curtains fell with a "plop," the frost on the window frames melted into droplets, sunlight poured in again, and birds resumed their song.

The color returned to the three people's faces, and the tension in their throats eased.

"This is incredible," Professor Henry murmured, picking up the black mandragora essential oil bottle. "What brand is this? How did it summon a true god? Or was it the quality of this obsidian? Whose tomb did I gather this soil from? Could it be an ancestor of the Dark God?"

While Professor Henry rambled on, Princess Margaret regained her composure. She turned to Seraphina with a warm smile, "That was terrifying. I didn't expect you to truly summon a god. This is something I'll never forget."

"I didn't expect it either. But perhaps it wasn't entirely my doing," Seraphina replied, removing her veil and hat, casually adjusting her hair. "Your earlier attempts might have stirred Him."

"Well, that's possible," Margaret conceded with a graceful nod, gesturing toward the door with a flick of her wrist. The sound of the bell signaling the end of class echoed through the tower, a welcome reminder that the ordeal was over.

She gave Seraphina a knowing look, her eyes twinkling with a mix of relief and amusement. "Shall we?" Margaret's invitation was as smooth as her composure, effortlessly steering them toward their next adventure—or perhaps a well-deserved escape.

"I saw your test results the other day," Margaret said with a smile that was equal parts friendly and mischievous. "I'm thrilled we ended up choosing the same course on our first day."

Seraphina, maintaining her composure, replied, "I saw an article about a museum exhibit on theology in the newspaper yesterday. It featured an ancient magic array relic. It looked fascinating, so I chose it. Honestly, I should've probably gone for the spell class instead."

Margaret's smile didn't waver. "Oh, is there such an exhibit? Relics don't really pique my interest, though. Many haven't been deciphered yet, so their value is limited. I'd rather dive into a book... Oh, sorry, give me a moment, I see someone I know."

Someone familiar?

Following Margaret's enthusiastic gaze, Seraphina's heart skipped a beat. Wasn't that the God of Light, Milos, himself? Had he returned to Burton?

As ever, Milos was impeccably handsome, his eyes cool and distant, the collar of his shirt concealing his Adam's apple with a chaste severity. He was wrapped up tighter than a winter's day, befitting the God of Light, whose conduct was as straight as a ruler.

"Lord Milos," Margaret chirped as she approached, "I'm delighted to see you again."

Seraphina's expression turned even more peculiar as she observed their interaction.

Yet Milos seemed uninterested in engaging with Margaret. He acknowledged her with a nod and cast a casual glance at Seraphina over Margaret's shoulder—a glance that was nothing more than a token of recognition. Seraphina knew she held no special place in the God of Light's heart.

"The museum has a new theology exhibit," Margaret continued cheerfully. "I'm intrigued by the ancient ruins featured. Bishop Saen has always admired your theological prowess. If I could attend the exhibit with you, I'm sure my understanding of magic arrays would deepen."

Seraphina: "..."

She was witnessing a masterclass in opportunistic learning.

"Sorry, I don't have time," Milos declined coolly.

"What a shame." Margaret's eyes flickered with mild embarrassment before she rallied with understanding, "That's alright, perhaps another time."

Milos nodded, then turned and made his way toward the dean's tower with purposeful strides.

"I was hoping to invite him to join us at the exhibit," Margaret turned back to Seraphina with a regretful look. "Since he's busy, perhaps we could..."

"Sorry, I don't have time either," Seraphina replied with a smile that didn't quite reach her eyes.

Margaret: "..."

"I'll be off, Your Highness." Seraphina gathered her skirts, politely excused herself, and swiftly headed toward the college gates.

She truly didn't have time—not with just a day and a half left to live. Those precious fourteen points were her lifeline, not to be squandered.

Ignoring Earl George's carriage, Seraphina took a detour down a different street, hailing a taxi to Bessen Road, the bustling commercial hub of the South District. She was on a mission to acquire the finest materials for her god-summoning preparations. Additionally, she needed to check the exhibition hall's hours, planning to exploit the little white sheep's generosity for all it was worth.

***

Seraphina had taken up a watchful position in the back garden. Just beyond the waist-high fence was Bishop Saen's garden, where Milos's quaint white residence stood. She had a strong suspicion that Milos had simply used the dean as an excuse to brush off Princess Margaret. Even if he truly had business with the dean, it wouldn't take long.

Sure enough, shortly after she settled on the bench, she heard footsteps approaching from the other side of the fence.

"Lord Milos," Seraphina called sweetly from across the fence, her voice like honey on a summer's day.

Milos glanced over. The girl before him was a vision in her goose-yellow silk dress, her blonde hair cascading like a golden waterfall. Her bright blue eyes sparkled with mischief, and her snow-white arms rested playfully on the fence. She was like a deer, bounding cheerfully from the forest, full of life and spirited energy.

He hesitated for a moment, then walked over to her.

"My little golden ball fell over there. Could you please help me retrieve it? I've been waiting forever for someone to pass by," she said with a charming smile, pointing to the small, hollow gold-plated ball lying near his feet.

It was a toy favored by the ladies of the court, often tossed for amusement, and sometimes adorned with precious gems. Milos bent down, picked it up, and handed it to her.

"Thank you so much," Seraphina said, reaching out. Her fingers brushed against his ever so lightly, a fleeting touch like a dragonfly skimming the surface of a pond or a butterfly kissing a flower.

Milos's lashes fluttered at the touch, and he quickly withdrew his hand. Seraphina, however, reclaimed her hand even faster, causing the ball to drop at her feet. She let out a soft complaint, her expression so innocently accusatory that it almost seemed as if Milos had been the one to initiate contact.

Expressionless, Milos met her gaze.

Seraphina stooped to pick up the fallen ball. "Why don't we visit the magic array exhibition together, Lord Milos?" she proposed.

Milos remained silent. His gaze drifted over her fair neck, revealed as she bent over, and the graceful outline of her shoulder blades beneath the thin fabric.

"Please?" She blinked, her lashes fluttering like the wings of a butterfly—a playful, innocent plea.

Still, Milos said nothing, his eyes fixed intently on her face.

"Come on, aren't we friends? Friends should stick together," Seraphina insisted, her voice sweetly cajoling as she twirled the golden ball.

"Stand up straight, no more twisting around," Milos finally replied, his voice tinged with a hint of exasperation.

"Will you join me if I stand up straight?" she asked, a playful challenge in her voice.

"Yes," he nodded, adding, "Stand straight and walk properly."

"Alright, then hold this for me," Seraphina said, handing over the golden ball with a smile as enticing as Eve offering the apple.

Although Milos was baffled by the connection between the golden ball and standing up straight, he accepted it without question.

Seraphina scaled the horizontal bar of the fence with the grace of a cat on a mission. The golden ball, truth be told, had absolutely no connection to standing upright; it was more of a pesky inconvenience as she maneuvered up and down. But now that Milos had finally agreed, she was determined to be at his side without a moment's hesitation.

Milos's eyes widened slightly, watching Seraphina scale the fence with the agility of a cat. She leapt down towards him with a radiant grin, her long, seaweed-like hair swirling around her like a golden halo.

For a fleeting moment, Milos was caught off guard by her brightness, her smile as dazzling as sunlight. Instinctively, he opened his arms to catch her, enveloping her soft, sweet-scented form.

"Host, five points," Little N's voice chimed in, transforming into a comically frantic squeal, like a rubber chicken in the midst of the unexpected embrace.

12

It was 3:30 in the afternoon, and the museum would be closing in just half an hour.

The sky was brooding, the wind whipping raindrops here and there like a temperamental artist. The threat of a downpour loomed large. Visitors began to drift away, and pedestrians scurried home, anxious to avoid being ensnared by the impending storm.

Seraphina meandered through the exhibition hall at her own pace.

The glass cabinets glimmered under the crystal lights, their contents—gray, ancient theological artifacts—seeming almost to murmur secrets from the past. Notes, divination tools, and rusted staffs lay dormant, exuding an air of history.

She examined them with a patience that belied her eagerness, while Milos followed with a calm demeanor.

The hug they shared in the garden had been like a pebble dropped into a lake: ripples spread and then vanished. Yet, even when ripples fade, the pebble remains. Seraphina knew that with enough pebbles, she could change the landscape entirely. Opportunities, after all, were hers to create.

"While learning about magic arrays today, I remembered the museum ad I saw in the paper," Seraphina said with a grin, stopping in front of the ancient magic array exhibit. "This place is enormous," she marveled.

Her fingers brushed over the description on the plaque, and her eyes widened in surprise. It was an ancient teleportation array. Was luck on her side so soon?

She pondered for a moment before turning to Milos, "Have teleportation arrays existed since ancient times? What's changed about them over the years?"

Milos nodded. "They're simpler now, but still challenging. Gathering materials is tough, and the failure rate is high. That's why most people stick to carriages, ships, or trains for long distances. Teleportation is an expensive affair."

"I have the materials. Could you teach me how to make one, Lord Milos?"

The maiden's eyes sparkled with a hint of apprehension at the thought of being refused, and she fiddled nervously with the folds of her skirt.

Milos hesitated, then nodded in agreement.

Seraphina's face lit up with a radiant smile, already planning to gather the materials with gold by tomorrow.

"I'll be moving out of Bishop Saen's house in two days."

"Eh?" Seraphina asked, surprised. "Where are you moving to? Are you leaving Burton?"

"I'm staying in Burton for now," Milos replied gently. "This journey helped me retrieve some old assets. I asked Bishop Saen to buy a house for me."

"I see," Seraphina nodded. It was a pity to lose the advantage of proximity, but visiting him without Saen's watchful eyes could yield some... interesting opportunities.

"Where should I find you once I have the materials?"

"72 Wisteria Road."

Seraphina committed the address to memory. She knew the street well—a prestigious area in Burton, where homes came with gardens and stables, not to mention a hefty price tag.

It seemed the God of Light had foreseen his own injuries and prepared a haven. What else, besides wealth, had he left for himself?

As she pondered, lightning cracked the sky, illuminating the museum's grand arched windows. Thunder rumbled, and raindrops the size of beans began to pelt down. The air turned thick with moisture, draping the museum in a watery gloom.

Seraphina glanced at the clock on the wall. It was four o'clock—the museum's closing time. Before she could ask Milos about their return, another flash of lightning struck, snuffing out all the candles. Darkness enveloped the exhibition hall as if night had descended in an instant.

Outside, the street fell eerily silent. The rain's patter on windows, the rumble of carriages, the chatter of museum staff—all vanished.

In the oppressive quiet and darkness, Seraphina instinctively moved closer to Milos. He gently pulled her behind him, holding her wrist with one hand while channeling spiritual energy into the small golden ball with the other. The ball flared to life, casting a brilliant light.

Seraphina blinked in astonishment. Magic, truly, was limitless. The once-ornamental golden ball had transformed into a glowing beacon.

While the light pierced the central darkness of the hall, the glass cases, windows, chandeliers, and display boards remained shrouded in shadow, unreachable by the light.

"Lord Milos..." she called out, her voice tinged with unease.

"Don't worry. I promise I'll get you out of here safely," Milos assured her, his gaze steady as a rock amid the storm.

Seraphina breathed a sigh of relief and instinctively moved closer to him.

But from the shadows, a figure emerged—a tall, pale young man with three pairs of massive black wings unfurling like a dark omen. He rose into the air, his eyes fixed on them with the morbid curiosity of the undead.

A fallen angel. Seraphina's heart skipped a beat as her grip tightened on Milos's arm.

Why did her luck always seem to run like this? When she was with the Dark God, the white birdmen were hot on her heels; now, with the God of Light, it was the black birdmen's turn to give chase.

The white birdmen? They were all about keeping things prim and proper, steering clear of any funny business. But the black birdmen? Oh, they were a fearless bunch, throwing caution—and decorum—to the wind.

She wondered how much power Milos retained after sealing most of his divine strength.

"Are you Milos? Even your name matches His," the fallen angel sneered. "Whether you are or not, you won't leave here today."

Milos merely smiled, a soft, confident smile. "I beg to differ."

The fallen angel's expression darkened, and his sinister aura seemed to rival even his master's.

Seraphina felt the murderous intent in the air prickling her skin. She was about to ask Little N to teleport them out when Milos pulled her close, whisking them from the center of the hall to a corner in the blink of an eye.

A "bang" echoed as the spot they'd just vacated exploded in a burst of dark green light, the stone pillars reduced to dust in the swirling chaos.

Milos's eyes narrowed slightly, and he crushed the glowing golden ball in his hand. The fragments scattered like stardust, rising and transforming into a cascade of golden lines that filled the air. As these golden lines passed through Seraphina, they felt warm—like sunlight bathing her skin.

But the fallen angel was less fortunate. His scream pierced the air as the golden threads shredded through one of his wings and punctured his body, leaving a trail of acrid smoke. His form flickered and retreated into the shadows, vanishing from sight.

Seraphina's eyes widened in wonder. Even with his divine power restrained, Milos could still cripple an angel.

She clutched his hand, ready for another swift escape. "Mi..." Her words faltered, surprise flickering in her eyes.

She glanced down at her hand, now stained with vivid red. Milos's blood. The exertion had taken its toll on him.

"Hush," Milos murmured, gently pressing a clean finger to her lips. The brief touch made him withdraw, a soft, fleeting gesture.

"Host, add one point," Little N's voice chimed in, ever the observer.

Seraphina: "..."

Milos's gaze shifted upward, his expression growing more serious. "There are more of them."

Seconds later, five ominous figures appeared in the air, their massive black wings casting long shadows. Their determined expressions made it clear they intended to bury the suspected God of Light here, even at the cost of their own lives.

"What a persistent bunch," Milos mused aloud, his tone calm. He turned to Seraphina, asking, "Will your parents worry if you're not home tonight?"

"Huh?"

"We might be away for a few days," he explained, as if they weren't facing a group of avenging angels.

"I'm sorry to interrupt," the leading fallen angel, Azale, interjected with irritation, "but you seem to be ignoring us."

"Let's not waste words, Lord Azale," another angel growled, "I want to crack his skull open and see if the bell tolls for a fallen god."

"We should wait for our master," Azale drawled, "Only a god can slay another god without facing a curse. If he truly is who we think..."

The mention of the Dark God's possible arrival startled Seraphina. She quickly shook Milos's arm, "My parents aren't here. Just an uncle."

Milos nodded, "I'll explain to him when we return."

"Think you're too late for an escape?" Azale taunted, his wings whipping up a whirlwind that sent floor tiles hurtling toward them.

Seraphina blinked, and in a flash, she found herself with Milos in the heart of an ancient ruin.

"Look at them," one of the fallen angels sneered, "thinking they can use that relic to escape. Does that dusty old thing even work?"

"Not unless you're a god," another chimed in. "No one else can coax magic from a fossil." The fallen angels laughed, circling in on the ruins like wolves closing in on prey.

"Hold onto me," Milos whispered.

Seraphina blinked, momentarily caught off guard.

"Apologies, the space here is quite... limited," Milos explained with a hint of a smile.

"Oh, no problem at all," Seraphina replied, grinning widely as she wrapped her arms around his waist, her head nestling against his chest.

The sweet floral scent clinging to her made Milos's heart race like a runaway horse.

"Host, one point," Little N's voice cheerily announced in Seraphina's mind. She couldn't help but smirk, tightening her grip slightly.

"And another point."

"Alright, hold on tight," Milos instructed.

"With great pleasure."

"Another point."

This was turning into a point-earning spree.

Milos's eyelashes fluttered, a flicker of regret crossing his mind for having reminded her to hold on tight. Catching his breath, he focused, squeezing the blood from his wound onto the teleportation array.

As soon as his blood touched the ancient symbols, a long-forgotten hum filled the air, like awakening an ancient machine. The teleportation array flared to life, casting an intense light that banished the shadows from the exhibition hall.

The fallen angels stared, dumbfounded, as their quarry vanished before their eyes.

Ten seconds later, one of them finally spoke, "I think he might actually be the God of Light."

"I doubt it," another countered.

"Why's that?"

"Would the God of Light allow himself to be hugged by a woman? I hear He's never even been bitten by a female mosquito."

"True," the fallen angels nodded in agreement. "Just like our master. The master doesn't allow hugs and has never been bitten by a female mosquito."

"Correction: no one dares hug the master, and no mosquito dares bite," Azale stated.

"Hush, the master is here."

A soft "pop" sounded in the air, and a long, lazy eye appeared, surveying the scene.

The once-chatty fallen angels fell silent, their boisterous conversation extinguished in the presence of their master.

13

The narrow, dark eyes surveyed the scene with cool indifference, prompting the fallen angels to kneel, their heads bowed in reverent fear.

Azale, summoning the last of his courage, spoke up, "Master, the one suspected to be the God of Light has used the ancient ruins to escape."

Cecil, seemingly unfazed, allowed a lazy smile to tug at his lips. "Naturally, you can't trap someone capable of wielding such relics. Even as a mortal, his power is beyond your comprehension."

A flicker of awe crossed Azale's eyes. So, the master had orchestrated all this to force the other party's hand, to reveal his true identity.

"Return for now," Cecil instructed. "The formation here will soon dissipate, and the Church of Light will notice the disturbance."

"Yes, Master."

As Cecil began to vanish, a thought seemed to strike him. "The house in Kvina County... No visitors yet?"

Azale hesitated, then shook his head.

"I see..." Cecil murmured, his voice barely a whisper.

***

As the light faded, Seraphina remained clinging to Milos's waist, savoring the feel of his solid form beneath her fingers. His strength was palpable—surely no problem for him to crank out 10,000 push-ups.

Milos glanced down, tapping her forehead lightly to nudge her back. "We've arrived."

"Oh," Seraphina said, releasing him with a hint of reluctance. "That was quick."

They stood in a misty forest, the air filled with the scent of wildflowers and grasses. In the distance, green mountains loomed, shrouded in the milky fog.

"Are we still in the South Continent?" Seraphina asked, looking around.

"Depenta Valley," Milos replied.

Seraphina blinked in surprise. Depenta Valley was indeed part of the South Continent, but on the verge of its borders. Beyond lay the Candis Mountains, and past them, the realm of the sea god.

Teleportation arrays usually responded to the user's subconscious desire—so why had Milos chosen such an out-of-the-way spot?

Milos surveyed the misty forest with an easygoing demeanor, then picked a direction and started walking, prompting Seraphina to fall in step beside him. "You seem to know this place well?" she asked, curiosity lacing her voice.

"My last long journey ended here," Milos replied, his tone casual yet tinged with something deeper.

Seraphina's surprise deepened. Of all places, she hadn't expected Milos to lead her to where he might have stashed his wealth.

"But why... did you choose this place?" she pressed.

"Because it's far enough," Milos said with a light smile. "I doubt the fallen angels would bother chasing us here."

Ah, so that was it. With his memory lost, Depenta Valley might be the only place name Milos recalled.

"We'll stay a day," Milos added as he walked. "I'll construct a new teleportation array before heading back to Burton."

"Do you have the materials?" Seraphina asked, a bit surprised.

"I have wealth," Milos replied with a chuckle.

Wealth? Seraphina's lips twitched with intrigue. Was she about to witness the God of Light's treasure trove? It was an unexpected turn of events.

As they made their way forward, the sun hung low in the sky, casting a dusky veil over the landscape. The thick summer grass obscured any clear path, complicating their route.

Milos pushed aside vines and pressed down the grass, making it easier for Seraphina to follow. His injured hand, though no longer bleeding profusely, was scratched anew by the grass, and fresh drops of blood began to fall.

Seeing Milos's injury, Seraphina quickly untied her skirt belt. "Lord Milos," she called out, rushing over with a determined look. Milos raised an eyebrow in surprise as she deftly began wrapping the belt around his hand.

"Just for now, until we find somewhere to properly treat it," she insisted, bending over to carefully secure the makeshift bandage. Her fingers worked gently but efficiently, and Milos found himself watching her with a new light in his eyes.

His typical stoic expression softened as he observed her serious demeanor and the way she fumbled slightly with the woolen fabric, like a cat tangled in yarn.

"Host, another one point to your favorability," whispered Little N.

Seraphina: "..."

In this tender moment, Seraphina mused over her accumulating "wealth"—a grand total of 19 points. Surely, she was quite the affluent one now, at least in the realm of favorability.

With Milos's hand tended to, they pressed on. After an hour, they stopped outside a massive cave. The interior was visible from the entrance, a shaft of light pouring in from a gap above, illuminating the swirling dust particles.

Seraphina frowned, feeling an inexplicable unease. The cave seemed to possess an uncanny ability to see through her every facade.

"Is this the place you mentioned, Lord Milos?" she asked with a wry smile.

Milos didn't answer right away. Seraphina noticed his demeanor had shifted—his once warm eyes now held a glacial indifference, as if he'd donned a cloak of ancient aloofness.

"What do you think?" he replied lightly, as if he were merely asking her opinion on a slice of cake.

He cast an illumination spell, and the cave walls glistened like wet tar. "A bit damp, thanks to a nearby waterfall. Quite the natural deterrent. I wonder how I found this place before…"

Seraphina's heart tightened. Whatever was happening to Milos, she knew she had to stop it. The God of Light couldn't awaken—not yet.

"Lord Milos," she said urgently, her voice laced with sincerity, "There's nothing here. Didn't you say you took your wealth? Let's go to a nearby village and get your wound treated."

"Treat my wounds?" Milos echoed absently, his gaze fixed on a particular spot in the cave.

"Yes, right here." She squeezed his hand, causing blood to seep through the light yellow silk ribbon.

The pain seemed to bring Milos back to the present. He glanced at Seraphina, a flicker of purpose returning to his eyes. "Just a moment. I need to collect some materials for the teleportation array, then we can leave."

"I really think we should go now," Seraphina urged, a determined edge to her voice.

Milos merely smiled and turned, walking to the cave's end. He pressed his injured palm against the wall, his blood absorbed like water into a sponge.

With a rumbling sound, an archway emerged from the stone, spilling forth a brilliant light, like the sun itself had taken residence behind the door.

"Follow me," Milos instructed, pushing the wall open. The light intensified, and Seraphina felt a shiver of foreboding as something ancient and powerful awakened.

She knew it was there, and she had to find it before Milos.

They stepped inside, revealing a cavern far larger than she'd imagined. A stone staircase descended into the unknown, surrounded by treasures so rare that stones overshadowed gold coins, which pooled at her feet like a lavish carpet.

"Let's see where the materials are," Milos muttered, uninterested in the gold, intent only on his task.

Seraphina's gaze roamed, searching for whatever had sparked her intuition.

A cold, piercing gaze seemed to cut through the light, making her shiver. Shielding her eyes with her hand, she squinted toward a corner cluttered with boxes. It was there, she was certain of it. Now, she just had to reach it before Milos did.

She glanced over at Milos, who was bent over, focused on something with his back to her.

Taking her chance, Seraphina lifted her skirt slightly and dashed toward the object that had caught her attention. Her hurried movements echoed through the quiet cave, the metallic clinks betraying her actions to Milos, who glanced over curiously.

In an instant, Seraphina's expression shifted to feigned curiosity. She adopted a casual tourist's demeanor as she sauntered toward the corner, all innocence and exploration. Satisfied, Milos returned to his task.

The closer Seraphina got to her target, the more the air seemed to chill and still. Her teeth chattered; her nails pressed crescents into her palms as she fought to keep her movements steady.

What could it be? Was it a gem-encrusted box? A scepter? Perhaps a gold salt bottle?

No, none of those...

Her eyes focused, calming as they landed on a spot where gold coins lay buried.

There it was.

She reached in, fingers brushing against something unexpected. Carefully, she extracted it—a letter, parchment worn and inked with dark cursive: "God of Destiny pays tribute to light."

Whatever its significance, Seraphina quickly crumpled it and shoved it into her bodice. For a fleeting moment, she imagined she heard the letter emit a tiny scream.

Whether from being stashed away or crushed into a ball, the ominous power surrounding it vanished, leaving her wondering why Milos hadn't discovered it before. She glanced at him; he was still engrossed in gathering materials, oblivious.

Milos maintained the disciplined habits he'd honed during his time as a god. Every action had a purpose, and he never squandered time on anything unnecessary. When he focused on collecting gold coins, his attention was solely on them. Similarly, when gathering materials, he paid no heed to the glittering temptation of gold. It was this focused efficiency that kept him from exploring the corner that might have intrigued him on any other occasion.

Having secured the last of his materials, Milos stood up, his coat pocket now bulging. "Ready to go? Did you find anything you liked?" he asked as he approached.

"No," Seraphina replied with a smile, hiding her secret. The item she fancied was already snug in her bra.

***

"I'll just pop to the bathroom," Seraphina said, grabbing a half-lit yellow candle and telling Milos before heading out and pushing open the door.

They were in a quaint, run-down hotel at the foot of Depenta Valley, boasting a grand total of two rooms—one already occupied, leaving them to share the other.

Nighttime money schemes could wait; Seraphina's mind was fixed on deciphering the letter.

The bathroom was down the corridor, shared and slightly shabby. Seraphina pushed the door open, set the candle on the sink, and eagerly pulled out the letter.

The envelope was already opened, indicating someone had read it. The reader? Clearly the God of Light himself, before he embraced mortality.

Under the dim, flickering light, she unfolded the letter and read:

"Please forgive my delayed reply. My apple tree has been infested with worms, and you know how vital apples are to me. I can't glimpse fate without them. Still, I've sorted out your destiny. No surprises, your choice was wise."

"Becoming mortal is the best way to conserve your power. The awakening clues you left are excellent, perfectly crafted. But beware of women—the sweeter they seem, the deadlier they can be. Fate suggests they might be your downfall."

The advice was sound, but alas, the habits of the God of Light had caused it to be overlooked.

Seraphina smirked and held the letter to the candle's flame.

14

After dealing with the letter from the God of Destiny, Seraphina washed off the lingering scent of smoke from her skin.

The letter had served as a stark warning: when the God of Light eventually regains his memory, he'll recall not just the letter but every detail of this past.

If by then their relationship was only marginally more than that of strangers, she'd lose any chance of getting close to Milos. The God of Light, under the watchful eye of fate, would never allow himself to be ensnared.

She scrutinized her reflection in the mirror. The cold water had washed away the dust, but it had also left her looking paler. With deft hands, she broke a twig from the window, lit it, blew it out, and used it to darken the ends of her eyebrows. A touch of rouge cream revived her cheeks and lips, bringing warmth back to her complexion. She discarded the bustle, letting her skirt fall naturally, accentuating her curves.

Her artistry was subtle, painting her beauty with a sweet, honeyed allure. The mirror now reflected a girl with rosy cheeks and eyes that were both innocent and seductive.

Satisfied with her appearance, Seraphina took the candle and stepped out of the bathroom. The old floorboards groaned beneath her feet, and the flickering candlelight cast her shadow in a graceful dance along the corridor.

As she pushed open the door to the room, her gaze fell on Milos by the window. Despite the exhaustion from battles and the long journey, he stood with his usual elegance, his posture upright, his expression as cool as the night outside. He turned at the sound of the door.

Seraphina, drying her hair with a towel, tilted her head slightly, causing her collar to slip and reveal a smooth collarbone and delicate shoulder.

Milos's usually steady gaze flickered, betraying a moment of distraction.

Not wanting the moment to linger, Seraphina quickly adjusted her collar, playing it off as a mere accident. "I need some ointment," she announced, hanging the towel on the door. She picked up a tray from a low cabinet and settled into the armchair next to Milos, reaching to untie the ribbon around his hand.

"I can manage," Milos said with a touch of resistance, moving to another chair.

Seraphina retracted her hand, leaning back to watch him struggle with the knot. Each loop she'd tied had resulted in a formidable knot, not easily undone.

She watched for a moment, then couldn't resist suggesting, "Why not just make it vanish, give it a..."

"Disappearing spell," Milos interrupted lightly. "If it were an ordinary bandage, I might. But this is your skirt—I intend to return it to you."

"Ah, I see," Seraphina nodded, grinning. "Let me help, then. I'm quite capable with these two hands of mine."

This time, Milos didn't argue. The stubborn knot had bested him after all.

As she leaned in to help, Milos caught the faint scent of roses from her hair, her cheeks as rosy as the blooms, her lips like the softest petals, exuding an intoxicating allure.

He turned his gaze resolutely to the old floral wallpaper, as if it held the most fascinating secrets of the universe.

Seraphina carefully untied half of the belt, revealing part of Milos's palm. Her head bowed, she focused on the stubborn knot, her breath warm against his fingers. Those elegant, slender fingers couldn't help but twitch slightly under her gentle ministrations.

"Host, one point."

Seraphina couldn't suppress a small, satisfied smile.

As she painstakingly worked the knot loose, Milos's expression grew increasingly tense. The tingling sensation on the back of his hand was unsettling, like a long-held taboo being tenderly unraveled. The sweet, floral scent of the girl beside him was like a serpent, slowly coiling around him.

"One point for the host," Little N chirped, sounding almost smug. "And another point! I'm a ruthless scoring machine. Yet another point. Host, are you planning to dawdle until tomorrow? Can't you tell my point-counting is slowing down? At this rate, even the God of Light will be lulled into numbness."

"I'm doing my best to speed up, but..." Seraphina muttered, brows furrowed in concentration. She hadn't quite grasped how merciless she'd been, tying so many intricate knots. Wouldn't it be just her luck to get ensnared in her own web?

Finally, after what felt like an eternity, she managed to untie the last knot. With practiced care, Seraphina cleaned Milos's wound, applied ointment, and bandaged his hand. She'd done this before with the God of Darkness and was quite adept at it.

"All done," she announced, tying a neat bow on the back of Milos's hand. Standing up, she stretched and wandered over to the mirror to dry her hair.

The sweet scent of roses faded, and Milos found himself staring at his bandaged hand. The numbness had gone, but a warmth lingered in his body. Rising, he headed for the door. "I'll go to the bathroom. You can take the bed; I'll be fine on the armchair."

"Host, are you planning to fleece him for more points later?" Little N inquired, with a hint of mischief.

"No, I've hit twenty-three points now. I'm saving them up for the little black sheep. If I gather enough, I can upgrade you," Seraphina replied, flopping onto the bed like a ragdoll."This subtle approach is truly a tightrope walk. I'm constantly worried he'll catch on to what I'm doing, yet equally concerned it might be too subtle to earn any points at all."

By the time Milos returned, Seraphina was sprawled on the bed, a thin blanket covering her, her pale arms peeping out. She was just about to bid him goodnight when he approached, his expression cool and unreadable. Lowering his gaze, he gently pulled the blanket up to her neck.

Seraphina: "..."

"Goodnight," Milos said simply, settling into the armchair and gazing at the fireplace with an indifferent look.

Seraphina pulled her arm out again, turned to face him, and smiled sweetly. "Goodnight, Lord Milos."

***

As the night deepened, the soft, even rhythm of Seraphina's breathing filled the room.

Perhaps it was her less-than-stellar sleeping posture, or maybe it was just the warmth of the room, but Seraphina had managed to sprawl herself across the blanket. As she turned over, her loose collar slipped down to her arms, revealing her entire shoulders and a generous expanse of her snow-white back.

Her long, seaweed-like hair clung messily to her cheeks, and a thin sheen of sweat on her forehead gave her complexion an even more delicate, rosy hue.

Across the room, Milos reclined in the armchair, maintaining his usual calm demeanor. His chin rested on his hand as he watched the girl sleep soundly on the bed.

He'd already covered her with a blanket three times, even wrapping her snugly once, like a croissant. Yet, each time, she kicked it off, sprawling out like a pancake.

In his mind's eye, an image surfaced: an angel draped in half a bed sheet, reminiscent of a classic oil painting. Yet even the angel, with her arms and legs artfully exposed in that timeless painting, hadn't stirred him quite like this.

She was like an irresistible strawberry cream cake, her metaphorical wrapping peeling away, practically holding up a fork and spoon, daring him with a playful "Come on, savor me."

Milos cast his eyes downward, his gaze landing on the blood-stained skirt beside him. With careful hands, he picked it up and smoothed it out. A simple flick of his fingers summoned a pure light that cascaded over the fabric, restoring it to its pristine state.

Raising the skirt to eye level, he scrutinized it from every angle, noting a few stubborn specks that refused to disappear. He repeated the cleansing light until the skirt gleamed, immaculate once more.

A dull "pah" echoed in the room, and Milos looked up to see the blanket on the floor, the result of another kick from the sleeping girl.

He retrieved the blanket and gently draped it over her once more, his gaze lingering as it journeyed from her slender ankles to her exposed back, along the elegant curve of her butterfly bones, up her graceful neck, and finally to her inviting lips, so vivid and tempting. She lay there with such trust, as if he could do anything he pleased.

Yet, he'd never crossed that line, and a quiet voice in his mind reminded him it wouldn't be right.

He moistened his lips, parched from the tension, and tucked the blanket securely from her chin to her feet. But as he turned away, her arm snaked out once again. With swift precision, he caught her wrist, gently tucked it back under the blanket, and ensured she was snugly covered once more.

The girl muttered softly in her sleep, her eyes tightly shut.

Milos returned to the armchair, his fingers tingling with the memory of her delicate, sweet scent—an aroma that seemed to seep into his very bones.

It was a long night, and sleep eluded him.

"Host, add three points," Little N chimed in.

Hmm... what's going on?

Uncomfortable.

It felt like something held her tightly, restricting her every move.

Uncomfortable and hot.

Seraphina struggled to lift her heavy eyelids, the old ceiling coming into view as her sleepy eyes adjusted. Sunlight streamed through the window, and she remembered she was in an inn at the foot of Depenta Valley.

Dawn had arrived.

She attempted to shift, only to find herself strangely immobilized, as if she'd been ensnared in a rubber hose.

"Awake already?" Little N's cheerful voice chimed in her mind. "You scored three points just by sleeping last night. Who knew you could earn points while lying down?"

Seraphina didn't respond, instead raising her head to assess the situation.

She found herself wrapped snugly in a blanket, rolled up like a spring roll.

To achieve this level of wrapping, one would have to place her at the edge of the blanket and roll her quite thoroughly.

"The handiwork of the God of Light," Little N commented. "Perhaps he was worried you'd get cold."

"It's summer," Seraphina said with a touch of exasperation.

She wriggled free from the blanket, feeling both amused and irked. The image of Milos rolling her up because he couldn't resist temptation flickered in her mind.

Once she freed herself, she stood barefoot in front of the dressing mirror. The girl staring back had a hint of annoyance in her eyes, her cheeks flushed as if she'd had a sip too many. Her skirt was damp with sweat, clinging tightly to her curves.

Seraphina inspected her reflection, thoughtfully adjusting the hair plastered to her cheeks. She had plans for this disheveled look.

Footsteps echoed in the corridor, prompting her to quickly remove her outer skirt, leaving only her corset and petticoats. The lacy corset connected to the layers of petticoats covered most of her, revealing just her snow-white shoulders and arms.

Milos entered with bread and tea, momentarily startled by her flustered appearance. His gaze flickered downward, lingering for a brief moment before he averted his eyes, "I brought breakfast. Once we eat, we can head back to Burton."

He walked past her with an impassive expression and set the tray on the low table.

"Host, add one point."

Tsk, if it weren't for the system pointing it out, she might have believed he was as unyielding as an iceberg.

Seraphina picked up her outer skirt, slipping it on. "Did you finish the teleportation array?"

Milos took a sip of tea. "I did. I didn't wake you because you seemed so peaceful. Once we're back in Burton, I'll teach you how to make one."

She adjusted her skirt, feeling a bit uneasy. "Honestly, I didn't feel like I slept well. I woke up this morning all wrapped up in the blanket and drenched in sweat."

"I rolled you up," Milos admitted, meeting her eyes. "You tossed in your sleep, and your clothes were slipping. I thought it best not to stare and covered you with the blanket. But I didn't account for the heat, sorry." He waved his right hand, conjuring a warm beam of light that enveloped Seraphina.

Seraphina felt a comforting warmth surround her, drying her clothes instantly and making them fall back into place.

"Forget it, I forgive you." Seraphina gave her skirt a modest tug, flashed a smile that could charm a dragon, and plopped herself down next to Milos. "We're friends, after all, aren't we?"

"Friends?" Milos echoed, his voice soft as the flutter of a moth's wings.

"Isn't that right?" Seraphina rested her chin on one hand, pointing at Milos and then herself. "Friends should stick together; we're the closest companions. Think about it, I was the one who stayed with you while fleeing those fallen angels, and we escaped here together."

"Your definition of 'friend' is unusual." Milos lowered his eyes, scooping half a spoonful of sugar into his tea and stirring it elegantly. "Bishop Saen also claimed to be my friend. But he has no intention of sticking with me, nor does he entertain the idea of having normal communication with me."

Seraphina blinked, momentarily surprised. Oh, normal communication. That must refer to their little accidental lip-lock when they first met—a bit of a diversionary tactic on her part. As for Saen, the old charlatan probably thinks friendship is a transactional affair. Apparently, he isn't the only one looking to capitalize on divine connections.

With a grin as innocent as a napping kitten, Seraphina declared, "Well, I'm different. I'm Lord Milos's most special friend."

Milos gave her a sidelong glance, as if she were a riddle wrapped in spring flowers, and wisely chose the path of silence. He was the type who never spoke with his mouth full, or while his plate still had a crumb.

Seraphina watched him with the intensity of a cat eyeing a particularly baffling contraption. No wonder there was always a ruler involved in the prayer ceremonies for the God of Light. It was as if He spent His days measuring Himself against His own divine standards, as rigid and precise as a Swiss watch.

Dethroning such a principled deity? Now that would be a feat akin to convincing a dragon to part with its hoard. Not impossible, but definitely requiring a fair bit of cunning and perhaps a touch of insanity.

*****

Back in Burton, Milos kept his word to explain her overnight absence to her uncle. Cleverly, he roped Bishop Saen into the tale, spinning a yarn about theological activities so grand it could quiet even the most scandal-hungry Countess.

Bishop Saen beamed, "Miss Doyle is the cleverest individual I've had the pleasure of meeting. I'm certain she'll bring great honor to your family in the days to come." Bishop Saen praised, practically glowing as he bade farewell to Earl George.

Count George's grin was so wide it threatened to split his face. For a noble of his standing, getting cozy with the seven archbishops was akin to scaling Mount Everest with nothing but a spoon. His eyes shimmered with pride as he gazed at his niece, the unexpected bringer of glory. "Feel free to attend such theological activities whenever you wish, my dear. Stay out all night if it pleases you. With God's light guiding you, what could possibly go wrong?"

The Countess, on the other hand, looked ready to combust from the inequity of it all. She'd barely returned late from the opera, and yet she was accused of tarnishing their noble name.

Seraphina watched Milos and Saen depart, then slipped back to her room, where her heart was set on a mission. She scooped gold coins into her handbag like they were candy, ready to procure a teleportation array and dash northward.

Two days had ticked by since she'd left the wounded Dark God in that apartment. Her conscience, as pure as freshly fallen snow, wouldn't let her rest knowing a deity was languishing. She had to offer care, a balm to his darkened soul.

The Dark God, deprived of affection, would yearn for even a flicker of light. Surely, he'd await her return. Delay too long, and he'd lose hope, rendering her efforts futile.

Timing was key, like seasoning a stew—too soon, and the flavor's off; too late, and it's burnt. Two days was the sweet spot: enough to stir impatience without tipping into despair. After all, what was too easily gained never seemed as sweet.

With determination in her step, Seraphina made her way to the Oak Street Tavern, seeking Lusahu, the mercenary leader from before. "I'm in the market for teleportation arrays. The more, the merrier."

The man behind the barrels blinked as if she'd just sprouted wings. "You're alive?" he stammered, then quickly corrected himself. "I mean, we thought you were a goner, blocked in a cave by monsters. We, uh... assumed the worst."

Seraphina's expression was as nonchalant as a cat in a sunbeam. Profit-driven alliances were hardly surprising. "No worries. I understand."

"Glad to see you're still kicking," Rosehu said, perhaps a bit sheepishly. "Now, about those teleportation arrays... They're tricky to make, high failure rate, and demand's through the roof—"

Seraphina casually opened her handbag, revealing a gleaming treasure trove of gold. Lusahu's eyes widened, glinting like a pirate's at a treasure chest. "Well, money talks, as they say."

"Fifty gold per array. I have two on hand. Need more? I can source them."

"Deal." Seraphina handed over the gold with a flourish. "Here's one hundred and twenty. I want two arrays. The rest is for hiring that diviner who impersonated me last time."

And with that, she set her plan into motion, a mischievous sparkle in her eye.

"That's easy." Lusahu snatched up the bag of gold coins with the eagerness of a squirrel hoarding nuts and nodded. "I'll bring her here right away."

***

Seraphina returned home with a purposeful stride, making a beeline for the kitchen where she retrieved a can of freshly made mushroom soup. Then, she trotted upstairs to change. She opted for a demure sheep's hoof sleeve dress with a collar that modestly covered her chin and layered it with a winter coat. After all, she was going to offer solace to a grieving young man, not tempt him into further chaos.

With a flicker of magic, the system cast a light that transformed her hair and eyes. A girl with black hair and eyes stared back at her from the mirror, her lips a vibrant red against her pale skin. She wore a coat of matching hue with a red scarf, striking a balance between well-behaved and slightly coquettish. Seraphina batted her long-lashed eyes with a hint of youthful mischief and adjusted her coat's corners.

"We can go," she declared, retrieving a small black pointed card from her pocket. This was the teleportation array to the north. She also tucked away a small golden pointed card meant for a return trip to the southern continent. Different regions had their own teleportation hues; the sea god's kingdom favored blue.

Seraphina tossed the pointed card onto the ground, and a circular dark magic circle unfurled. Wisps of black smoke filled the room with alarming speed. She cast a glance at the small garden below, where the disguised diviner was admiring the blooms. She would ascend once Seraphina departed.

She stepped into the magic circle with haste, lest the maids mistake the smoke for a fire hazard.

The black fog enveloped her vision entirely, like stepping into a premature night. But the darkness was fleeting, soon giving way to the soft glow of dusk, where night prepared to drape its cloak.

This was Kvina County of the North, where seasons and time danced to a different rhythm than the South Continent.

Seraphina tugged her scarf tighter against the biting wind and briskly exited the narrow, dim alley.

The small apartment was nearby, but she didn't rush. First, she stopped by a bakery to buy bread with ham. Paired with the mushroom soup, it was a dinner crafted with care for the Dark God.

Upon reaching the apartment, she looked up at the room with mint green curtains—it lay dark and still, as if holding its breath.

"Host, it looks like the Dark God won't come back," her internal skeptic chimed in.

"No. He will definitely come," Seraphina asserted, confidence in her voice as she carried her basket into the shadowy apartment entrance.

A faint, otherworldly light seeped in, casting enough glow to dilute the corridor's shadows. Seraphina squinted at the door numbers, placing the basket at her feet. The old door seemed to merge with the corridor's darkness, its bottom gap hinting at vacancy.

She knocked gently, but silence answered back.

Undeterred, she knocked again, the "dong dong" startling a lone black feather dangling from the door.

Seconds ticked by before an unseen force descended with the silence of snowfall, illuminating the dark room with unexpected brightness.

"Who is it?" A low voice rumbled through the wooden barrier.

Who indeed?

Only someone who brings warmth.

16

A soft rustling broke the silence in the room. The door creaked open to reveal Cecil, standing half in candlelight, half in shadow, like some dark angel caught between realms.

Seraphina tilted her chin up, pulling down her scarf to reveal her face, her smile brimming with a mix of relief and delight. "You're still here? That's wonderful."

Cecil's response was as silent as the grave, his eyes—hidden beneath a tousle of black hair—gave nothing away. He neither invited her in nor shut her out, standing there like a stoic statue.

Seraphina could sense the undertone of resentment in his demeanor. Cecil was like someone who had just caught a glimpse of sunlight, only for it to vanish before he could truly bask in its warmth. She had left him in that apartment, a solitary figure amidst shadows, without so much as a word about his well-being. Had she not returned, she feared he might have shut yet another door within his already barricaded heart, growing even more skeptical of love and kindness.

"I brought food," she chirped, lifting the basket. "Bread I bought and soup I made myself."

Cecil's gaze lingered on her before he silently stepped aside, granting her passage into his dim sanctuary.

Once inside, bathed in the flickering candlelight, Seraphina noticed the bandages still wrapped around his torso. They bore the familiar marks of her handiwork, untouched and unchanged.

His exposed skin was a honeyed canvas of strength, highlighted by broad shoulders, muscular arms, and a lean waist—a veritable storm of temptation.

Seraphina quickly diverted her gaze, her heart racing as if it were in a marathon. That body was a siren's song, whispering promises best left unheeded.

"Haven't eaten yet?" she asked, bustling past him to the window, setting the basket on the small round table.

As she unpacked the bread and mushroom soup, she noticed a fine film of dust covering the table, windowsill, armchair, and candlesticks. Clearly, Cecil had left shortly after she had.

Keeping her observations to herself, Seraphina continued unpacking the meal. "I could've been here sooner, but it was my first time making soup. Took longer than expected. Hope you like it."

Cecil leaned against the door, arms crossed, watching her with the wary curiosity of a stray cat, unwilling to approach the hand that fed it.

Once the food was arranged, Seraphina tightened her scarf and picked up the basket.

Cecil, catching her swift departure, allowed a faintly mocking smile to play at his lips as he reached to open the door.

"I'll just pop downstairs for bandages and ointment," Seraphina paused beside him, adding, "You really ought to change those. It's not good to leave them on too long."

Cecil's expression wavered, subtle shifts disrupting his cold facade.

"And," she added, eyes earnest, "drink the soup before it gets cold. I can't run faster than it chills." Seeing his reluctance, she gave him a gentle push towards the table.

Ignoring the tableware, she grabbed a teacup, washed it in the bathroom, and filled it with steaming mushroom soup. Handing it to him, she said, "Here you go. I used plenty of white mushrooms and milk."

Cecil regarded her, unmoving. But after a tense pause, likely unable to conjure a reason to refuse, he accepted the cup. As his fingers curled around it, his lashes fluttered, and warmth seeped into his chilled hand.

"You need to finish it all," she instructed with a bright smile, gesturing a large circle over the table. With that, she picked up her basket and headed out.

Once outside, Seraphina gazed at the night-cloaked sky, exhaling deeply. Things had gone as planned. Each time Cecil's expressions veered towards sarcasm or resistance, her nerves had danced on edge. But now, relief unfurled within her like a banner in the breeze.

In this era, pharmacies were as rare as unicorns. If you fell ill, you had to summon a pharmacist to your home, which could be quite the ordeal given how few and far between they were. They were scattered across the city like stars in the sky, leaving grocery stores to occasionally stock minor medicines for convenience.

Seraphina procured fresh bandages and healing ointments from the grocery store downstairs. Rather than hurrying back, she indulged in a leisurely browse through the shop, her fingers trailing over beautiful porcelain, embroidered collars, vibrant lace, coconut shell egg rolls, and satin shawls with a distinctly northern flair.

"Host, aren't you going back to the apartment?" Little N inquired, puzzled by her dawdling.

"Yes," Seraphina replied, flicking a satin shawl adorned with golden dots that shimmered against the pink fabric. "But not immediately. I'll return in a little while."

"Why?"

"Like I mentioned before. Sugar that comes too easily isn't sweet. When something is too readily available, it loses its value. I want him to appreciate its worth while waiting. It's classic hunger marketing."

"Wow, host, I'm starting to feel unworthy of you. You must be amazing to be paired with an SSR system," Little N mused, feeling a bit ashamed.

"So you need to upgrade quickly," Seraphina chuckled, selecting a set of inexpensive silverware and a pale yellow tablecloth. Fifteen minutes had passed since she left the apartment, a suspenseful interval designed to provoke curiosity about whether she was returning.

When Seraphina knocked on the door, it opened the moment her knuckles brushed the wood, as if someone had been waiting on the other side.

Cecil maintained his lukewarm demeanor, though Little N's report on the point increase betrayed his true feelings.

"Host, add two points."

Ah, the darkness that stands in opposition to the God of Light, Seraphina thought with a faint sigh. The two deities had been entwined in love and hatred since time immemorial, even matching each other in their feigned expressions.

Seraphina carried the tableware to the bathroom, washed it, and placed it on the low cabinet. "I bought new tableware; you can use this to eat," she said, glancing at the untouched food on the small round table.

Cecil's current behavior was much like a seasoned street cat—wary and suspicious, conditioned by harsh experiences to distrust those who offered him sustenance.

Seraphina wondered what the dark god had been like as a youth. Surely, his transformation into the sensitive, suspicious, and brooding figure he was now had roots in his past.

"This soup is perfectly safe. I made it myself," Seraphina offered, feigning a wounded expression. She scooped up a spoonful, sipped it, then stuck out her tongue at him, "See? I'm fine."

Cecil's eyes flickered with interest. Her lips were a vivid red, her teeth pearly white, and her tongue small and endearing — far removed from the thick, oily tongues he despised.

He harbored no love for humans. To him, they were akin to the gods of the divine realm, skilled in deceitful speech aimed at extracting favors. Consequently, he had decreed strict divine laws in the North, where liars faced the penalty of tongue removal.

Yet, he found no reason to despise this human girl. She exuded warmth and fragility, like a harmless little creature that piqued his curiosity.

Following his impulse, he reached out, seizing Seraphina's hand and drawing her closer.

Seraphina's eyes widened in surprise as Cecil's indifferent yet handsome face filled her vision. Her jaw was gently pried open, and his fingers brushed against her tongue, exploring with a tender touch. Her face flushed, and she instinctively leaned back, prompting him to stop.

"What... what are you doing?" Seraphina demanded, wiping her mouth with the back of her hand in indignation.

"Your tongue is very nice. I wanted to touch it, so I touched it," Cecil remarked, as casually as if he were discussing the weather forecast.

Seraphina blinked, momentarily stunned. His logic was as imperious and straightforward as a decree from the heavens themselves—light should exist, and thus it was willed into being. Overbearing and utterly beyond reproach.

She realized that gods were creatures of freedom and whimsy, unbound by the constraints that governed mortal behavior. Unlike the stringent God of Light, many deities acted on impulse, driven by desires as capricious as a summer breeze. Their actions were instinctive, akin to a human's thoughtless decision to crush an ant. It was a collision of dimensions, a clash devoid of reason.

The Dark God, Cecil, was a perilous entity, embodying death and wielding immense power. His actions followed his own code, unfettered by human sensibilities. Over countless millennia, unchecked by restraint, darkness had thickened around him. It was the post-era humans' plea for self-discipline that he faced now.

"This isn't right," Seraphina asserted, seizing the chance to impart a lesson on proper conduct. "You did that without my consent, and it's quite rude. It makes me angry. Imagine it the other way around—how would you feel if I suddenly touched your tongue?"

Cecil frowned, puzzled by her words. Consent was a foreign concept; his actions were never contingent on others' approval. Yet, her hypothetical scenario intrigued him. With surprising earnestness, he pulled Seraphina's hand towards his lips, offering, "Would you like to touch it? If you do, you're welcome to. I won't be upset."

The candlelight, filtered through the crystal lampshade, cast a magical glow over his black hair. His eyes, beautiful and enigmatic, shimmered like stars in an abyss—dangerous yet irresistibly tempting.

Seraphina found herself momentarily lost, captivated by Cecil's striking features. His face was a masterpiece, a blend of raw strength and ethereal beauty that seemed to draw her in like a siren's song. She was completely absorbed, her thoughts adrift in the depths of his enigmatic gaze.

It wasn't until she felt the unexpected, warm sensation of her fingers being engulfed by his mouth—yes, his actual mouth—that she snapped back to reality. The strange, damp heat jolted her from her daydream like a bucket of ice water, firmly yanking her back to the present.

"This isn't right," she protested, yanking her hand back as if she'd just touched a live wire, scrubbing it against her clothes with the vigor of someone trying to erase a mistake. "You shouldn't just go around touching people willy-nilly, and you definitely shouldn't let others touch you like that."

"But you touched me first. I thought you were enjoying it," he replied, with a grin that could melt butter—or start a small rebellion.

"I didn't enjoy it at all," Seraphina huffed, her irritation swirling like a tempest. What was this? Trying to seduce the god of light was already a Herculean task, but dealing with a dark god? She hadn't anticipated this. Was this supposed to be seduction? What on earth had she unwittingly sparked in this mysterious, shadowy deity?

Cecil's handsome face wore a look of profound confusion.

After his return to the underworld, he found himself in an uncharacteristically pensive mood, seeking the sage advice of fallen angels. With all the gravitas of one asking the secrets of the universe, he inquired, "What does it mean if a woman kisses me or—heavens forbid—strips me bare?"

The fallen angels, seasoned connoisseurs of earthly affairs, exchanged knowing glances before offering their profound insights:

"It means she desires your body," one said, with a wink that could have toppled kingdoms.

"She wants to mate with you," another added, with the kind of certainty usually reserved for death and taxes.

"Let her touch you; she'll be more drawn to you," the third chimed in, as if explaining the intricacies of a fine wine.

***

"I thought you returned because you were interested in my body," Cecil said, crossing his arms and leaning against the wall with a lazy grace. He stared at her, this girl who possessed the light he craved. He didn't mind a small price for it, especially since the price brought a peculiar pleasure—one he was eager to explore.

But now she claimed she didn't enjoy it, and he was left pondering what to do.

<u>17</u>

"I'm not interested in your body," Seraphina proclaimed with all the righteousness of a saint standing in the middle of the room.

In truth, she was more interested than she'd care to admit, but that wasn't the prize she had her eye on. Her grand mission was to mend the sinister god and steer him onto the path of righteousness. Yet, somehow, things were veering off course like a drunken sailor on a stormy night. The dark god appeared to be paddling straight towards the sea god's domain, and that was a cosmic no-no if ever there was one.

Cecil, leaning casually against the bathroom door frame, folded his arms and raised a brow, his captivating peach eyes perplexed. "What do you want?"

I want you to be a good person, she thought.

"I don't want anything," Seraphina insisted, her eyes shining with a kind and pure light that could make even angels doubt themselves.

"I was just worried you might be dead," she whispered. "After I left you here that day, I kept seeing you in my mind, covered in wounds. We fought zombies and monsters together, and we faced that terrifying white angel."

"We escaped two crises together. In my heart, I already see you as a companion. Even if it's one-sided, I really don't want you to get into trouble. So I couldn't help but come to check on you, that's all."

Cecil watched her in silence for a long moment, before a soft laugh escaped him.

How could there be kindness without strings attached?

In his world, the law of equivalent exchange ruled with an iron fist. Whatever he took, he was bound to repay. It was as if he ran the universe like a divine bank teller; every answered prayer came with its own cosmic transaction fee. What his believers gained, they lost something in return, balancing the scales as if the universe itself was keeping a meticulous ledger.

"Very well. Let me know when you figure out what you want from me," he said, moving to the armchair by the round table, picking up a soup spoon as if it were a scepter.

"The soup's cold, don't drink it," Seraphina urged.

"This soup is specially made for me, I will drink it," Cecil replied smoothly. "As for the temperature, that's easy to fix."

With a flick of his wrist, the cup of cold soup warmed in his hand, steam curling up in lazy tendrils—a divine spell in action.

Seraphina, conceding defeat, sat across from him, resting her cheeks in her hands. "Why didn't you drink it while I was out shopping?"

"I've lived in the Hades... Mendes Swamp for a long time. My hands are colder than most. Holding a warm cup is comforting, so I held onto it a bit longer. And just as I was about to drink, you returned."

Ah, so that's why...

Seraphina inwardly cursed herself over her earlier lapse in judgment. If she hadn't put on that little soup-sipping show, complete with the tongue-out finale, would she have triggered the dark god's peculiar quirks? It was like she'd accidentally discovered a hidden feature in a mystical app, and now she couldn't quite figure out how to toggle it off.

Cecil finished the soup in the cup, then the rest from the pot, not leaving a single drop. To be fair, there were only two tea cups' worth—not exactly a feast.

"Still hungry?" Seraphina inquired, holding out a piece of bread like an olive branch. "I should have picked up a stove while I was out, you know, so I could whip up some steaks and make more soup... Oh, not a fan of bread?" she noticed as he declined, setting it down like a rejected peace offering.

"I don't like to eat store-bought," Cecil replied, his tone carrying just a touch of disdain, as if the bread had personally offended his culinary sensibilities.

Ah, so he prefers a personal touch.

"Got it, next time I'll bake you bread myself. My baking skills are legendary," Seraphina boasted shamelessly.

"Host, you're quite the braggart," Little N chimed in, arms crossed.

Seraphina ignored the comment and pulled out ointment and fresh bandages from her basket. "Let's change your dressing. By the way, I don't know your name yet?"

"Cecil," the black-haired young man replied earnestly. "My last name is quite a mouthful, so just remember Cecil."

Seraphina was so surprised she could barely control her expression. The Dark God had actually revealed his true name, dropping it into conversation like it was nothing. But she didn't want to know.

If he'd used an alias, she would have gladly committed it to memory. But now, as a subject of the Dark God, she couldn't exactly pretend ignorance of His name.

"Uh... your name is the same as the great Dark God," Seraphina said, her face as stiff as a board.

Cecil smirked ever so slightly. "And you, what's your name?"

"Seraphina Doyle."

"Seraphina Doyle," he repeated, committing it to memory with the seriousness of a knight swearing an oath.

"Well, don't forget it," Seraphina said with a smile, her eyes skirting over the bandages wrapped around his body. "Should I help you remove those, or do you want to do it yourself?"

Cecil moved his fingers slightly, and with a flash of light, the bandages vanished into thin air. What lay beneath were wounds that defied healing. Deep and shallow, they revealed dark flesh and blood that seemed to pulse with a barrier, holding the blood at bay.

Seraphina only managed a quick glance before averting her eyes, her heart thundering in her chest. Although she was allowed to look upon the god, the raw power was overwhelming.

If one dared to look directly at a god without permission, these wounds, teeming with divine flesh and blood, could consume them with a mere glance.

"Wash up first, and I'll apply medicine," Seraphina said quickly, focusing on the night sky beyond the window to steady her racing heart.

Cecil nodded and headed to the bathroom. Within seconds, the sound of running water filled the air.

Seraphina turned in surprise, staring at the bathroom door. Her intention had been for him to use a cleansing spell, not to take an actual shower.

Ten minutes later, Cecil emerged, clad in trousers with his upper body bare. A dark green towel hung around his neck as he used it to tousle his hair dry.

His disheveled appearance carried a kind of careless elegance. The grotesque wounds on his body had a broken beauty, highlighted by the glistening water droplets.

His arms were a masterpiece of form, muscles flowing with a kind of effortless grace. His waist was equally striking, lean and taut. In the candlelight, his pale skin took on a warm, honeyed hue.

Seraphina found herself unable to look away from Cecil. But to her surprise, her heart didn't feel like it would explode this time. A closer look revealed that the barrier over his wounds seemed thicker.

Cecil picked up the green ointment, unscrewed the cap with a practiced motion, and handed it to Seraphina.

She took it, dipped her fingers into the balm, and asked him to turn around.

Cecil complied without a word.

Without the barrier of power, the blood and flesh in the wounds were clearly visible, like magma flowing through a volcano, slowly churning within Cecil's body.

This is the flesh and blood of the gods, she marveled internally, applying the ointment with gentle precision. As her fingers touched the wound, she felt the skin quiver beneath her touch.

"Does it hurt?"

"It hurts quite a bit," Cecil admitted with surprising honesty.

"How did you get so badly injured?" Seraphina asked as she moved to another wound.

"My mortal enemy has always been merciless," Cecil replied, almost as if it were a casual observation about the weather. "It's not surprising. Our existence is defined by devouring one another. The darkness seeks to engulf the light, and the light strives to banish the darkness."

Uh... I really didn't want to hear that, Seraphina thought, her internal monologue spiraling into mild panic. I don't want to know who you truly are. It's much easier to think of you as just Cecil, the guy who doesn't like store-bought bread, rather than a cosmic force locked in eternal battle.

Seraphina quickly clamped her mouth shut and focused on applying ointment to Cecil's wounds. Treating the back was simple enough, but when it came to the front, things got a bit trickier. Last time, she had applied the ointment with her eyes tightly shut, under the guidance of Little N, when Cecil was blissfully asleep. This time, however, she felt the full weight of Cecil's gaze, his eyes keen and ever-watchful.

She lowered her eyes, acutely aware of Cecil's breath warming the top of her head. As she worked on his collarbone and chest, that warmth seemed to intensify, as if his skin was heating up under her touch.

"Last time, you applied it to me like this," Cecil chuckled softly, his voice tinged with a trembling breathlessness.

"Yeah," Seraphina replied, her voice steady despite the nervous flutter in her chest.

"Fortunately, I was asleep. If I had caught you daring to desecrate my body like this, you'd likely be in the underworld by now."

"Would you really kill me?" Seraphina asked, a note of curiosity in her voice.

"I'd have broken your neck. But not now," Cecil said, his gaze fixed on her delicate fingers as they moved over his chest. His black eyes seemed to be shrouded in a mysterious fog, his voice rough.

"Why not now?"

"Because you brought me here when I was injured. You left me food. You returned to take care of me and even made me soup..."

Seraphina paused, realizing that these small acts of kindness had somehow brightened Cecil's world, despite his dark nature.

Once the ointment was applied, she carefully wrapped him in fresh bandages.

"Dong—" A low, resonant bell tolled in the distance.

The wide, proud streets of the North were cloaked in dusk. Buildings, like solemn sentinels, stood quietly under the pale starlight. In the stillness of the night, only the intermittent toll of the bell broke the silence. Twenty-two chimes marked ten o'clock. Kvina County had entered its nightly curfew.

This was the law set by the Dark God. At this time, no one was permitted to wander outside. The North, neighboring the underworld and the abyss, harbored mysterious powers unmatched by other lands. Night bred fear, and fear turned into monsters. Even a substantial city like Kvina County couldn't escape the natural order.

"Ah, it's already night curfew," Seraphina remarked, turning to peer out the window in surprise. The streets below were deserted, shops shuttered tight. Gas lamps cast their glowing light, as if trying to fend off the monsters lurking in the shadows.

"Indeed," Cecil agreed, following her gaze. To him, the law was perfectly reasonable.

"I can't go home," The girl grumbled, a trace of annoyance in her voice.

"Host, do you even have a home in the North?" Little N chimed in, lacing its words with a healthy dose of sarcasm.

"Then just stay," Cecil suggested, as if it were the most natural decision in the world. "There's a bed here; you can sleep in it."

"Not so proper?" Seraphina mused, inwardly rejoicing at the unexpected offer of a place to stay. "If I take the bed, where will you sleep?" Perched in an armchair all night like the God of Light? That would be so embarrassing—I can't have two gods keeping watch.

"I'll sleep on the bed too," Cecil replied with straightforward logic. "It's a double bed; it can certainly accommodate two people."

Seraphina: "..."

His reasoning was impeccable, leaving her without a single argument in return.

<u>18</u>

"**G**o wash up first, we'll talk about the bed when you come out," Cecil said, and almost immediately, the sound of water rushing filled the bathroom.

Seraphina hurriedly opened the door, eyes widening as a stream of steaming water appeared out of thin air. It was like the air itself had torn open a portal to another realm, pouring water into the bathtub until it nearly spilled over the edges.

"Okay, okay, it's going to be full," Seraphina said, a hint of panic in her voice.

"Yeah," Cecil drawled lazily from where he leaned against the door frame, and just like that, the water flow ceased.

"Divine magic is amazing," Seraphina marveled, staring at the clear water, mist curling above it like a milky veil. It was as if he'd conjured it out of nothing.

Cecil gave her a sidelong glance. "I remember when we were in the Misty Forest, you said you were a gold hunter. You should know a bit about divine magic, right?"

Seraphina nodded. "Of course. Well, sort of."

"What I know is pretty basic. You know, knowledge costs gold, and I'm still on the golden path to earning more. So, spells and divine rituals, I'm not exactly an expert."

Cecil pondered for a moment. "Do you want to go to Mok Yak to learn dark divine arts?"

"No, I prefer to learn on my own," Seraphina replied brightly, stepping into the bathroom and closing the door behind her.

Mok Jak was a seminary in the north, known for specializing in dark divine arts. It was a rare opportunity, but Seraphina had her hands full. Once the sea god line opened, her schedule would be even tighter.

"Host, you just earned three points," Little N said gleefully. "One point each time you applied the ointment. Added to your previous 29 points, we have a total of 32 points now."

"31 points," Seraphina corrected as she slipped out of her skirt, hanging it on a hook before carefully stepping into the bathtub.

"Huh?"

"Today, I used one point to extend my life for three more days."

"Oh, right. I forgot."

Seraphina submerged herself into the hot water, leaving only her head above the surface. Each breath sent gentle ripples across the water. "I'll head back to Burton tomorrow morning."

"Ah, so soon?"

"I have a class the day after tomorrow. I can't let the divine magician who covered for me do it again. Plus, I made plans with Milos to learn the teleportation array. I can't delay anymore; I need to gather all the materials."

"Host, you're like a spinning top."

"No choice. If I don't keep up the pace today, I'll be off-kilter tomorrow. And don't forget, there's still the SSR," Seraphina said, her voice tinged with determination.

"Who is that SSR?"

"I think I have an idea who one of them is," Seraphina mused.

"Are there several SSRs?" Little N gasped.

"Of course not, there's only one SSR. But its power isn't as simple as yours, just changing hair and eye color. An SSR could alter appearance, even gender. If that's true, we're in deep trouble. There are no clues, so we can only gauge based on the malice they have towards me."

"Host, you're thinking way ahead," Little N said, feeling slightly ashamed of his own limitations.

"So, Little N, you need to up your professional game," Seraphina said, standing up from the water. She reached for a towel, drying herself off before dressing meticulously, fastening each button with care. After all, she couldn't be as casual with the Dark God as she was with the Light God; everything needed to be properly covered.

When Seraphina emerged from the bathroom, she found Cecil lounging on the bed, deep in thought. As soon as he saw her, he patted the spot next to him with a casual invitation that made her heart skip a beat.

Seraphina took a moment to assess him under the dim light. Despite the haphazard bandages crisscrossing his body, they did nothing to diminish his allure. His taut arms, chiseled abs, and the suggestive play of muscles beneath the wrappings were enough to make anyone's temperature rise. She pressed her lips together, feeling as if the air was saturated with seductive undercurrents.

"That... is not right," Seraphina stammered, her voice wavering like a leaf in the wind. "We're just ordinary companions. Only couples, lovers, brothers and sisters share a bed..." What on earth was she saying?

"I'd better sleep in the armchair... Ah!" she exclaimed as an invisible force twined around her waist, gently lifting her. The sudden weightlessness made her gasp, and she found herself floating toward Cecil, who sat propped against the headboard, one arm behind his head, the other beckoning her with a mere flick of his finger.

Before she could collide with him, Cecil caught her, effortlessly settling her beside him. With a chuckle, he said, "You talk so much. Are you sure you're from the North?"

Seraphina tried to sit up, but the invisible force held her in place. Resigned, she lay flat, protesting weakly, "This isn't about the North. We should be decent, restrain our actions, not cause trouble for others..." Suddenly, darkness enveloped her, cutting her off mid-sentence.

"Go to sleep," Cecil murmured.

There was a soft rustling in her ears, and Seraphina felt the comforting weight of a down quilt settle over her. Cecil lay down beside her, his presence both reassuring and slightly unsettling.

"Did you put out the candle?" Seraphina asked, surprised.

"Yeah."

"But..." she began, remembering the North's tradition of keeping lights burning through the night to ward off evil spirits.

"Don't worry," Cecil said lightly. "No one dares to come here."

Of course, Seraphina thought, relaxing as she remembered who she was with. Who would dare provoke the Lord of the North, the god who dwelt in the underworld and embraced the darkness year-round?

Perhaps it was the warmth of the quilt, or the immense power of the god beside her, but sleep soon claimed her, and she drifted off, her eyelids growing heavy.

Cecil listened as her breathing became slow and even, indicating she was deeply asleep. He sat up, gazing out the window with a lazy grace.

How could the God of Darkness sleep in the dark? He extended his hand, drawing the night closer until it curled around him like a loyal pet.

A distant, shrill cry pierced the air, snapping Seraphina awake. She sat up, realizing the force around her waist had vanished.

"Don't worry," Cecil's calm voice reassured her. "Someone broke the rules and ventured out, only to be attacked by evil spirits."

Seraphina looked at him, surprised by his composure. Even though someone had dared to flaunt his rules and paid the price for it, the gods' indifference still sent a chill down her spine. It was one thing to hear about divine detachment, but witnessing it firsthand was an entirely different ordeal.

She slipped out of bed and padded barefoot to the window, pressing her hand against the glass to peer outside. Suddenly, a sharp pain bit into her palm. She drew back with a wince, seeing blood welling from where her skin had been torn.

"Be careful," came Cecil's languid voice from behind her. Seraphina turned to find him standing there, seemingly appearing out of nowhere. "Stay close to me. Without candles, the darkness will consume you."

He wrapped a strong arm around her waist, pulling her away from the window.

Cecil took her hand, brushing his fingertips over the wound. A cool white light flickered, and tiny buds of new skin began weaving over the cut.

"Healing is a magic of light. I'm not very skilled at it, so it might take a moment," Cecil said, his focus on her palm as he layered the healing spell. Her hand was as soft and pale as the fingers he had once—regrettably—tasted. He wondered if it would taste the same now.

But he refrained, recalling her dislike for unsolicited touches.

"Host, you just earned an SSR coin," Little N chimed in.

"What's an SSR coin?" Seraphina asked, blinking in confusion.

"Let me see. I was just as baffled. I first stumbled upon this," Little N, a self-proclaimed expert still learning the ropes, muttered as it scurried off to investigate.

After a good ten seconds, it returned with a triumphant air. "Aha, that's the trick! R and SR levels get a boost from those favorability points. But SSR levels? They need SSR coins—those nifty things you earn when you tweak a god."

"Like, say, turning the Dark God into a good god. Each step he takes towards the light earns you SSR coins. And these coins? They're the golden ticket. They not only upgrade me but also let you trade for high-level blind boxes."

"What's all that about?" Seraphina asked, intrigued.

"Remember the low-level blind boxes? One point of favorability buys you one, with a mere 1% chance of snagging a high-level item. But a high-level blind box? That's a guaranteed win with a 100% chance of a high-level goodie, and even a 10% shot at a hidden limited."

"Wow, so cool!" Seraphina exclaimed, her eyes practically sparkling with excitement. "I can't wait." She clutched her small but precious collection of props tightly, only two in her possession so far, each too valuable to waste on a whim.

One was a piece of plasticine with the magical ability to replicate anything—ideal for duplicating powerful divine arts and a potential lifesaver when the chips were down. The other was a charm that could make someone see only her for 24 hours—a clever little trick she intended to use against the sea god.

"But where did that coin come from?" Seraphina inquired, curiosity piqued.

"Beats me," Little N admitted sheepishly. "That's top-secret R-level intel."

"Guess I'd better level you up fast."

After their chat, a sudden hush fell over Seraphina. She peered out the window, puzzled. "Why did the shouting stop?"

"Maybe they got eaten," Cecil commented, his focus on her palm as casual as discussing someone eating an orange.

The Dark God's indifferent tone made the night feel even more frigid. Seraphina shivered, glancing up. His gaze was icy, his expression as cold as the night, only softening when he looked her way.

"Get some more sleep," Cecil suggested. "Dawn's still a ways off."

Seraphina's initial thrill of earning SSR coins faded, the realization hitting her that the powerful god had only cracked open a sliver of darkness for her. She still had a long journey ahead.

She lay back down, tossing and turning as sleep eluded her. Whether it was the fatigue from her travels or the whirlwind of recent events, she couldn't tell.

Cecil turned on his side, his dark eyes lazily observing her. "Can't sleep?"

"I'll fall asleep soon," Seraphina replied, quickly shutting her eyes as she felt his arm brush against her, wary of any peculiar antics.

The black-haired god watched her, his voice a soft murmur, "Are you scared?" He shifted closer, a protective presence beside her, warding off the night's chill like a great, gentle beast.

"Don't worry, I promise that sort of thing won't happen to you."

Seraphina opened her eyes, meeting the god's gaze, his proximity a strange comfort. She decided to warn him in advance, "I'll head home at dawn."

"Alright," Cecil replied in a deep, resonant voice. "Will you come back?"

"I will."

After all, how else could I conquer you? She thought with a quiet determination, feeling the challenge stretching before her like a vast, uncharted map.

Dark God: I want love, lots of it. Just for me... Only look at me, just me... His thoughts whispered into the night, a plea masked beneath his stoic exterior, yearning for the warmth he dared not openly seek.

19

At dawn, Seraphina stepped out of the apartment and into the bustling streets of Kvina County. After a night of eerie silence, the town had returned to its usual lively self, as if the shrill cries of the previous night were nothing more than a dream. The people of Kvina had grown accustomed to this life—born in darkness, yet living in the light.

As she made her way down the street, a woman in a black robe approached, looking every bit the fierce warrior with dark hair piled atop her head. She seemed like someone you wouldn't want to cross paths with on a bad day.

Seraphina instinctively gave the woman a wide berth, quickening her pace toward the distant alley as if her life depended on it.

As they passed, the black-robed woman came to an abrupt halt, turning with the eerie grace of a predator. Her eyes, cold and calculating, locked onto Seraphina's retreating figure like a serpent sizing up its next meal, lingering until Seraphina disappeared from view.

"What an impressive one," the black-robed woman mused, her voice carrying the chill of winter.

"It seems your strength pales in comparison to hers," a rough voice chimed in with a mocking edge. "While you're busy currying favor, someone might be getting awfully cozy with the Dark God."

"Shut up," the woman snapped, her eyes darkening like a storm ready to unleash its fury. She strode into the apartment, each step echoing with an unspoken threat.

The corridor shivered as a sudden chill swept through, heralding the arrival of her massive black feathered wings. They tore through her robe with a fierce elegance, unfurling from her back with a slow, menacing grace. The wings rose and fell like the calm before the storm, then folded neatly against her back. As if imbued with life, her robe seamlessly knitted itself back together, concealing the fearsome power beneath.

***

Meanwhile, Cecil had returned to his usual form, now clad in a tight black robe that glistened with a dim silver sheen, reminiscent of cold moonlight.

The door swung open, and the black-robed woman entered, kneeling at his feet, her demeanor respectful and poised.

"Master, I believe we've located Him—Milos, the God of Light. He remains in Burton, but it seems he hasn't regained his memory."

"Yeah," Cecil replied, his tone indifferent.

The woman waited, but when no further response came, she dared to glance up. The handsome god was absentmindedly toying with an empty medicine bottle, his fingers graceful and lazy.

She sniffed the air subtly, catching the scent of mignonette. It was the fragrance of the ointment humans used for healing, and it was clear who had applied it.

"Master," she ventured cautiously, "I detect the scent of a human—I..."

Cecil's gaze snapped to her, cold and unyielding. She immediately prostrated herself, trembling as if she'd glimpsed the relentless chill of hell itself.

"Vasali, you seem to have misunderstood," Cecil said slowly, "I elevated a wild angel to serve me, not to grant her the right to scrutinize my affairs. Servants are to remain grounded, never raising their eyes without permission. Some matters are beyond your purview."

"Master, I meant no intrusion, only concern for your welfare... I swear it won't happen again." The black-robed woman pressed her forehead to the cool floor, shivering with a plea for mercy. But the silence above her stretched on, unbroken.

"He's been gone for a while," the rough voice echoed in her mind.

"Why didn't you tell me sooner?" she snapped, raising her head in frustration. Sure enough, the Dark God was nowhere to be seen—likely back in the underworld. Gods roamed where they pleased, answerable to no one.

"You went astray from the start. All that risk for a mere sliver of loyalty."

The black-robed woman's expression grew grim. "I didn't err. How else could I approach Him if not as His subordinate?"

"Not a subordinate—a servant," the voice mocked.

"I won't be a servant for long." She stood, pacing the room. The basket of bread and the empty medicine bottle Cecil had held were gone.

She pursed her lips, recalling similar bottles she'd seen in the temple, placed near the throne. It was only a matter of time before such trash cluttered the place.

***

Seraphina bustled through the streets of Burton, dusk draping the city in shadow, a cloth bag of supplies slung over her shoulder.

The abrupt transition from the North's daylight to the South Continent's night left her momentarily disoriented. She had attempted to purchase a teleportation array earlier but failed to acquire one for the North. Instead, she gathered a hodgepodge of materials, hoping to persuade Milos to craft one for her.

"I doubt the God of Light will be inclined to make a teleportation array for the North," Little N commented.

"He will definitely do it," Seraphina said nonchalantly, waving a hand as if brushing away the very notion of doubt. Her real concern lay elsewhere.

"How many coins are needed to upgrade to SSR?" she asked, cutting to the chase.

"Fifty," replied Little N.

"So I have to convince the three gods to make forty-nine changes just to get these coins?"

"Not necessarily," Little N explained, trying to sound like the wise sage he wished to be. "If a god makes a particularly big change, you could rake in a bunch of coins all at once. It's like your favorability points or heartbeat index—varies every time based on the drama level."

"Got it," Seraphina nodded, decisive as ever. "Give me a high-end blind box."

"A what?" Little N blinked, wondering if he'd misheard.

"A high-end blind box," Seraphina repeated, her tone leaving no room for debate. "The SSR upgrade is a distant dream; let's focus on the now. Maybe a blind box can solve my current troubles."

"Hmm, that does make sense."

With a flash of light, Seraphina's hand felt the pleasant weight of a long, vertical box, shimmering with a high-end luster that screamed quality.

"I'll open it," she declared with infectious energy, tearing into it with gusto. A golden light spilled from the box, turning her eyes to molten gold.

"Hidden limited!" Little N shrieked in excitement.

"Calm down," Seraphina said, her smile wide and knowing. She tipped the box, and out rolled a dainty blue glass bottle, no bigger than her finger. Inside lay a gummy candy shaped like a mermaid.

The bottle read: "Dream Pills: Designate one person to consume this pill, and they will become a child of the sea and have an encounter with you."

A child of the sea, huh? Exactly. Men transform into mermen, women into mermaids—those forbidden creatures with their alluring human upper bodies and mesmerizing fish tails.

Thinking of the romantic tale of drinking a magic potion in pursuit of true love, Seraphina allowed a mischievous smile to curve her lips. "Looks like I've found a way to get the sea god ashore."

She turned the bottle in her hands, noting the empty line for a name. So that's how it worked—just write the sea god's name, and he'd unknowingly swallow the pill. Then, he'd be hers to deal with.

Seraphina felt a peculiar thrill about the Sea God. Her hometown had been under his dominion, after all. Now, she was about to meet the old village chief himself, and she found herself eagerly anticipating the encounter.

She slipped the dream pill into her pocket, her fingers brushing against something soft. A spark of excitement lit up her eyes as she pulled out the unexpected item.

Six feathers, three white and three black. She had left these for Cecil last time, but not only had he returned them, he'd added three more. Just whose feathers had he plucked this time?

"Wow," Little N commented in bemusement. "Host, you're truly a master at feather plucking—in every sense."

Seraphina chuckled, tucking the feathers back into her pocket before striding toward the residence of the God of Light. Today's plan had changed. She no longer wanted a teleportation array for the North; she wanted one for the Kingdom of the Sea.

***

"You want to learn how to make a Teleportation Array for the Kingdom of the Sea?" Milos asked, surprise coloring his voice. "Not many people go there. The Sea Kingdom isn't large on land; it's mostly sea."

"I'm not planning a visit. I just want a blue brand. The color of the Sea Kingdom Teleportation Array is beautiful," Seraphina replied, resting her elbows on the table and cradling her chin in her hands, watching Milos sift through the bag of materials.

Milos had moved to a spacious house with a garden, free from the intrusive presence of Big Saen's lightbulb, much to Seraphina's relief. She watched him pick out blue crystals, his slender, deft hands moving with a grace that made her a tad envious.

"I'll help you pick," she offered, pretending to be helpful. Her fingers occasionally brushed his, ostensibly by accident.

Milos lowered his gaze, his long lashes fluttering slightly. The fleeting touch of Seraphina's fingers took him back to the moment when she applied ointment on his hand. The skin seemed to remember, tingling where it had been touched.

Milos raised his eyes, only to see her face focused and earnest, seemingly oblivious.

"Host, add one point," Little N chimed in, noting the subtle rise in favorability.

"Don't mess up," Milos said lightly, his voice as calm as ever.

"I'm not messing up. I'm just helping," Seraphina replied, feigning innocence as she reached for another crystal, her fingers accidentally-on-purpose brushing against the porcelain again.

This time, her fingers were caught in a firm grip. She looked up in surprise to find Milos holding her hand with a steady expression, his other hand still calmly sorting through the rough stones. She tried to pull her hand back, but his grip held her in place.

Though it could be seen as a way to keep her from causing mischief, there was something undeniably provocative about his approach. If the God of Light had a point system, this would surely be racking up the scores.

Seraphina smiled, propping her cheek on her free hand as she watched Milos. His eyes remained impassive, seemingly engrossed in his task, but the increasingly sluggish pace at which he selected blue crystals betrayed his distraction.

After Little N reported two point increases, Seraphina called out sweetly, "Lord Milos."

Milos didn't lift his gaze, merely responded with a soft "um."

"These crystals should be enough, right? I remember you mentioned needing 22, but you've picked more than twice as many," she teased with a smile.

Milos finally looked up, his expression still composed. "The teleportation array has a high failure rate. It's wise to have extra materials as a backup."

Seraphina: "..."

Would the God of Light really botch a teleportation array?

Time slipped by, and an hour later, the pointed blue card was complete, glowing softly in the room. Outside, the city lights shimmered like a sea of stars.

"It's late, go home," Milos said, handing her the blue card

Seraphina cast a wistful glance at the dark night outside, a hint of reluctance tugging at her. She'd donned a particularly daring skirt today, one that showcased more of her assets than usual—a strategic choice meant to make a lasting impression. She wasn't quite ready to depart until she'd hit that coveted 40-point mark in her little game of charm and wit..

"Can't I stay here? It's so dark outside, and I don't have a carriage. I'm too afraid to go home alone."

"No," Milos replied, unyielding. He picked up a yellow pointed card and handed it to her. "This is the teleportation array for the southern continent. Use it to teleport home."

Seraphina: "..."

What kind of extravagant gesture was this? Using a teleportation array card worth fifty gold just to send her home? She would have preferred to walk and save this card.

"Okay," she said, taking it reluctantly. She knew she couldn't push him too far; the ice was breaking bit by bit, but she wasn't ready to leave just yet.

She took her sweet time packing her things, all the while sneaking glances at Milos, who stood nearby with his arms crossed and an air of patient endurance. His long lashes cast shadows like crow feathers over those cool, clear eyes of his. His face was so exquisitely handsome, it practically invited a gentle teasing, as if daring anyone to try and ruffle his serene demeanor.

On a whim, she stood on tiptoe and quickly pecked Milos on the lips. "Consider it a thank-you gift."

Milos's eyes widened in shock, his heartbeat instantly thrown into chaos.

"Host, two points!" Little N squealed. "How did you manage that at the eleventh hour?"

Seraphina smirked, "My days in sales promotion back in school taught me well. Always observe, seize opportunities, and create value."

Little N chimed in, "I've learned something new today."

Milos blinked, his gaze lingering on her bright red lips. After a thoughtful pause, he murmured, "Isn't that just normal communication between people? Why would it be considered a thank-you gift?"

Eh? Well, he had a point there.

20

Seraphina returned home using the teleportation array, landing with the grace of someone who'd done this more times than she cared to count.

Lily, the diviner who often stood in for her, was lounging on the sofa in the bedroom, engrossed in a newspaper. She looked up, startled. "I thought you'd be gone for a few more days."

"I have classes tomorrow," Seraphina replied, tossing her handbag onto the low cabinet. She turned to see Lily swiftly undoing the belt on her dress, watching as the face that mirrored her own began to melt away like wax.

"Sorry about the short notice," Seraphina said with a grin, "but it looks like you can't take a break just yet."

Lily raised an eyebrow. "You just got back, and you're leaving again?"

"Of course," Seraphina said, rifling through the closet for a blue skirt with a wide hem. "I won't be long. I'll be back before morning classes."

"You're always on the go," Lily remarked, her half-melted face slowly reassembling itself. "Oh, by the way, I have some news."

"What is it?"

"I had a special visitor today," Lily said with an amused smile. "Princess Margaret, the capital's own rose."

"What?" Seraphina turned sharply, a prickle of unease running through her. "What was she doing here?"

"Nothing much," Lily replied, twirling a lock of hair around her finger. "We just chatted about fashion and the latest trends. But you should be cautious. Margaret kept studying my face very closely."

"People might not notice, but I do. As a pretender, I pay a lot of attention to how others look at me. I'm always on the lookout for any sign of detection. Margaret was trying to figure out if we were the same person."

Seraphina lowered her gaze, hiding the storm brewing inside her. Margaret was observing her?

"Would Lusahu betray our secret?"

"No, we're bound by a three-party contract. The world's will enforces it—anyone who breaks it pays with their life."

"Understood." Seraphina's expression returned to calm. "Please handle it if she comes back. I don't want my friends finding out."

Footsteps echoed in the corridor. "Miss Seraphina, dinner is ready."

"I'll be down shortly," Lily replied, perfectly mimicking Seraphina's voice. She patted Seraphina's shoulder with a reassuring smile. "Don't worry, everyone has secrets. I'm no exception." With that, she slipped out to dine in Seraphina's place.

"Host, do you think we've been discovered?" Little N asked, worry seeping into his voice.

"Most likely," Seraphina mused. "Margaret is definitely the SSR. It's her identity in front of the God of Light. I had my doubts, but her visit confirmed it."

"As for her role in the North, there are two possibilities. Either she hasn't managed to get close to the God of Darkness and just happened upon me, or she's already mingling with him, becoming someone he knows well."

"Mingling with the Dark God?" Little N was aghast. "Who could she be?"

"I suspect she might be an angel," Seraphina said thoughtfully. "In my history of gods class, I studied their pasts and found the Dark God differs from the others."

"Other gods only take hereditary angels as their servants, but the Dark God accepts both hereditary and wild angels, making him the one with the most. Could it be that the SSR has a powerful ability to transform, like adding wings to its host?"

Seraphina continued to piece her theory together. "Even if she's become an angel, she might not possess complete angelic powers. But she's definitely not weak—she's a system-selected tasker. Next time, I'll ask Cecil how many angels he's got. Though, I've got a pretty good guess who she is."

"Who?" Little N prompted eagerly.

"It's the woman we saw when we left the apartment today," Seraphina concluded. "Her stern expression and the aura she exuded were anything but ordinary."

"I think she's crafting a persona—a fallen angel character. After all, we all wear different masks for different gods. But she's easy to spot because she's such a dramatic performer."

"Wow," Little N exclaimed, thoroughly impressed. "Host, allow me to shower you with a barrage of thumbs-up praise!"

Seraphina chuckled and stretched her arms. "Now that we know who she is, we're not stumbling around in the dark anymore. We'll head to the Sea Kingdom after divine arts class tomorrow."

"Host, I still have a question. Will she expose us to the Dark God?"

"I doubt she'd dare," Seraphina replied with a confident smile. "She has a mouth, and so do I. Neither of us wants a mutually destructive showdown. She'll likely just keep trying to trip me up, hoping I'll slip."

"What should I do then?" Little N asked, a bit anxious.

"Oh, we'll figure it out," Seraphina said casually, adjusting her skirt in front of the dressing mirror. "For now, let's deal with the sea god and then head to class."

"Wow, host, we just hopped from the North to the Southern Continent, and now you're off to the Sea Kingdom? You're basically an air travel expert."

Seraphina grinned, pulling out the small blue teleportation card. "Just my professional skills as a time management master."

Little N: "..."

***

As soon as the teleportation light faded, Seraphina was greeted by the scent of the sea and the sound of waves crashing. The smell was identical to her hometown's, evoking a sense of warmth and familiarity.

The halo vanished, revealing the moonlit sea and a starry sky, the rushing wind binding them together into one vast expanse.

Facing the sea breeze, Seraphina walked to a massive black reef and surveyed her surroundings. Aside from the sea and rocks, there was nothing but desolation—not even a solitary tree.

Waves crashed against the reef, breaking into milky white foam. She set her lantern on the reef and fished out the small blue bottle. In the weak light, she carefully penned the name of the sea god, Iblis Rhea.

The moment her quill paused, the glass bottle flared with light and then quickly dimmed. Darkness reclaimed the scene, and Seraphina noticed the mermaid candy had vanished from the bottle.

She waited for five minutes, but nothing changed.

As the minutes ticked by, Little N grew restless. "Host, is it a dud?"

Seraphina chuckled. "The target is a god; he might have some resistance. Plus, with all those eyes watching beneath the sea, the pill probably needs the right moment to cast its dream."

Just as she finished speaking, the sea surged, and a brilliant light leaped up.

Before she could discern what it was, it splashed back into the sea, sending up a spray of water.

Seraphina's heart raced with anticipation. She knew the moment had arrived. She jumped off the reef, stepping carefully onto another low rock as she made her way toward the commotion.

The nearer she got to the water, the slicker the rocks became, making her progress precarious. Cold seawater splashed her face as she reached the lowest rocky beach. There, at the junction of two large reefs, lay something resembling a giant fish, draped in gently swaying seaweed.

Seraphina approached cautiously, aware that mermaids could be aggressive. Stopping five steps away, she slowly raised her wind lantern.

The soft glow illuminated the rocky scene and unveiled the sea god Iblis.

Seraphina's eyes widened in surprise. She had always pictured the sea god as a composed young man, his expression eternally indifferent, a reflection of his perpetually satisfied desires.

But the figure before her defied that image: a youthful, handsome face tinged with the boyishness of a teenager. His upper body was human and bare, while his lower half boasted a dark blue fishtail. He couldn't have been more than 18 years old. So this was what the sea god looked like in his younger, medieval days — a blend of youthful charm and ancient mystique.

He seemed uncomfortable, his hands sinking deep into the gravel. His upper body was slightly raised, and in the dim light, his thin waist and taut, pale skin exuded a dangerously alluring presence. Water droplets traced a path along his sharp jawline, glided down his chest, and disappeared into the shimmering scales of his fishtail, adding a touch of ethereal beauty to his otherwise perilous appearance.

Seraphina leaned closer, perhaps dazzled by the light. The boy's ice-blue eyes, previously hidden beneath his bangs, slowly opened, like a turbulent undercurrent beneath the calm sea, threatening to unleash a storm.

"It's you..." Iblis rasped, his voice low and hoarse. His eyes shifted from confusion to focus, locking onto Seraphina as though replaying incoherent fragments in his mind.

Today was supposed to be a day of celebration—his birthday, with all of Atlantis in revelry. Yet, after drinking a bit too much, he ventured out for a walk, only to find his head spinning as he tumbled into the coral.

And then, the transformation began—a terrifying change as his massive fishtail split into smooth legs, like a knife slicing through him, leaving him trembling. He'd taken human form before, but never with such agony.

Iblis roared and thrashed in the seagrass, a voice echoing in his ears, "This is the potion you desired. Drink it and you can pursue the one you love. Fail to win her love, and you will dissolve into sea foam."

Iblis: "..."

What in the depths was happening?

"Oh, I forgot to mention. You traded your voice for the potion, and now it's time to collect your voice."

His eyes widened, veins standing out on his forehead as a piercing force clawed at his throat. He bit his lip, fighting desperately against it, while flashes of impossible images surged in his mind.

He and his brothers, singing on the sea, guiding fishing boats. A figure fell from a massive ship, and he swam to rescue her.

The human girl, beautiful and pale, with sun-bright hair, lay unconscious in his arms. He pushed her ashore, took one last look, and returned to the sea.

Love at first sight, they said. He sought the sea witch for a potion to become human and follow his heart. But the price was his voice.

Fish shit! He had lovers aplenty, why would he sacrifice himself for just one? And when did this witch even show up in the sea?

Iblis fought desperately, but his strength was a mere fraction of what it should have been, dulled by the alcohol.

Yet he was still a god. He managed to preserve both his merman form and his voice. But that strange power had robbed him of his amphibious nature. He could no longer breathe like humans.

Now, he was suffocating, stranded on the shore.

Water, he needed water—someone had to sprinkle water on his gills.

He looked at Seraphina, discomfort etched in his eyes, and begged hoarsely, "Please, water first..."

Seraphina: "..."

It seemed that all gods, in their divine irony, couldn't escape the predicament of being caught short in the very element they were meant to command.

21

The sea under the moonlight was whipped up by the wind, and the cold stars were embedded in the night sky like the countless eyes of the gods watching over the world.

Seraphina stood frozen, watching in shock as the boy collapsed again, gasping for breath. His webbed fingers dug deep into the sand and gravel, so fiercely that blood began to seep out.

"Water... If you don't give it to me, I will really die," the boy rasped, his voice hoarse with desperation.

Seraphina, acting quickly, smashed her wind lantern on the reef, using the remaining half to scoop water from the shore just a few meters away. She hurried back, pouring the water over Iblis's gills.

"More, more..." Iblis lay on his back, his neck arching into a graceful curve. As he regained some strength, his palm began to emit a silver light, pressing against his throat to restore his ability to breathe air.

Seraphina made several more trips, dousing his gills with water until they gradually disappeared, the fine fish scales on his neck giving way to smooth, human skin.

His breathing steadied, his expression grew serene, and he began to survey his surroundings. His gaze finally settled on the busy girl, his water-blue eyes filled with curiosity.

"Are you okay?" Seraphina asked, breathless from her efforts.

"Princess?" Iblis propped his head on his arm, his voice no longer dry but carrying a lazy clarity thanks to the water.

Seraphina shook her head. "You've got the wrong person."

"How could I mistake you? I remember your face." A sly smile tugged at Iblis's lips as he suddenly reached out, grabbing Seraphina's calf and pulling her close.

She yelped as she fell onto him, her knees striking the rough gravel and her hands landing on his wet, slippery fishtail. The tiny scales nipped at her palms like hungry creatures.

"Apologies, my body's still in self-defense mode," Iblis said with a smirk.

His aqua blue eyes sparkled with mischief, reveling in the discomfort he caused her.

"Tell me, how did you manage it? How did you shove that bloody experience into my head and toss me from the sea floor?"

Iblis studied Seraphina's face, amusement dancing in his eyes. " Seems you know my tastes. Even in Atlantis, you're exceptional."

He leaned in closer, his voice a slow, seductive whisper. "Who sent you? Cecil, Milos, Davaskova, or Yabloni? I bet it was Cecil. He's the one for precise, uncompromising strikes. Milos is more methodical. Plus, he and I have a history."

"I cut off the underworld's water supply, and he retaliated by closing the gates to sea-borne souls. Those souls returning to Atlantis caused chaos. You know, humans fish so much, the sea's dead outnumber grains of sand. Atlantis was nearly suffocated in a gray fog for a time."

Seraphina struggled to her feet, inspecting her wounded palm. She whispered a denial, "I don't know any of them."

"Tsk, what an adorable little liar you are," Iblis chuckled.

Seraphina realized he had seen through the dream pill's effects. As a native, she knew this astute god well. The sea god had maintained peace on both land and sea for millennia, never allowing his realm to be marred by war. His intelligence was anything but superficial.

She had never expected to trick him with the pills from the start. After all, when the strange power erupted, she was the only one left standing on that dark beach. It would be hard to convince anyone that it wasn't her doing.

The pills were merely a means to an end—a way to lure him up from the seabed. The real work, however, lay elsewhere.

Watching Seraphina clutch her injured hand, the young man chuckled. "Does it still hurt? Let me take a look."

"You're quite delicate. You made me bleed too. How could I not feel pain?" He gently took her hand, bringing it to his lips, and began to slowly lick the beads of blood.

Seraphina winced, feeling as if countless tiny thorns were scraping her skin, causing more blood to ooze. It was clear he wasn't holding back the barbs on his tongue—a mermaid's tongue was notorious for such things—and he seemed intent on punishing her.

A streak of bright red blood glistened at the corner of Iblis' mouth, his aqua blue eyes gleaming with excitement. His strong arms encircled Seraphina's waist, preventing her escape. "Human blood. Now I understand why those crude sharks are so fixated on it. It's quite a treat."

He pinched her chin with his webbed fingers, a mocking smile playing on his lips. "Planning to drain my precious little girl before I turn into sea foam? You know, if you can't have something, sometimes it's best to destroy it."

Seraphina lay limply against Iblis, her breath shallow. Her eyelashes fluttered, and her pale face took on a delicate, fragile appearance, while her bright red lips looked as tempting as blossoming flowers.

"Trying to tempt me?" Iblis murmured, his gaze growing colder.

He'd spent enough time onshore; his patience was wearing thin.

"Still not going to spill your secrets?" He chuckled, leaning in so his lips brushed her earlobe. "Maybe I should accept Cecil's little gift. Unless you plan to tell me how you managed to drag me out of the sea..."

But suddenly, the young god's taunting words ceased. His eyes widened as he clutched his chest. His heart thundered violently as something spread rapidly through his veins, an uncontrollable emotion flooding him, making him tremble.

The girl before him became the only light in his darkness, the lone half-bottle of water in his desert, the small fire in his winter snowstorm, drawing his gaze irresistibly.

This was wrong.

Terribly wrong.

Iblis clutched his chest, battling against this inexplicable surge of emotion. But the heat in his blood only intensified, racing up from his neck to his tailbone, a numbing, insatiable feeling that he couldn't suppress.

His eyes grew hazy, and the fingers gripping her chin began to relax, tenderly caressing instead.

He closed his eyes uneasily, took a breath, and opened them again. The girl's face filled his vision, his eyes blazing with intensity. He just wanted to keep looking at her, to keep her close.

How could she be so beautiful? He wanted to embed her in his eyes forever.

"You can only see me": A spell that binds someone's interest solely to you. Duration: 24 hours. No side effects. All he desires is to see you; without you, it's as if his very air is gone.

Seraphina shed her fragile facade, standing up to casually wipe the excess powder from her palm. She had taken advantage of Iblis's distraction to crush the spell powder and apply it to her wound. She originally intended for him to get it on his own injured hand, but fate had a sense of humor—he had licked it up with his tongue.

It was, undeniably, a catastrophe of his own making.

"Where are you going?" Iblis clung to her legs as if they were his life raft, his eyes wide with the kind of fear that only a god caught in the snares of his own emotions could muster. The omnipotent being was positively unraveling, unable to fathom a world where he couldn't tether her to his side.

Seraphina, with an air of mischievous command, lifted his chin. Instantly, his face tilted up, displaying those ocean-blue eyes brimming with adoration as radiant as the sun itself, waiting for her touch like a guppy hoping for a splash of water.

She laughed, a sound like silver bells. "I'm off to find the Dark God. Didn't you say he sent me?"

Iblis turned ashen, his disbelief as tangible as a slap. His heart twisted so fiercely he feared it might just up and explode. What did that brooding deity have that he didn't? How could anyone possibly outshine him?

"Stay with me," he implored with a voice tender enough to melt icebergs. "I'll double whatever he offers. Atlantis? It's yours. Or perhaps the southern continent? I'd conquer it just for you."

The scene was almost comical—like a mighty overlord presenting a world map and declaring, "See this? All of it, yours for the taking."

Seraphina caressed his cheek, her gaze softening as she peered into his eyes. "But I don't like you," she said, each word a delicate dagger.

I don't like you.

The declaration hit Iblis like a tidal wave, leaving him pale and reeling. The god who had never once stumbled in the treacherous game of love suddenly tasted heartbreak, and it was as bitter as he'd feared.

Jealousy flared like wildfire, stoking his resentment towards Cecil. Loss clawed at his insides, leaving him feeling like he was about to crumble into the sands beneath him.

"What... what can I do to make you like me?" he pleaded, desperation lacing his voice.

Seraphina's eyes drifted skyward, catching the verdant glow that signaled it was time to leave.

With a firm resolve, she pried his hands from her legs with all the grace of a queen dismissing a courtier. She retrieved the teleportation array, ready to whisk her back to the southern continent.

The golden card blazed to life, a beacon of her imminent departure.

Iblis' eyes widened in sheer panic as he scrambled to stop her, clawing at the sand with hands that lacked the power to defy fate.

Curse this wretched fishtail, heavier than a ship's anchor and twice as stubborn.

He summoned his divine light, a desperate bid to morph his tail into legs. But alas, his earlier struggle against those blasted dream pills had sapped his strength. The traitorous tail remained obstinately unchanged.

Damn it all, these legs have a mind of their own! They refuse to transform when it's crucial and then go rogue, changing willy-nilly at the most inopportune times. It's enough to drive a god to madness—or at least to question his life choices!

22

In the grand, sunlit hall, the spell class professor was in the midst of demonstrating a healing spell. Everyone was hanging onto every word like it was the last piece of chocolate in the box.

Seraphina lowered her eyes, her quill a blur as she hastily captured the professor's key points in her notebook. In a world where antibiotics and anesthetics were as mythical as dragons, a quick-healing spell wasn't just a convenience—it was a lifeline, a promise of fewer hours spent wincing and more time spent plotting her next adventure.

For instance, her hands and knees were currently swaddled in gauze, each bandage a testament to her need for a little magical healing.

Her encounter with the sea god had been a calamity of epic proportions—an unexpected tragedy where both parties came away licking their wounds.

What started with the simple intention of using a dream pill to coax him ashore had spiraled wildly out of control.

Her plan had been simple: lure the sea god ashore with a dream pill, use a bit of magic to make a lasting impression, and then let him chase after her with the urgency of a fish out of water. However, gods have a pesky habit of being, well, godlike. Even the slickest tricks and the highest-level props couldn't fully contain his divine might.

Now, with his memory restored, the sea god was likely fuming. A god nursing a grudge was not unlike a storm at sea—unpredictable and quite the spectacle.

He would undoubtedly pull out all the stops to track her down.

But that was perfectly fine with Seraphina. At least she knew she was steering this chaotic ship in the right direction.

A pretty face might flit through his thoughts like a passing breeze, but an unforgettable memory? That was the real prize, and she was certain she'd etched herself into his mind like a sailor's tattoo.

"You're studying very hard," came a voice as sweet as sugar. It belonged to Princess Margaret, who seemed determined to befriend Seraphina no matter how frosty her reception.

"Hmm," Seraphina replied, eyes still glued to her notes.

Margaret leaned in, offering unsolicited advice on the spell with the enthusiasm of a self-appointed expert. "You know, it"s all about the timing. From here to here, slower down⋯"

Nope.

"When you see the spiritual power outline the wound, don't rush. Observe."

Nope.

"And then speed it up here to finish."

All wrong.

Seraphina glanced up at Margaret with a smile so disarming it could charm birds right out of their trees. Sure, Margaret's method promised to heal a wound faster than you could say "abracadabra," but its durability was about as reliable as a house of cards in a windstorm—more flash than function.

Had her trickery already begun?

"Ah, I see. I'll remember that," Seraphina said, her voice as sweet as honey.

A bell tolled in the distance, signaling the end of class. Textbooks were snapped shut, and students flowed out of the room like a tide retreating to sea.

Seraphina stood, and Margaret naturally fell into step beside her, continuing her monologue about healing techniques. Seraphina listened with half an ear, her mind whirring through her schedule. She'd met with the light yesterday, and facing the sea god again so soon was a bit too ambitious—even for her. Darkness would have to wait, too. Two days should do it.

Free time. A rare treasure. What to do with it?

"Seraphina, hey..." Margaret's lace-gloved hand waved in front of her eyes, snapping her back to the present. "Sorry, I got distracted. What were you saying?"

Margaret's expression darkened momentarily. She'd just shared a wealth of dubious healing tips—ones that might have been more at home in a comedy than a textbook — and Seraphina had missed it all. For Margaret, it was like offering a treasure trove only to find it unappreciated.

She forced a smile, preparing to repeat herself, but Seraphina cut her off with a raised hand. "No need, I've got it all," she said, her gaze fixed on something—or someone— behind Margaret.

What do you mean? I haven't even begun my spiel, Margaret thought, her expression turning stormy as Seraphina darted away with the grace of a gazelle.

"Lord Milos—"

Seraphina's voice carried across the hall as she approached a figure beside the statue of the god of light. Milos stood there, a thick tome in hand, exuding an aura that could rival the sun's brilliance. His demeanor was usually as icy as a winter morning, but when he saw Seraphina, a warmth thawed his frosty exterior.

Margaret pursed her lips, the shadow in her eyes quickly masked by a practiced smile. She followed in Seraphina's wake, determined to remain in the orbit of the captivating Lord Milos.

"What happened to your hand?" Milos asked, eyeing Seraphina's left hand, which was wrapped in enough gauze to suggest she'd taken a tumble off a cliff rather than a mere misstep.

"Oh, just a little fall," Seraphina replied with a nonchalance that could rival a cat's disdain for water. "No worries, though.

We covered healing in class today. Her Highness Margaret shared a nifty little trick with me. Perfect time to practice, right?"

"What trick?" Milos inquired, a skeptical brow arching.

"Well... something about speaking slower on the 'n' and speeding up at the 'r'. And pausing while outlining the wound," Seraphina recalled, her brows knitting together in concentration.

"Isn't that right, Your Highness?" she asked, turning to seek Margaret's confirmation, only to find her gone as stealthily as a shadow at noon. A sly smile curled her lips.

"That's incorrect," Milos said, frowning slightly. "It might appear healed, but one wrong move and it'll split wide open again."

"Ah?" Seraphina feigned confusion, blinking innocently.

Milos cast a glance at her hands, bundled like loaves of bread. "Untie them."

"Milos, are you going to help me heal?" Seraphina teased, mischief dancing in her eyes. "But what about my knees, thighs, and waist? They're also a bit banged up."

Milos hesitated, momentarily taken aback. "You fell that hard?"

Seraphina: "..."

Trying to flirt with him was like trying to catch smoke with bare hands—he was just so literal.

"Come over here. Let me see," Milos said, gesturing towards a nearby grove and heading in that direction.

Seraphina followed, curiosity piqued. " LordMilos, why are you at the academy today?"

"Borrowing a book," Milos replied, his tone as light as a breeze.

Seraphina's eyes flicked to the thick tome he carried. It was an ordinary compendium of divine law, penned by the God of Light. Such books were commonplace enough, but anything bearing the God of Light's name made her skin prickle as if ants were marching over it.

She remembered the letter from the God of Destiny, hinting that the God of Light had left behind clues to regain his memory. Was this one of them?

"This book isn't rare. It's available in any bookstore. Why come here to borrow it?" Seraphina asked, her voice steady, her smile serene.

"I heard the Inoway Academy has a copy marked by the God of Light himself. It's just a legend, though no one's found his notes yet. It crossed my mind yesterday, so I thought I'd check it out."

"I see..." Seraphina replied, though her heart felt a chill despite the sun's warm embrace.

It seemed undeniably a "clue." She couldn't let him get his hands on it.

As they chatted, they reached the grove. Ancient trees formed a natural canopy, their leaves filtering the sunlight into a dappled mosaic on the ground. Thick shrubs and hedges enclosed the area, offering privacy that was perfect for tending to injuries away from prying eyes.

They settled beside a sturdy oak. Milos laid Seraphina's hand across his knee, deftly unwinding the bandages. Beneath was a paste of light green, covering a palm that looked as though it had tussled with something fierce and lost.

"This isn't from a fall," Milos noted, examining her hand with a keen gaze. "It looks more like punctures from a mermaid's scales and mouthparts."

Mouthparts?

Seraphina's expression froze for a moment. The sea god certainly wouldn't appreciate that description; it was clearly a tongue, she thought with an inward chuckle.

She shook her head, feigning innocence. "Mermaid? I've never seen one! I injured myself on some sharp rocks by the sea."

Milos glanced at her but let the matter drop. He focused on her hand, murmuring a spell. Light flared, and the wound vanished as if it had never been, leaving Seraphina no chance to witness the miraculous regrowth.

"Wow, that's amazing." Her smile was as bright as the sun, eyes twinkling with admiration.

Milos allowed a small smile. "Did you catch my demonstration?"

"Huh? That was a demonstration, not just showing off?" Seraphina asked, eyes wide with playful incredulity. "It was so fast—who could possibly catch all that?"

Milos chuckled softly. "I recited the spell aloud for your benefit. Normally, it's not necessary."

"Really?" Seraphina batted her eyelashes with feigned innocence.

"Any other places?" Milos asked, his tone steady and undistracted.

"Yes, here," Seraphina replied, having anticipated his question. With a flick of her wrist, she lifted the hem of her skirt to reveal the wound on her knee.

As Milos bent down to inspect it, she leaned in, her voice a soft whisper in his ear, "If you lift it a bit higher, you'll find the wound on my thigh."

Milos, unflappable as ever, simply focused on removing the gauze from her knee, showing no reaction to her innuendo.

Seraphina stood there, unfazed, while internally, her personal scoreboard ticked up—"One point for the heartbeat value," she mused. Milos, the master of mixed signals.

"This is definitely a wound from a sandy fall," Milos said softly, untying the gauze with care.

"Same thing happened earlier," Seraphina chimed in breezily.

Milos remained silent, delicately tracing the wound with his fingers. Seraphina's skin tingled under his touch, prompting her to nudge him lightly. "Stop touching it," she teased.

Lowering his gaze, Milos examined the jagged edges of the wound. This wasn't from ordinary sand but a rocky beach. Recalling Seraphina's request for a teleportation array to the Sea Country, he asked softly, "Did you go mermaid hunting?"

Eh?

Seraphina's eyes widened in surprise.

Leaning against the sturdy oak, Seraphina pondered Milos' expression. The wound on her knee had betrayed her secret— he knew she'd been to the Sea Country. But mermaid hunting? Ah, the charmingly straightforward logic of Milos. He must have assumed she was tagging along with gold hunters, a plausible cover given the forbidden allure of mermaid hunting.

His self-fashioned explanation had her predicament neatly resolved, a twist she hadn't anticipated.

"Oh, don't ask," she replied, feigning embarrassment as she turned her head away.

With a gentle touch, Milos healed her knee, leaving it as good as new.

Seraphina, wary of further scrutiny, decided against revealing the marks on her thigh and waist. She couldn't risk him identifying them as mermaid-induced.

"Anything else?" Milos inquired.

"Oh, no need for those. Just minor bruises, really. They'll heal in a couple of days," Seraphina assured him, hastily smoothing down her skirt.

Milos didn't press further. He rose and helped Seraphina to her feet.

"You've got classes this afternoon, so I'll head home," he said.

Seraphina watched him go, her gaze lingering on the divine law code. With no immediate plan to thwart his investigation, she nodded.

Once Milos disappeared from view, Seraphina heard the rustle of clothing behind her. Before she could react, a powerful presence enveloped her, pulling her into a firm embrace.

Her nose collided with a gem-studded button, sending a sharp pain through her senses and tears to her eyes. Looking up, she found herself face to face with Iblis, his smile edged with playful mockery.

"So here you are," he said with a grin, "I've been searching everywhere for you."

Seraphina's heart skipped a beat as she glanced toward the direction Milos had gone, worried he might return.

"Hey."

Iblis's voice, tinged with displeasure, drew her attention back. A strong finger lifted her chin, forcing her to meet his aqua-blue eyes, which twinkled with amusement.

"Ah, tears already? So adorable. Are you that moved to see me?" he teased.

Seraphina blinked up at him, her eyes glistening. "I dare not move," she replied, her voice a mix of defiance and resignation.

23

A gust of wind swept through the woods, bending the rushes to the ground and sending the leaves of the beech trees into a symphony of rustling. The branches creaked and groaned, sharp sounds cutting through the air as the entire sky over Burton was seized by the fierce winds.

Iblis glanced upward, his lips curling into a scornful smile. "Even in the absence of the God of Light, Burton's vigilance is impressive. They've sensed the presence of a foreign god."

"Are you leaving?" Seraphina asked, her voice laced with hopeful anticipation.

"Of course not," Iblis replied, his eyes glinting with mischief. "I've just found the one who has captured my interest. How could I leave without doing anything? Don't worry, as long as the God of Light remains absent, those old bachelors of light won't detect me."

Seraphina: "..."

Her concern wasn't about whether the Church of Light would discover him.

"You... you should let me go first," Seraphina said, squirming uncomfortably to free her arm from his grip.

Iblis chuckled, releasing her arm as he leaned back against the tree, folding his arms. "Are you from the South Continent?"

"Yes," Seraphina replied, rubbing her sore arm and looking up at him. Iblis stood taller than her, his short brown hair catching the breeze in a way that made it dance.

He looked at her with a blend of youthful softness and intense focus, but a closer look into his eyes revealed an indifference, as though nothing in the world truly held his attention.

"So, being from the South Continent, why have you turned away from the light and toward the darkness?" Iblis inquired with a sly smile.

"You could say I was sent by the Dark God," Seraphina said, avoiding a direct answer. "I've never admitted it, though."

"Oh, is that so?" Iblis chuckled, clearly unconvinced.

"Who was that person just now?" Iblis suddenly asked.

"Ah?" Seraphina feigned ignorance.

"Your lover?" Iblis guessed.

Seraphina blinked innocently. "He... is just the academy's pharmacist. You know, we often get hurt while studying divine arts, so every academy has someone like him."

"I don't like him," Iblis said lightly. "He called my tongue a mouthpart. That word displeases me. The last time I heard it was from the God of Light, and I nearly flooded Burton in my anger."

Seraphina: "..."

Again with the God of Light.

Iblis looked at her with a hint of displeasure. "And you, you haven't seen monsters like mermaids, right?"

Uh...

Seraphina, caught in her own web, felt embarrassed.

"Well, it's just for interrogation purposes," she reasoned. "I can't admit to hunting mermaids. In fact, I have a deep respect for them."

Iblis laughed, "Alright, little liar with sharp teeth."

The distant bells chimed melodiously, signaling the end of the break as students returned to class.

Seraphina's mind was on the "Divine Law Code" that Milos had taken. She didn't feel like attending class; she just wanted to retrieve it. But Iblis didn't seem easy to shake off.

"Can I leave?" she asked tentatively, biting her lip.

"Of course, you're free to go," Iblis nodded gently.

Seraphina looked at him in surprise, not expecting him to be so agreeable.

Taking a cautious step back, she said, "Then, I'll be going."

Iblis merely raised his chin, watching her with a bemused interest.

Grateful for the unexpected permission, Seraphina turned swiftly and ran out of the woods, her skirt gathered in her hands.

Her heart pounded in her chest as she sprinted faster than she ever had, spurred on by a newfound sense of urgency. She'd always failed short-distance running tests in school, but clearly, she just needed a little motivation.

Once out from under the shadow of the trees, she was bathed in warm sunlight again, and a sigh of relief escaped her lips.

She touched her back and found her clothes damp with sweat.

"Host, why did sea god let you go so easily?" Little N asked.

"Who knows?" Seraphina replied, puzzled. Logically, what she did yesterday could have warranted severe judgment in Atlantis—a clear act of blasphemy.

Yet Iblis had let her go after a few casual questions. The stroke of luck seemed too good to be true, leaving her wary of hidden traps.

"So what should you do now?"

"I think I should deal with Milos first," Seraphina decided after a moment's thought. "I don't want to hear that the God of Light has returned to the temple tomorrow morning."

"How will you get it back?" Little N asked.

"Well..." Seraphina frowned, running through several plans in her mind, none of which seemed foolproof. She realized she'd have to play it by ear.

Instead of heading straight to Milos, Seraphina first went to a fruit store to buy a basket of fresh strawberries, then made her way to his house.

Milos lived in a house with a sprawling garden—a common feature in the area, with most homes being three-story off-white buildings with large courtyards.

Milos' garden was particularly lush. Flowers bloomed everywhere, even in the cracks of the walls, and sunlight seemed more abundant here than anywhere else.

He truly was the God of Light.

Seraphina pushed open the white courtyard door. Milos didn't employ servants, yet the house was immaculate, everything in its place as though guided by an unseen hand.

She entered the living room with the strawberries. Milos wasn't there, but she knew that from the moment she entered, the house itself was watching, alert to any unusual activity.

So she sat quietly in an armchair, placing the strawberries on the low table and waiting for him.

Ten seconds later, she heard footsteps on the stairs.

Turning, she saw knee-high boots descending first, followed by long legs clad in mustard-colored breeches, a simple white shirt with rolled-up sleeves revealing strong arms, and lastly, Milos' stoic face.

He appeared as composed as ever, which reassured Seraphina. No clues had been found, and he remained the familiar Milos she knew.

"Don't you have class this afternoon?" he asked as he walked down.

"I was supposed to, but the strawberries at home ripened, and Uncle George asked me to pick some for friends. You're my only friend, Lord Milos, so I came here," Seraphina explained, pushing the basket toward him. "Strawberries are delicate. I wanted to come in the evening, but they wouldn't be fresh by then."

"So you skipped class?" Milos asked, his brow furrowing slightly.

"Lord Milos, you'll teach me the same thing, won't you?" Seraphina replied with a bright smile, holding up a finger as if to seal the promise. "Just this once, I swear," she added, her tone playful and lighthearted. She hoped her sincerity and a bit of charm would soften him, coaxing him to indulge her just this once.

Milos glanced at her slender white fingers, then lowered his gaze and asked, "What were you supposed to learn this afternoon?"

Did he agree to teach her?

"Magice of Illumination," she replied cheerfully.

"Alright." Milos sat in the armchair next to her, picking up a quill and writing in the air. A thin, fiery light streamed from the quill's tip, forming words that floated in mid-air.

"All freshmen learn Illumination when they start. I'll teach you something different," Milos said.

"Why different?" Seraphina asked, intrigued.

"This spell is called Expel Darkness. It brings light like Illumination, but it also burns dark creatures."

Seraphina's heart skipped. "Like when you used golden light on the fallen angel in the museum?"

Milos nodded. "Almost. You can't pierce an angel yet, but you can scorch their skin."

"Wow, I'd love to learn that," Seraphina said eagerly. "It sounds really useful."

"Yes, it affects both dark creatures and theologians who follow darkness."

Oh, then I can't use it on Cecil, Seraphina thought.

Milos taught with dedication, and Seraphina learned with equal fervor. Within an hour, she managed to conjure a small light orb the size of a marble, rotating slowly in the air and emitting a soft glow.

"This… won't even light up my face," she remarked.

"Practice is key." Milos sat beside her, watching the light orb with her.

"How long until I can make it as bright as a candle?" Seraphina asked.

"I'm not sure," Milos admitted. "I don't remember. I don't even know how I know this magic."

"I'm sorry," Seraphina said, her eyes soft with apology. "I forgot."

"It's alright," Milos replied lightly.

Milos always exuded an aura of omniscience, as if nothing was beyond his grasp. Sometimes she forgot he'd lost his memory. His words reminded her of her purpose.

"Did Lord Milos find the God of Light's handwriting in that book?" Seraphina inquired, feigning interest with a curious tilt of her head.

"I haven't read it yet," Milos replied, his tone calm but thoughtful.

"Really?" Seraphina feigned disappointment. "I wanted to see what the handwriting looked like."

"I'll get it now." Milos stood and went upstairs.

As she waited, Seraphina washed a plate of strawberries. Each one was plump and red, a light touch enough to make juice spill.

What a delicate fruit, she mused, placing the plate on the table.

Milos came down with the Code of Divine Law in hand. Before he could open it, Seraphina quickly extended her hand and, with a smile, said, "Let me see." She had a nagging feeling that Milos must not look inside the book. His ability to perceive what others could not made it imperative to keep it closed.

Without hesitation, Milos handed the book to her.

Seraphina took the book, but instead of opening it, she ran her fingers over the cover with a trace of caution. As she did, a palpable sense of danger seemed to seep from the book, as if it were mocking her with a silent sneer.

It reminded her of the unsettling nature of the God of Destiny's letter. With a resigned sigh, she squeezed the cover, leaving behind two crescent-shaped nail marks. "I didn't realize the academy had such an ancient book. If I had known, I would've borrowed it before Lord Milos."

"Princess Margaret helped me borrow it," Milos explained. "I mentioned it to Bishop Saen, and she happened to be there and volunteered to retrieve it."

Seraphina's expression turned sour. "Princess Margaret... She doesn't seem to like me much. If it weren't for your reminder today, I might have botched the healing spell with her added 'ingredients.'"

A flicker of doubt passed through Milos' eyes. "Have you offended her?"

Seraphina shook her head. "I don't remember."

After a moment of silence, Milos advised, "Stay away from her in the future."

Seraphina couldn't help but smile at his seemingly protective gesture. "Let's not read this book, okay? Lord Milos is my friend, and I want to distance myself from Princess Margaret now. There's no reason for my friend to be involved with her."

Milos glanced at the book, hesitating. It was clear he was eager to find clues about his lost memories within its pages.

"Please, is it okay?" Seraphina pleaded, hugging his arm and leaning against him. Her proximity and soft demeanor made Milos, who was deep in thought, stiffen slightly.

Milos lowered his gaze to Seraphina, who was looking up at him with a hint of grievance in her delicate eyebrows. Her sweet breath softly brushed against his chin and Adam's apple, causing the air around them to feel suddenly dry and charged.

Seraphina waited anxiously for his response, but when none came, she began to consider another approach. Just then, she heard Little N cheerfully report, "Host, add one point. Your Lord Milos was moved in silence again."

Eh?

"Okay," Milos finally relented.

Eh?

Two surprises hit Seraphina at once, like receiving an unexpected gift package. She beamed, raising the book triumphantly. "I'll help you return it to Princess Margaret." But in truth, she had no intention of letting the book linger where it didn't belong. The stove is its true home, after all. It felt only right to consign it to the flames, where it could no longer pose a threat or serve as a temptation.

Milos nodded, but after a few moments, he asked, "I promised you, so what will you give me as a thank you gift?"

"Thank you gift?" Seraphina was momentarily startled, gesturing to the washed strawberries on the table. "Will these do?"

"I'm afraid not," Milos replied lightly, his eyes briefly flickering to the book on her lap, hinting that he could change his mind at any moment.

Quickly, Seraphina hugged the book tightly and reached for a strawberry, offering it to him. "Try it first, don't rush to refuse." Seeing him hesitate, she took a bite to demonstrate. "Look how big and red this strawberry is."

She bit into the strawberry, and its bright red juice flowed over her lips, making them appear even more inviting. Seraphina's lips, already rosy and fair, now seemed irresistibly sweet.

Milos's gaze lingered on her lips for a couple of seconds, his usual cold demeanor giving way to a deeper, more thoughtful expression.

Sensing his shift, Seraphina lightly tapped her lips with her finger. "Oh, I suppose this can't be a thank you gift, just as you said earlier. It's simply a normal exchange between friends."

Having achieved her goal, Seraphina stood up with the book in her arms, ready to leave.

Milos, seemingly having anticipated her move, allowed a small smile and stood to escort her out.

Just as she was about to leave, Seraphina turned back, stood on her tiptoes, and gently touched Milos' lips with hers. As he instinctively tried to pull away, she placed a hand behind his head, threading her fingers through his soft hair, and gently drew him closer for a soft, fleeting kiss.

"It can't be a thank you gift, but it can be a normal exchange," she whispered, her voice sweet and a bit mischievous.

Milos's eyes widened slightly in surprise, his heartbeat suddenly racing uncontrollably.

***

"Host, that was amazing! Just a peck, and you gained three points," Little N exclaimed, spinning with joy.

"I was surprised too. I thought it would only be one point, but three is quite the bargain," Seraphina replied with a smile. "By the way, how many points do we have now? Let's see how close you are to upgrading."

"Forty-one points~ But it'll be forty by tomorrow," Little N replied.

"Oh, time to exchange points for life again? Time flies," Seraphina remarked, a bit nostalgic.

"Host, will you go to the Dark God tomorrow? We're only ten points short."

"Yes," Seraphina said, smiling as she entered Count George's house. The maids, busy preparing dinner, curtsied as she passed. Seraphina nodded in acknowledgment and headed to the kitchen.

It was the only place with a fire in the summer. On her way home, she had flipped through the book and found nothing miraculous. The book seemed to serve no purpose but to make her uneasy.

Standing before the blazing fireplace, Seraphina tossed the book into the flames without hesitation. Using the fireplace tongs, she pushed it deeper into the fire.

With a whoosh, the flames roared higher, consuming the book. Seraphina stayed until she was sure it had burned to ashes.

As she walked down the corridor, a thought crossed her mind. If she destroyed all the clues left by the God of Light, could he still regain his memory? For a god who couldn't remember, would her mission be considered successful or a failure?

"What do you think, Little N?"

"I don't know," Little N admitted, feeling inadequate.

"Never mind, maybe we'll find more detailed rules after you upgrade," Seraphina said casually, reaching to open her bedroom door. She felt sticky from sweat and wanted to shower before dinner.

"Are you back?"

The moment she opened the door, Seraphina saw a familiar figure in the armchair by the window—the nightmare of a boy. She instinctively wanted to retreat and slam the door, hoping to wake from this nightmare.

The young man barely moved a finger, and the door seemed to freeze in place as if set in stone.

"Running away when you see me?" Iblis sneered.

"Of course not," Seraphina replied, quickly thinking on her feet. "I just wanted to close the door so no one sees you. You didn't exactly come in through conventional means, did you?"

Iblis chuckled, releasing his hold on the door, which closed and locked itself.

"What are conventional means?"

"Like the front door," Seraphina suggested.

"I came through the front door," Iblis said seriously.

"But you weren't invited in by the owner, were you?"

"Oh, then no," Iblis replied with a smile. "I come when I please, and I can ensure no one notices my presence."

It was the same kind of domineering arrogance typical of gods.

"I remember," Seraphina said, leaning against the wall and watching him warily. "You said I could leave."

"Yes, of course," Iblis nodded. "I respect your legs; they can go wherever they like. Now it's your turn to respect mine."

Seraphina frowned. The logic was sound, but something felt off.

"This is my bedroom. Naturally, I respect your legs, they can go wherever they want. But entering my room should require my consent, right?"

Iblis smiled. "Who tossed me from the ocean floor yesterday without my consent?"

Oh... she had forgotten.

Recalling her "misdeeds" from yesterday, her confidence waned.

She hadn't expected Iblis to confront her so soon. She had hoped to leave a lasting impression on him—but not while he was still angry and vengeful. She thought she had at least ten days before he'd calm down.

"What did you do to me the second time?" Iblis asked, resting his chin on his hand, his gaze unabashedly fixed on her. "Why do I suddenly feel so enamored with you? I can't bear to be away from you. You probably don't realize, but after you left, it was like I was a fish out of water."

You are of course a fish out of water, Seraphina thought.

Iblis's eyes narrowed. "You're probably thinking that I was a fish out of water, right?"

"Wow," Little N exclaimed. "He's the smartest god I've ever encountered. Uh... Can he hear your thoughts, Host? If so, that's bad. I'll be exposed."

"Why don't we test it?" Seraphina said, staring at Iblis.

Savage fish! Savage fish! Savage fish!

Iblis's expression remained unchanged, his gaze still heavy upon her.

"Host, did he hear it or not?"

"Alas, I don't know."

Suddenly, there was a sound of hurried footsteps in the corridor, followed by a knock on the door. "The hot water is here."

Seraphina was slightly startled, remembering her request for a bath.

But...

She turned to look at Iblis.

"Open the door," Iblis instructed lightly. "They can't see or hear me."

Seraphina shot him a skeptical glance but decided he wasn't playing tricks. She opened the door.

The maids came in, carrying several large buckets of hot water into the bathroom. In no time, the tub was filled with steaming water.

Once they left, Seraphina locked the door. Then she realized—why lock it? To keep intruders out while she bathed? But wasn't the biggest "intruder" already here?

"Humans bathe like this?" Iblis asked, strolling into the bathroom with curiosity. He picked up the soap, touched the rubber duck floating in the tub.

"Never seen it before?" Seraphina asked.

"No," Iblis replied, sniffing the cologne on the sink. "I rarely visit the land. We Atlanteans soak in seawater year-round and don't need baths."

"Oh," Seraphina replied absently, tugging at her sticky skirt.

"When are you leaving?"

"Leaving?" Iblis echoed with a smile. "The bathroom or this house?"

"Both."

"I'll leave once you tell me what I want to know," Iblis said, starting to unbutton his shirt.

"Sure, let's talk. Why are you undressing?" Seraphina instinctively covered her eyes.

Iblis sneered, "Why pretend? Haven't you seen my body?" He shrugged off his shirt, revealing a smooth, muscular chest.

"Don't get any ideas. I've been out of the sea too long. If I don't soak, my body dries out."

Seraphina covered her eyes with one hand, peeking through her fingers. It was dark last night, so she hadn't seen him clearly. Now she could appreciate that sea god had quite the physique.

His body was that of a young man, slim but not slender, with broad shoulders and a narrow waist forming a perfect inverted triangle. His arms showed lean, strong muscles, and his legs were straight and well-proportioned.

Ah, he bathed without even removing his pants? Seraphina mused, watching as Iblis settled into the bathtub. The tub was small, and his legs stretched beyond its edges. A shimmer of light flashed, and the black breeches transformed into dark blue fish tails, gracefully swaying like a giant fan.

Iblis leaned back, casually placing his hands on the tub's edge. His neck arched elegantly, like a swan's, as droplets trickled down his Adam's apple.

He luxuriated in the water for a while, before sneering lightly, "I guess you must be disappointed not to see my legs."

"Not at tall," Seraphina replied, lowering her hand from her eyes and openly observing the merman in the bath.

"Really?" Iblis smiled faintly, "I don't care much for this form. But I've always been accommodating to girls. If you wish to see, I don't mind changing it for you."

"I really don't want to," Seraphina replied, a thought suddenly striking her. "I heard humans aren't supposed to look directly at gods without permission."

"That's true, but I'm different," Iblis said nonchalantly. "I reside in Atlantis, and sometimes many small, mindless fish swim into the temple unknowingly."

"If I adhered strictly to that rule, half the fish in Atlantis would perish." He turned his gaze to Seraphina, "Consider yourself fortunate. Otherwise, bringing me ashore would have turned you into a pulp."

"You could easily kill me," Seraphina ventured cautiously, testing his intentions.

"How could I kill you?" Iblis turned his face, resting his chin on one hand, his smile lazy. "I traded my heavenly voice with a sea witch for this opportunity..."

Seraphina was momentarily speechless.

"You should cherish it," Iblis added as his tail vanished, replaced by two slender legs dangling over the tub's edge. Before Seraphina could discern any details, his black breeches reappeared.

"Ahhh, Host, did you see it clearly?" Little N exclaimed in shock.

"No," Seraphina replied, slightly disappointed but relieved.

"Hahaha, I saw it clearly. Not only did I see it clearly, I also took a screenshot," Little N chimed in, sounding quite pleased with itself. "It's a pity that my level is too low to share it with you."

Seraphina blinked in surprise as Iblis stepped out of the bathtub. She tried to keep her expression neutral, but her mind was buzzing with Little N's gossip.

"What do you think?" Little N asked eagerly.

"Hmm... very good," Seraphina replied.

"Be more specific," Little N urged.

"It's majestic and magnificent," Seraphina replied, biting her lip to suppress a giggle.

"What's that laughter about?" Iblis asked, glancing at her with a curious expression.

Seraphina tried to maintain a straight face but couldn't help the slight upturn of her lips. "Oh, it's nothing," she said, waving a hand dismissively. "Just a little inside joke."

Iblis raised an eyebrow, clearly intrigued. "An inside joke, huh? Care to share?"

She shook her head, still smiling. "Maybe another time. It's more fun to keep some things a mystery."

Iblis snapped his fingers, a subtle light enveloped him, and the water vapor instantly evaporated from his skin. He pulled his shirt from the hanger and snapped his fingers again, causing the water in the bathtub to vanish and refill itself.

"Go wash," he instructed lightly, carrying his clothes out.

Seraphina watched him leave, a bit surprised. She hadn't expected to get a bath with clean water. She had assumed he would leave her with the used bathwater.

Quickly, she rushed over to lock the door, even though she knew it was futile. If Iblis wanted to see something, a mere lock wouldn't stop him.

***

Feeling refreshed after finally rinsing off the sticky grime, Seraphina emerged from the bathroom in a simple white silk dress, her snow-white calves exposed. She felt like a flower freshly washed by rain, exuding a clean fragrance.

Iblis, lounging in an armchair, lazily raised his eyelids, eyeing her calves for a few seconds before looking away.

Seraphina tied her hair in front of a mirror, put on earrings and a gemstone necklace, and donned a big puffy skirt. "I'm going downstairs to eat," she announced.

"Okay, let's eat together," Iblis said, standing to follow her. Seeing she didn't move, he turned with a lazy smile, "Why aren't you leaving?"

Seraphina hesitated. "How are you going to eat with me? Why don't I bring you some bread later?"

"I don't eat leftovers, and I'm not your pet," Iblis said, pulling her gently but firmly toward the door. "You have to get used to it," he whispered in her ear, his voice clear, "We will live together for a long time."

"How long?" Seraphina asked, her tone wary.

"So long... that the person behind you can't help but come to you," Iblis replied, a slow smile spreading across his lips.

At the dining table, Count George and his family sat in their finery, each glittering with jewels. Their poise reflected their noble dignity.

After Seraphina sat down, the butler began serving dishes. Each person received two peeled emerald prawns, and the main course consisted of twelve dishes, served in small portions, enough to satisfy everyone by the end.

Seraphina, feeling hungry, picked up a shrimp with her fork, only to find her hand guided to the left. Surprised, she turned to see an extra chair beside her.

Iblis sat there, holding her wrist, easily guiding her hand to deliver the shrimp to his mouth. He even licked her fingers in the process.

Seraphina's heart raced wildly, and she quickly glanced around to gauge everyone's reaction.

But everyone was absorbed in their meal, the servants were in a daze, and no one seemed to notice her peculiar predicament.

"Don't worry, no one can see your abnormality," Iblis assured her.

Seraphina's face paled as he ate another piece of shrimp from her hand. Afterward, he lifted her hand and gently traced her fingers with his tongue.

"Are you a dog?" she couldn't help but quip, as it seemed like he was licking the plate clean after eating.

All eyes turned to her in astonishment.

Iblis laughed heartily, "Sorry, I forgot to mention. You can't talk to me because I didn't block your voice."

"Are you talking about me?" asked Rose from across the table, feeling insulted. Hadn't she just eaten a bit faster?

"Of course not," Seraphina replied quickly. "I'm memorizing a new spell."

"A new spell?" Robus eyed her suspiciously. "We didn't learn such a spell in our classes."

"I learned it on my own. Watch," Seraphina said, shaking the fork gently. "Are you a dog?" she whispered, all while giving Iblis a firm kick under the table. He managed to suppress his laughter and, with a subtle flick of his fingers, conjured a small light that made the roast chicken on the plate emit a "clucking" sound.

"Oh, it says it's not," Seraphina explained with a calm demeanor, as if it were the most natural thing in the world.

The table erupted into murmurs of surprise and amusement, Count George even clapping his hands in delight. "Remarkable! Is this magic?" he exclaimed.

"What's the purpose of this spell?" the Countess inquired, her eyes narrowing with suspicion.

"Well..." Seraphina hesitated for a moment, thinking quickly. "It's to ensure we're not eating something we shouldn't be, like dog meat. The same spell works for chicken or fish, helping us verify our ingredients."

As she spoke, she marveled at her own quick thinking, managing to twist the situation into something plausible.

"Incredible!" Count George praised, giving her a thumbs up. The others at the table, despite their skepticism, offered polite nods of approval.

The Countess looked displeased. She had hoped to criticize Seraphina's table manners, but Seraphina had slipped through her grasp.

"Those three ladies don't seem to like you," Iblis noted with a glint of interest in his eyes. "It's not surprising; you're quite a handful. But I like you a lot."

Seraphina pondered his words, wondering if there was any truth to his compliment. Yet, there were no points gained in her favor, so she dismissed it as another one of his sweet nothings. She understood that for the Sea God, the real satisfaction lay in the game of wits and banter, not just in the words themselves.

Her goal was clear: to keep his interest piqued without letting him feel as though he'd won. It was a delicate balance, engaging with him just enough to keep the dynamic intriguing while maintaining her own ground. She knew it was a game— a game she couldn't afford to lose.

Perhaps because Seraphina couldn't fight back verbally, Iblis leaned closer. He propped his chin on one hand and guided Seraphina to feed him, while his other hand gently caressed her waist.

As she fed this fish baby his beloved seafood, Seraphina retaliated by pinching the tender flesh inside his arm, showing him that while she couldn't argue, she could act.

"Seriously, you blew my mind," Iblis said, rubbing his arm where Seraphina had pinched him. "No wonder the one behind you chose you to approach me. I'm trapped by you. A wild rose with thorns."

Seraphina couldn't help but smirk at his words inwardly . "A wild, obstinate merman".

After dinner, they returned to her room.

Seraphina changed into her nightgown. Tomorrow, she planned to ditch him and head north. She needed to warm another god with her presence! But first, she had to figure out how he had found her so quickly.

"How did you find me?" she asked, watching Iblis as he roamed the room.

"It's simple," Iblis replied casually. "Your teleportation array is golden, your hair is golden, which suggests you're from the southern continent. Of course, it could be a decoy. But I've tasted your blood, and that makes it easy to track you."

Seraphina's heart skipped a beat. Wasn't that like having a tracking device implanted?

She combed her hair in front of the mirror, observing him subtly. "Is this a special mermaid ability? If a mermaid tasted many people's blood, could he distinguish them all?"

If he said no, she'd find a way to spike his soup with chicken blood, duck blood, or anything else.

"I've only tasted your blood," Iblis said lightly. "I'm not a true merman, nor am I interested in human flesh. My true form doesn't look like that. The merman appearance is just for fitting in with Atlantis."

"Much like the God of Light you believe in, his true form isn't human. He adopted a human guise for easier rule."

"If you're thinking of adding something to my food, I advise you to give up. I won't be fooled. Just as you thought, tasting too much blood dulls the senses. So, I don't plan to taste anyone else's blood. I won't let you confuse the taste. If you try anything, I won't hesitate to drink your blood again."

He stopped behind Seraphina, looking at her reflection in the mirror.

He was tall and thin, his eyes raking over her reflection as though peeling away layers to reveal the tender fruit beneath.

Seraphina's long eyelashes fluttered slightly, but she quickly feigned ignorance and continued combing her hair.

Iblis scanned the room again and whispered, "The tip card."

Seraphina's heart skipped a beat as she saw a small object fly from her skirt pocket in the mirror. It was the southern continent's teleportation array. She lowered her eyes slightly.

"Wow, host, he really used this trick," Little N remarked in surprise. "Good thing you gave Lily the northern land's teleportation array in advance."

"I just didn't want the maid to find it while cleaning. So I always have Lily bring it to me," Seraphina said thoughtfully. "It seems he suspects a connection with the Dark God. Of course, I do. I not only know the Dark God, but also the God of Light."

"I'm going to sleep, good night," Iblis said calmly, returning the yellow card and heading to the bathroom.

Seraphina's eyes widened in surprise, unsure why he was going there. Was he going to sleep in the tub?

A few moments later, she heard the sound of splashing water.

She glanced over and saw him transformed back into a mermaid, lounging lazily in the water-filled tub, swishing his tail, looking utterly at ease and almost blowing bubbles.

"Want to join?" Iblis asked with a smile. "There's room here."

"No, thank you," Seraphina replied, leaning back and stretching out on her bed with satisfaction.

***

As dawn broke, Seraphina tended to her baby fish at the dining table, just as she had done during last supper. With her task complete, she hopped into the carriage bound for school.

Seraphina was unsure what had transpired—perhaps something orchestrated by Iblis—but somehow, Count George had arranged for an extra carriage.

This meant Seraphina once again had her own private ride, sparing her the company of her cousins.

Iblis was like her shadow, accompanying her in the carriage, during classes, and even at meals.

By midday, Seraphina concocted a reason to slip away to Shell Road for lunch. Not only was the city library there, but so was Lily, who worked there. Seraphina was keen to shake off Iblis and delve into the library's resources on what to do if one ended up marked by a mermaid. And while she was at it, she planned to work on her disguise with Lily's help.

"I'm feeling peckish," she declared, trying to sound casual.

"Didn't you just have something to eat?" Iblis queried.

"I was feeding you!" Seraphina retorted, enunciating each word with a hint of exasperation. She furrowed her brow, feigning discontent, "I've been with you for just a day and I'm already famished. I really fancy a little cake." She gestured towards the afternoon tea spot nestled behind the library.

With a chuckle, Iblis obliged, "Alright, go ahead and eat."

"I'll go alone," Seraphina insisted.

"Why's that?" Iblis pressed.

"Because..." Seraphina's mind raced for a plausible reason.

"Ah, you're off to see the pharmacist to change your medicine again, aren't you?" Iblis suggested with a knowing smile.

Pharmacist?

Seraphina followed his gaze, puzzled, and saw a tall figure in a white robe making his way towards the library.

Quite dashing, she mused, squinting slightly.

As he drew nearer, his features sharpened, revealing the striking coolness in his eyes.

Her eyes widened in recognition—Lord Milos?

Iblis smirked at her, then cupped his hands around his mouth to call out, "Hey there—Mr. Pharmacist!"

"Don't shout," Seraphina hissed.

<u>24</u>

"**M**r. Pharmacist—"

A shout echoed from afar.

Milos didn't break stride, nor did he feel the need to glance over. After all, he wasn't a pharmacist, and the shout wasn't directed at him.

"Don't shout such nonsense." Another voice, softer yet unmistakable, sweet as honey, reached his ears.

Milos halted abruptly, his icy gaze cutting through the path to the two figures by the flower bed.

There stood a girl in a light green puffy skirt, vibrant as a dandelion, trying earnestly to stifle the boy beside her with her lace-gloved hands.

The boy appeared lazy, effortlessly pulling her into a gentle hold, resting his chin atop her head, chuckling softly at some private joke.

The sky darkened suddenly, the bright sunshine vanishing, casting a shadow over Seraphina. Realizing something was amiss, she glanced up. There was Milos, standing at the stairs, his gaze colder than ever.

Her heart skipped a beat, sensing trouble. She wriggled free from Iblis's embrace and rushed towards Milos.

"Lord Milos—"

Her cheeks flushed, blue eyes wide with worry—a rare sight, for she was usually all smiles.

Milos looked down at her, the coldness in his heart melting slightly, though his expression remained stern.

Iblis sauntered over, amusement playing on his features.

Seraphina, catching him in her peripheral vision, felt a pang of dread. Worried he might call out "Mr. Pharmacist" again, she quickly interjected, "This is Lord Milos, a friend of mine."

Oh really? Pharmacists can be called Milos too?

"Milos?" Iblis chuckled, his gaze flickering over Milos's face before returning to Seraphina. "Apologies, I thought you were introducing me to the God of Light."

"It's the only name I recall," Milos replied flatly.

Fearing they might delve into the topic of amnesia and inadvertently alert the sea god, Seraphina swiftly intervened.

"What's wrong with sharing a name with the God of Light? You're called Iblis, same as god of sea," she retorted, tugging on Milos' sleeve. "Are you heading to the library? I'm going there too."

Iblis looked momentarily speechless. I am the real sea god.

Inside the bright library, Seraphina and Milos stood by the shelves, flipping through books. Iblis took one glance and, finding it dull, wandered off.

Seraphina discreetly instructed Little N to monitor Iblis's movements and alert her if he approached.

Milos, detached, his lashes casting shadows over his eyes, picked up a couple of books, ready to leave. A slender arm stretched out before him, halting his path. His gaze shifted slightly, then paused.

"Lord Milos."

Her soft, pleading voice softened his stern gaze.

"What's the matter?"

"This library is enormous, and I don't know where to start," she admitted. "Since you recognized the mermaid bite instantly, I thought you might know."

"If, hypothetically speaking, a mermaid drinks your blood, they can track you easily. How can one remove that mark?"

Milos was taken aback. "Have you encountered a mermaid?"

"No, not exactly. But my wound was from a mermaid bite. I heard they can mark you, and I'm concerned..."

Seeing her genuine fear, Milos's demeanor softened. "Don't worry. Mermaids can't come ashore or stay out of water for long. Just avoid that sea area. But even if you get close, it won't matter much. Mermaids won't just sip on your blood. If there are too many of them, it will scramble their memories."

"But I'm still worried. What if it comes through the sewers? I've heard of mermaids in sewers... eating people..." She fiddled with her skirt's fabric, her brow furrowed in worry.

Milos softened his tone, "If you're truly scared, there's a way to temporarily mask your scent. But against a powerful mermaid, the effect won't last long. Was the mermaid who bit you a divine magician?"

"Possibly," Seraphina nodded uncertainly, "He wasn't caught, anyway."

"Take citrus peel, purple star stone powder, white fresh, and Esk grass roots, with a touch of dragon bone powder. Boil into a brown concoction and drink it. For ordinary mermaids, it masks the scent for a month. For higher-level divine magicians, half that time, and even less for more powerful ones."

What is this concoction? I've only ever heard of citrus peel.

Her eyes, as blue as a cat's, gazed up at Milos, laced with a hint of playful pleading. "I can't make it myself."

Milos didn't respond immediately, merely gazing at her with a cool detachment.

Seraphina reached out for his hand, his gaze shifted downwards, but he didn't pull away. Encouraged, she continued softly, "Alchemy formulas are often private. Even if they're in books, they're like what you told me—just ingredients, no measurements or steps. I can't possibly make it."

"Lord Milos, please help me. I'll collect it from you once you're done. I promise there'll be a thank-you gift this time."

Milos considered her for a moment before asking, "The person with you, who is he?"

"Oh, him," Seraphina replied, a little flustered, "A relative from the countryside. My mother was missing me and sent him to check on me. He's not quite right in the head, so don't mind his odd remarks."

"A relative," Milos's gaze lingered on her face, "Alright, I'll help you with this."

Seraphina's face broke into a bright smile, "Thank you! I'll come by tomorrow afternoon?"

"Yes," Milos nodded, a subtle smile touching his lips.

Sunlight streamed through the grand window, Seraphina shaded her eyes with her hand as the overcast sky cleared.

"One point for the host," Little N chimed in.

Where did this point come from? Good deeds must be contagious, Seraphina thought, her heart alight with happiness.

"Who are you calling stupid?" A chilly voice interrupted her reverie.

Seraphina didn't need to turn to know it was the sea god, Iblis.

"Little N!"

"Host, he teleported here. I only registered his presence when you heard him," Little N stammered.

"I wasn't referring to you," Seraphina turned, soothing the agitated young god, "You're the cleverest."

Milos's gaze shifted from Seraphina to Iblis and back again, "Remember to come by my place tomorrow." With that, he turned and left, books in hand.

The young god's voice dripped with sarcasm, "Relatives from the countryside, huh? not quite right in the head?"

"I was wrong," Seraphina pleaded softly.

She sighed in relief only after Milos had gone.

"Who is he?" Iblis queried, leaning against a bookshelf, his expression stern.

"The pharmacist Milos," Seraphina replied with a knowing smile.

"Come on, don't act like that," the boy suddenly closed the distance between them, "I know he's not just that."

"Oh, really? Then who do you think he is?" Seraphina asked, taking her time with each word.

"Probably your lover," Iblis drawled lazily, "though you don't seem to be hiding it very well."

His aqua blue eyes glinted like crystals, as if he already knew her secrets. "The way you're so attentive to him, I suspect his identity is far from ordinary."

"Get lost," Seraphina said, shoving him away with a cold look.

Iblis lost his balance momentarily, catching himself against the bookshelf.

"What's your deal?" he grumbled.

"Just getting a book," Seraphina replied, reaching behind him to grab a title, her voice playful. "You're in the way."

Iblis glanced at the book she picked up, "How to Care for Piglets"?

He chuckled, his earlier displeasure vanishing as he playfully pinched her cheek, "I might just fall for you."

No heartbeat points, not genuine.

"Host, you just earned a point!" Little N exclaimed in surprise.

Seraphina was equally taken aback, feeling the joy of a thrifty person finding a lost coin.

When she went to register the book for borrowing, Seraphina discreetly slipped a note to the administrator, Lily, under the guise of adjusting her book.

Lily, accustomed to her boss's mysterious ways, retrieved the pre-prepared Northland teleportation array, opening the note only after Seraphina had left.

"Dear Lily, let's meet at the alley behind Oak Street Tavern at 5 p.m. tomorrow. Don't forget the teleportation array."

"Do you really intend to borrow this book?" Iblis asked as they exited the library.

"Of course. I mentioned it before—my family lives in the countryside south of Burton. We've got a farm, so it doesn't hurt to learn more."

"I thought you were a divine magician?"

"I haven't taken the exams yet. I'm on the path to becoming one. Besides, caring for animals doesn't conflict with that. I've been feeding you, haven't I?"

Iblis paused for a moment before catching on, his expression shifting to amusement, "Well played. And let's not forget your four counts of blasphemy by the seaside."

Seraphina furrowed her brow, "Why four?"

"The seaside blasphemy was excessive, so it's counted as one; calling the mermaid a monster is one; saying I have a bad brain is another; and comparing me to an animal you feed is the fourth."

"Oh, I see. Four counts, huh? You're quite petty."

With everything squared away, Seraphina was in high spirits, chatting with Iblis as they approached the carriage. As they neared, she spotted Robus and Rose waiting impatiently.

"Why are you so late? We almost went in to find you," Robus said, sounding irritated.

"What's going on?" Seraphina asked directly.

"Her Royal Highness invited us to play cards. You know, it's considered rude to be late," Rose explained.

"Princess Margaret?" Seraphina inquired.

"Who else?" Robus replied. "Of course, it's her."

"Why the sudden invitation?" Seraphina pressed on.

"During lunch, we were discussing poker, and Her Royal Highness showed interest. We asked if she wanted to play, and she hesitated but agreed, saying she couldn't just visit someone else's home. So naturally..."

"We're going to the palace," Robus and Rose finished together, excitement evident.

Seraphina nodded thoughtfully, "And what does this have to do with me?" She hadn't heard her name mentioned.

"Don't be silly," Robus chided. "You can't play cards with just three people. As soon as Father heard, he insisted we bring you along. It's a great opportunity. Not everyone gets to visit the palace."

Seraphina sighed. It seemed Margaret hadn't orchestrated everything, but she had to tread carefully, especially since dealing with an SSR was no small feat.

"I really don't want to go. I've been at the library all afternoon, and I'm exhausted..."

"Are you trying to embarrass the Doyle family?" Robus said, displeased. "Officials have already recorded our names at the palace. If one of us doesn't show, it'll be seen as disrespect to the royal family."

"Father won't be pleased either," Rose added.

"Alright, alright," Seraphina relented, a headache brewing.

Once in the carriage, she turned to Iblis, "Will you come with me?"

Iblis didn't answer immediately, instead asking with interest, "Are you afraid of the princess?"

"No, not afraid, just not fond of her," Seraphina said, choosing her words carefully. "And she doesn't like me much either. But if you come along, I'll feel better." She looked up, her vibrant blue eyes shining with trust.

"Don't try to sweet-talk me," Iblis chuckled, gently pinching her chin. "I know you can't wait to send me back to Atlantis."

Not quite, you're one of my flock too. I'm thrilled to discover you can be sheared today.

***

In an elegant room, servants busily arranged tea and snacks. Near the window, a small table draped in silk hosted an intense card game.

Seraphina played distractedly, making frequent mistakes, but she didn't mind much. Playing cards wasn't her main concern.

Iblis lounged beside her, one hand on the back of her chair, tapping the red king, "Play this."

After another round, Margaret set down her cards, rubbing her temples, looking weary.

Robus took the hint, "It's past five. We should excuse ourselves."

"Yes," Rose chimed in, "You must be tired after such a long game. You should rest."

Margaret smiled, appreciating their consideration. The perks of being a princess meant others anticipated your needs without a word.

Seraphina exhaled in relief—it was finally over. She placed her cards down and bid farewell to Margaret alongside her cousins.

Margaret nodded with a smile, accepting a glass of juice from a maid, taking a sip before setting it aside with a tired gesture.

As Seraphina departed, she overheard a maid suggesting Margaret take a nap.

Everything seemed normal, perhaps Margaret really was just interested in cards. Maybe she was overthinking.

Back home, she indulged in two cups of black tea, finally feeling satisfied.

Iblis leaned on the table, watching her with a lazy curiosity, "Is that why you didn't touch the desserts or juice at the palace? I'm curious, what did the princess do to you?"

"She hasn't done anything yet, but that doesn't mean she won't in the future," Seraphina replied, peeling and eating an orange.

Iblis chuckled, "Want me to drag her to the ocean floor for you?"

"Too cruel," Seraphina said, separating the orange segments, "Even though I don't like her, I never intended to harm her..."

Before she could finish her sentence, her eyes widened as a blinding white light enveloped her. Iblis, acting on instinct, pulled her close, and together they were drawn into the light.

Back at the palace, the cards on the table glimmered briefly. Margaret smiled, brushing her fingers over them, selecting a heart and a spade.

"Huh? Another person got caught in it," she mused.

The card designs morphed into portraits of a male and female.

"Probably just a servant who happened to be nearby," a gruff voice echoed in her mind.

"Good thing I used high-level items to deal with her," Margaret said with a smile. "She left my place safely, everyone saw it, so no one can point fingers at me."

"Exactly," the voice agreed. "Even if she disappears, no one will suspect you."

"Will she really end up in the card world?" Margaret asked.

"Of course. Once she touched the cards, her presence was recorded. After she got home, we activated the gateway to the card world, pulling her in."

"And then?"

"Then you burn it," the gruff voice chuckled.

"She won't escape, will she?" Margaret inquired.

"No, everything in the card world is made of paper. There's no water, and the air is dry. She'll be drained in less than half a day and remain trapped forever, unable to interfere with us again."

Margaret leaned back with satisfaction, "I should have listened to you sooner."

"It's not too late," the voice assured her, "as long as you leave the thinking to me. It's clearly not your strength."

"I'll rely on you from now on," Margaret said, holding the cards near a candle flame, watching as they blackened and curled.

"Of course, my SSR title isn't just for show."

***

Seraphina landed in a haystack. Before she could regain her bearings, Iblis materialized above her, landing heavily. They rolled down together, startling the grazing sheep, which bleated and scattered.

"Get up! You're crushing my skirt," Seraphina panted, turning her face away. Iblis seemed to enjoy this, his breath tickling her neck.

Iblis propped himself up, his hands on either side of her head. "Why worry about your skirt now? Shouldn't you be more concerned about where we've been taken?"

"My immediate concern is not being crushed by you," Seraphina retorted, pushing him away with all her might and sitting up.

"Ungrateful," Iblis said lazily. "If I hadn't used magic to lighten your fall, you'd have been flattened."

Seraphina stood, brushing the hay from her clothes. A lamb, sensing the danger had passed, returned to nibble on the grass.

Frowning, she reached out to stroke it, exclaiming, "Why does its wool feel like paper?"

She touched other sheep, her eyes growing wider with each one. "This one too, and this one." The sheep, uncomfortable with her probing, scampered away.

Iblis plucked a piece of straw, twisting it until it unfurled into a sheet of pale yellow paper. He grabbed a sheep, tearing it apart with a swift motion.

To Seraphina's shock, the sheep split in two, revealing paper-made organs that fell out without any blood.

The bisected sheep bleated, examining its paper innards.

"This..." Seraphina stared at the paper lamb parts at her feet, speechless.

"This is the world of cards," Iblis explained calmly. With a wave of his hand, light shimmered, and the paper organs reassembled inside the sheep, restoring it. The lamb stood, inspected itself, and fled.

"Card world?" Seraphina repeated, bewildered.

"Yes, a realm governed by cards. Kings, queens, soldiers—all cards. Everything else is paper: the subjects, the sun, sky, mountains, trees, wind."

"How did we end up here?" Seraphina asked.

"I'm not sure. There are no doors to the card world. Even gods can't access it. It's a closed realm. But some records mention humans visiting, though most perished here. Some, however, managed to escape."

"Escape?" Seraphina felt a twinge of unease.

Iblis licked his lips, "Haven't you noticed how parched we're getting? There's no water here. The card world dries out anything moist."

"I'm not thirsty," Seraphina shook her head. "I just drank two glasses of water."

"I should have thought ahead," Iblis admitted, a hint of regret in his voice.

"What now? Can you get us out?"

"I have to, even if I can't," Iblis said, glancing at her. "I'm more vulnerable to dehydration than you. This air is leeching my moisture."

Seraphina noticed Iblis's labored breathing and fatigue, realizing he was in worse shape than he let on.

"I'm worried you'll be dried out before I figure a way out," Seraphina said, concerned.

"Oh, I'm not worried," Iblis replied, breathing heavily.

"Why not?"

"Because..." Iblis's gaze lingered on her lips. "We have you, the human-shaped fruit."

He suddenly reached for her, pulling her close.

Seraphina gasped as she fell back into the haystack.

This position allowed Iblis to cage her beneath him.

Seraphina struggled but couldn't break free. His face drew nearer, her internal alarms blaring.

"Where should I start? I hear human lips have an irresistible taste," he mused, his voice teasing, "I haven't tried them yet..."

His rough fingers traced her lips, sending shivers down her spine.

"No, no, no." Remembering his thorny tongue, Seraphina quickly covered her mouth with her hand, blinking rapidly.

"Please, Lord of Sea, even emergency rations should be consumed slowly. Bite me and I'm done for."

"Now I'm Lord of Sea?" he grinned lazily, "Too late."

He leaned in, and Seraphina instinctively closed her eyes, pressing her hand firmly over her mouth.

In the next moment, a warm pressure enveloped the palm of her hand. Seraphina's eyelashes fluttered immediately.

It wasn't as painful as she had anticipated. Instead, it was soft and gentle, like clouds and cotton candy.

It felt moist, warm, and just a tad ticklish.

25

Seraphina closed her eyes tightly, one hand covering her lips, the other resting on Iblis's shoulder. She felt something touch her palm. Unlike the previous gentle sensation, this was more supple, more forceful. It was moist, with tiny soft thorns grazing her palm repeatedly, causing an itchy, tingling sensation.

Her eyelashes fluttered as she realized what it was. Her plan to charm and manipulate Aquaman without yielding anything tangible had backfired; she was being taken advantage but without earning any heart points. Just as she resolved to resist, a sharp pain pierced her palm—the tiny thorns had turned rigid, puncturing her skin. Warm blood welled up and was swiftly swept away by the tongue before it could spill.

Seraphina's eyes flew open, and there was Iblis, his face close to hers. His eyes, obscured by his brown bangs, were dark and turbulent, like a stormy sea. He held her wrist firmly, preventing her from moving, as his lips transitioned from licking to sucking, drawing a stream of blood into his mouth. Her palm throbbed with a numbing pain.

Just as she was about to fight back, she heard Little N's voice, "Host, hold on, one SSR coin."

"An SSR coin?" Seraphina was startled, a hint of excitement mixing with the pain.

"I don't know how, but something in him shifted because of you," Little N explained.

"What did I change in him?" Seraphina pondered. "He's only tasted my blood once before. This second time—is it a sign of loyalty?"

She felt her logic was a bit stretched.

"Seems like it," Little N agreed. "Winning over the sea god requires his loyalty. Eating only the host's blood suggests a form of loyalty."

"In that case, we have many firsts to explore," Seraphina said, amused.

"Ahem, host, please remain dignified," Little N chided gently.

Seraphina speculated, "I now know how to earn points: each first experience needs repeating to signify loyalty. Though stingy in appearance, he's rather generous—awarding SSR coins instead of mere heartbeat points."

"So, should he continue?" Little N prompted.

"Will more sucking yield more coins?"

"No."

"Then make him stop."

Iblis noticed Seraphina's slight trembling and paused, switching from sucking to gentle licking. The tiny thorns on his tongue softened, brushing her wound tenderly like feathers, eventually coming to a stop.

Seraphina's eyes glistened with unshed tears.

Iblis withdrew, his light brown lashes fluttering, revealing bloodshot eyes tinged with satisfaction. He examined Seraphina's palm, marked with tiny punctures, blood seeping anew.

"Apologies, I got a bit carried away," Iblis murmured, his thumb glowing softly as he traced it over her wounds. Tiny buds sprouted, closing the punctures as if they were living things. As the healing magic worked, the intense dark blue in his eyes lightened, restoring their usual clarity.

Seraphina's tears, initially an attempt to induce guilt, flowed freely now. She hoped they'd serve as a deterrent against future incidents. After all, her periods only came once a month.

The girl's body shook slightly, tears pooling at the corners of her eyes, cascading down her cheeks. She looked vulnerable and endearing.

Iblis seemed taken aback, leaning down to press his lips to her tear-streaked cheeks, softly kissing away the moisture until he reached her earlobe.

His warm breath, tinged with the scent of blood, left goosebumps on her skin, causing her to shiver more.

"You're relentless, even stealing tears," she accused, voice trembling.

Iblis chuckled, his laughter rumbling against her neck. "Didn't you know I'm parched?" His voice was hoarse, laced with amusement.

"You've made me smell of blood," Seraphina huffed, pushing him away.

Her tears, her carefully summoned emotions, had been wasted. She'd delved into all the tragedies stored in her mind to summon them.

The boy's eyes sparkled with amusement. "I might have felt guilty before, but not anymore," he teased.

"Get off me," Seraphina grumbled, more frustrated now.

"Alright, alright," Iblis relented, standing and offering his hand to her. "Come on, don't be mad. Let's go find the Paper God."

"The Paper God?" Seraphina echoed, intrigued, accepting his hand to rise.

"Yes," Iblis explained, "just like us, the Paper God is a creation of this world. The God of Light exists because of light, the God of Darkness from darkness. Similarly, the Paper God created this world."

"Really?" Seraphina's curiosity piqued. "You think we can ask him to let us out?"

"Yes, reasoning with intelligent beings is usually straightforward," Iblis replied.

Seraphina snorted, "Flattery won't increase your favorability with me."

Iblis smirked, "You can't blame me for what happened. Dehydration made me uncomfortable, and you provoked me. I intended to scare you, but the blood's taste triggered my instincts."

"Your blood was delicious, so I lost control. As for the tears, I salvaged them to avoid waste. I've got an idea: next time I'm thirsty, you should cry—whether from fear or sorrow, it doesn't matter."

"Can you taste emotions in tears?" Seraphina asked, surprised.

"Yes, I'm especially sensitive to liquids. It's innate. But this was my first time tasting tears. In Atlantis, tears merge with seawater instantly."

"You've never tasted tears?" Seraphina's eyes widened in astonishment.

"No. Why?"

"Nothing, it's just... delightful," Seraphina grinned, another SSR coin secured. In her mind, Little N was already celebrating.

Iblis eyed her curiously. "You're happy I've never tasted tears?"

"No," Seraphina replied, still smiling. "You mentioned if I don't want to bleed, I should cry. Of course, I'm glad to have found a way to survive."

"Is that so," Iblis murmured, a slight curl to his lips. "Cry now."

"Huh?"

"I'm thirsty again."

"You just drank my blood," Seraphina protested in disbelief.

"Indeed," he admitted, frowning as black scales appeared on his neck. Light flickered as he pressed his hand there, suppressing the scales. "We need to hurry before my true form emerges."

"True form?"

"My true form," Iblis said softly.

Seraphina recalled his words about mermaids resembling Atlantis' creatures. His true form likely referred to his original form.

What could those black scales signify? Given his title of sea god, she guessed a sea serpent.

Ugh... Best not to reveal your true form; she feared she might cry from fright.

They descended the hillside, passing trees and flowers crafted from paper, remarkably lifelike. Even the wind and sun were paper creations.

Thin golden paper strips dangled in the air, while the wind was a massive, wavy paper strip. Absent the looming threat, it might have been a charming journey.

Time passed, and Seraphina's throat burned. Her earlier tea had long been metabolized, leaving her parched enough to consider drinking her tears.

Compared to her, Iblis fared worse. His water affinity made the paper world particularly hostile. Less than twenty minutes in, dark scales covered his neck and arms. His eyes grew increasingly shadowed, frequently darting to her lips and throat.

"Can't you create water?" Seraphina asked, wary.

"No, I've tried," Iblis replied, his gaze heavy with thirst.

"Why do you keep staring at me?" Seraphina hugged herself defensively, fearing another bloodletting.

Iblis chuckled, "I thought of a way we could both get water."

Seraphina felt a mix of incredulity and curiosity as she looked around the paper city. Despite knowing something was amiss, the dryness in her throat compelled her to engage with Iblis. When he lifted her chin, urging her to open her mouth, she realized his intent was to share water through a kiss. She clamped her mouth shut, refusing to comply with such a bizarre plan.

"Are you kidding me?" she asked, her voice edged with disbelief.

Iblis's impatience grew. "Hurry up, I don't want to force you. I'm really thirsty."

Seraphina, ever resourceful, tried to offer an alternative. "How about tears? I could cry some for you."

He frowned, dismissing the idea. "I don't want tears. Who knows what kind of sad thoughts you're conjuring up—they're too bitter."

"Maybe I could think of something funny and cry from laughter," she suggested, trying to lighten the mood.

"Enough nonsense," he replied, pulling her into a firm embrace. The warmth of his breath on her neck sent a shiver through her, a reminder of their precarious situation.

"Fine, I'll let you drink my blood," she relented, extending her wrist toward him. "But don't take too much—I'm anemic."

Iblis hesitated, looking at her slender wrist. Though the sight of her blood vessels tempted him, her reluctance to kiss him stirred an unfamiliar irritation.

"You'd rather bleed than kiss me?" he asked, his voice laced with a hint of hurt.

"Yes," Seraphina replied firmly. "In Atlantis, maybe it's different, but humans only kiss people they like. I don't like you."

The words stung, and Iblis's expression faltered briefly. Memories of their encounter on the beach flashed through his mind, echoing her rejection. Yet, instead of anger, he felt something akin to longing.

"Host, two points," Little N chimed in, amused by the unexpected emotional exchange.

Seraphina was perplexed. Why was he affected by her words?

Iblis's demeanor shifted. "I'll remember—I only kiss those I like."

Seraphina blinked, unsure why this declaration seemed significant. Shouldn't Iblis, the god of the seas, be immune to such sentiments?

Determined to change the subject, Iblis offered a solution. "You don't want to walk all the way to the capital, do you?"

"Why didn't you fly before?" Seraphina asked, curious.

"I was determining the direction. The driest air indicates the city's location," he explained.

"Do paper gods live in cities?"

"Gods are elusive," Iblis said, his gaze softening as it lingered on her. "Except, apparently, to you."

Seraphina feigned ignorance, "Why head to the city, then?"

"To stir up trouble," Iblis replied with a mischievous grin. "Force Him to reveal Himself."

***

The paper city was unlike anything Seraphina had seen. Buildings of all sorts—houses, churches, towers—stood delicately crafted from cardboard. Despite their fragile appearance, the city thrummed with life as paper people went about their daily routines.

Seraphina marveled at the paper products adorning shop windows, pondering the permanence of paper cosmetics. Would they be akin to tattoos on these paper faces?

The arrival of two humans sent the paper citizens into a frenzy. Screams echoed as they dropped their belongings and retreated indoors, slamming doors in their wake.

"Are we that terrifying?" Seraphina mused aloud.

"They fear our blood," Iblis explained with a chuckle. "A past incident left them wary."

Seraphina nodded, understanding the paper people's caution. "What should we do now?"

"If you were me, what would you do?" Iblis asked, curious about her perspective.

"I'd head to the palace or church to make a scene," Seraphina replied thoughtfully. "Draw the gods' attention."

"Exactly my thoughts," Iblis said, pleased. "Let's disrupt the palace. I know how you feel about such places."

Seraphina took his hand, a faint light enveloping them as they vanished and reappeared in the palace.

The playing card king and his court were in the midst of a performance. Unlike the paper citizens, they were part of the cards themselves, with only their limbs protruding.

A loud crash interrupted their act. Looking up, they saw two very real, very three-dimensional humans peering through the newly created hole in the roof.

"Humans! Humans!" the cards shrieked, scrambling in panic.

"Protect the king!"

"Someone stepped on me!"

"Hide under the carpet!"

Seraphina leaned over, taking in the chaos below.

"Careful," Iblis warned, pulling her close as they descended. The sudden drop startled her, and she clung tightly to him, her soft breath tickling his collarbone.

Iblis slowed their descent, savoring the unfamiliar, sweet scent that clung to her. It was a far cry from the salty, bitter air of Atlantis, and he found himself wanting more.

"Host, another point," Little N announced.

Seraphina, still wrapped in Iblis's arms, was puzzled by the day's events. His reactions seemed random yet consistent, adding layers to his character like a puzzle she was eager to solve.

Once they landed, Seraphina quickly extricated herself, taking in the pandemonium. The king and queen clung to each other, surrounded by guards wielding paper shields and swords.

"Are there only a few cards here?" Seraphina asked, observing the scene.

Iblis nudged a lump under the carpet with his foot, causing it to tremble. A muffled cacophony of breathing and whispered prayers emanated from the hiding cards.

"Don't get blood on me!"

"Me neither!"

Seraphina found their fear amusing but unnecessary. She wasn't here to harm herself.

"Excuse me," she addressed the Ace of Hearts, "do you know where the Paper God is?"

The room fell silent as her question hung in the air. The playing cards exchanged glances, their fear giving way to curiosity.

"So you seek the Paper God," one guard said, relaxing and dropping his sword. Even the queen resumed fanning herself, the tension dissipating.

"Yes, I wish to meet the Paper God. Is there a problem with that?" Seraphina asked, unfazed by their reactions.

"Indeed," said the Ace of Hearts, with an air of dramatic flair that only a card could muster. "Every human who stumbles in here wants an audience with the Paper God. Some, though, prefer to vent their frustrations on the city—toppling houses, tearing paper limbs. So, you can imagine our relief when you said you just wanted a meet-and-greet with god."

Seraphina nodded thoughtfully, as if the idea of paper carnage was just another Tuesday for her. "Ah, I see. Well, we're just trying to find the exit from this origami wonderland."

"Simple enough," interjected the Jack of Diamonds, who had appeared with all the subtlety of a stage magician. "I'm the archbishop here, and only I can lead you to the God. Wait right here." And with that, he scampered off, presumably to divine guidance or grab a snack—who could say?

The Queen, not to be outdone in this parade of oddities, pointed her dainty folded fan at Seraphina. "I remember you," she said with a knowing smirk. "You're the one who consistently bungled good hands at cards."

Seraphina blinked. "How could you possibly know that?"

"Oh, darling, as queen, I flit between decks in the human world with grace and aplomb. I watched you and your three friends play that day. You had such promising cards, yet..." The Queen sighed, reminiscent of a disappointed teacher. "I lingered because I adore children, but when I awoke, I found the girl with the rose setting the cards ablaze. Naturally, I fled."

Seraphina's mind whirled. Margaret, with the rose—of course. Advanced props must have been involved in her sudden arrival here.

"Follow me," announced the Jack of Diamonds upon his return, before Seraphina could dwell too long on Margaret's machinations.

But the Queen wasn't finished. She called after Seraphina, her voice tinged with a rare seriousness, "Do you know why most people who wander in never find their way out?"

Seraphina shook her head, genuinely curious.

"The closer you get to the Paper God, the drier the air becomes. Many have been reduced to husks before reaching the exit," the Queen explained, her voice dripping with reluctant sympathy.

Understanding dawned on Seraphina. "Ah, so that's the trick. Thank you for the heads-up. But if staying means a slow demise, I might as well face the challenge head-on."

"Indeed," the Queen said, with a sigh that suggested she'd seen this all before.

***

The Jack of Diamonds led them to the grand entrance of the hall—a temple dedicated to the Paper God. As Seraphina stepped closer, she felt her skin begin to tingle and tremble, as though every drop of moisture was fleeing her body at an alarming rate, vaporizing into the dry air.

Her resolve, however, stayed intact. After all, she had a god to meet—or outwit—and a way out to find.

The Jack of Diamonds looked like he'd just spent an afternoon sunbathing in a desert without sunscreen. His papery skin was cracking like old parchment. "I won't be seeing you off. You're on your own," he declared, and with a dramatic flair, spun on his heel and bolted like his life depended on it.

"This is a disaster," Iblis muttered, his palms glowing as he valiantly attempted to shove the rebellious scales back under his skin. "Forget you, even I can't step foot in that temple."

Seraphina eyed the persistent scales that popped back up like stubborn weeds. "What happens if you revert to your true form?"

"The Paper God will send me packing," Iblis replied casually, like discussing the weather. "He despises me. Without my charming presence, He'd have carte blanche to extend His domain far and wide."

"far and wide," Seraphina murmured, realization dawning. "You mean our world."

"Precisely. But alas, every world has its own set of rules. Just as my powers are stifled here, the Paper God's would be similarly leashed in our realm. So naturally, any deity with a penchant for water is not exactly on His Christmas card list."

"Got it," Seraphina said, frowning as she inspected the scales on Iblis's arm, clearly wishing she could steamroll them.

"Little N, I want to open a blind box," Iblis announced out of the blue.

"Now?"

"Yes, because who knows if I'll get another chance."

"Fair enough. What caliber are we talking about here?"

"I'm thinking... trash-tier blind box, the kind that costs me a single point of favorability."

Little N raised an eyebrow, "..."

"Blind boxes are a gamble. I'll start with the favorability points, then move on to the SSR coins. Who knows, maybe Lady Luck will smile on me."

"You've got a point. Visualize it, Host. Otherwise, where are you going to stash all your loot?"

"Right."

Seraphina blinked, and suddenly a blind box manifested in her mind, its drab exterior screaming mediocrity. With a flick of her mind's eye, the box vanished, leaving behind a lollipop with a less-than-promising label: 'Bad Luck Lollipop, enjoy a full day of misfortune with every lick".

Next!

"Crying Doll: Weeps 24/7, guaranteed to dampen your spirits."

Next!

"A nondescript hand cream, changes color at a whim."

Out, all of you! Begone!

Seraphina was on a roll, opening blind boxes like a kid tearing through presents on a sugar high. Each one was more ridiculous than the last. Just as she was about to upgrade to a high-end blind box, a shimmer of silver caught her eye. Suddenly, there it was: "Shower, fill a bucket of water every minute, perfect for a brisk, cold shower. Side effect: catch a cold. "

Well, if that wasn't enough to tug at the heartstrings. She was almost misty-eyed.

This little gem of a prop was practically a tearjerker, with side effects so gentle they might as well come with a lullaby. What could possibly solve her dilemma more effectively than a shower? Those twenty favorability points were a steal.

Seraphina turned to Iblis, beaming like she'd just won the lottery.

"What's got you grinning like a Cheshire cat?" Iblis inquired, reaching over to check her forehead. "Are you delirious?"

"Nope, check this out." Seraphina whipped out the shower and gave it a click, and voila—their own little rainstorm.

Iblis blinked at the shower in disbelief, "Why are you..."

"No time for chit-chat," Seraphina cut him off. "This shower's like a sprinkler on a timer. Once it's on, bucket of water every minute."

Without another word, Iblis grabbed Seraphina's hand, and they sprinted toward the temple.

As they neared the temple's entrance, the air got so dry it could rival a desert. Inside, the shower's spray turned to steam, leaving just enough water to dampen their skin.

Sensing their arrival, the Paper God turned. Towering at a dizzying four or five meters, he sat on a high stool, wielding a pair of silver scissors. Sheep, rabbits, trees, and paper people were snipped into existence, only to vanish once they hit the floor of the pristine white temple.

The air was thick with fluttering paper scraps, like a blizzard of confetti.

At the far end of the temple, a door beckoned, radiant with light. Instinctively, Seraphina knew it was their ticket out of there.

A breeze drifted in from the door, turning the paper storm into a frenzy.

Seraphina and Iblis bolted for the exit without hesitation. The shower was in overdrive, gushing water as if its life depended on it. But the paper scraps kept coming, and the shower's stream started to dwindle.

With five meters to go, the shower sputtered to a stop.

Seraphina felt like she'd been stuffed with desiccant; her skin was parched, her strength evaporating. Her very bones seemed ready to crumble.

Those last five meters stretched on like a century. Her eyes fixed on the door, desperate, but her limbs refused to cooperate. Iblis was faring worse, his essence at odds with this place, moisture evaporating rapidly.

Just two steps shy, he collapsed.

Seraphina rushed to support him, fumbling with the shower, but its timer wasn't up, leaving the room devoid of water.

"Just two more steps," she urged, dragging him inch by inch. The door was so close, a whisper of cool breeze beckoning them to freedom.

The Paper God snipped away, the room thick with paper shards, the air growing ever drier.

Iblis clutched his chest, struggling to contain the power surging within. His arms and neck were rapidly covered in black scales, threatening to erupt. Seraphina feared he had mere seconds before he burst.

The Paper God glanced over, and Seraphina quickly wrapped her arms around the half-conscious Iblis, shielding his transformation. She shook the shower desperately, praying for even a trickle of water. Just a little more, and he could hold back the change.

When the scales on Iblis's neck started to spread, Seraphina made a bold move. She reached out and touched the scales. Instinctively, they bit her hand, drawing blood.

Seraphina didn't hesitate. She sucked on the wound, then pressed her lips to Iblis's, forcing his mouth open and passing the blood to him.

Iblis jerked to life, instinct taking over before consciousness returned. He wrapped one arm around her waist, the other cradling her head, deepening the kiss. He clung to her, drawing the blood greedily.

Seraphina winced as the thorns on his tongue re-emerged, sending a shiver down her spine. She carefully avoided them, tears streaming down her face, mingling with the blood at her lips, and swallowed by him.

Then, maybe after a dozen heartbeats, the shower on the ground sprang back to life, drenching them like salvation itself.

Seraphina felt Iblis's lips part from hers, and a warm, gentle hand stroked her waterlogged hair.

She opened her eyes, meeting the gaze of the young god.

His eyes were a clear, serene blue, as gentle as the sea itself.

26

Seraphina and Iblis found themselves perched on a precarious cliff overlooking the sea. The darkness wrapped around them like a comforting cloak, with only the stars and a shy crescent moon daring to pierce the night. The wind, salty and damp, whipped against them, carrying the scent of the ocean and the promise of a new beginning. Behind them, the door shut with a finality that sealed away the parched world they'd just escaped.

Seraphina exhaled, the tension leaving her body like a deflating balloon. Her legs, as if finally realizing the ordeal they'd been through, gave way beneath her, and she sank to the ground. The pain she'd conveniently ignored during their escapade surged back with a vengeance, her hand felt like a bonfire that had spread up to her forearm. Tears, unbidden, flowed freely.

Iblis reached out, as if to pluck starlight from the sky, illuminating Seraphina's hand with its gentle glow. He frowned at the sight.

"Why is it so serious?" he asked, concern etching lines across his usually serene face.

"What do you think?" Seraphina replied, her voice a mix of frustration and pain. Her hand was a disaster zone—scales had bitten deep enough to expose bone, and the sight made her stomach lurch.

Iblis knelt beside her, his fingers weaving a pattern of light that danced over her skin. Under its touch, granulations sprouted around the wound, like tiny soldiers ready to mend the breach, but they hesitated, unsure.

"What's happening?" Seraphina asked, puzzled. "Shouldn't the healing spell weave them together?"

"This isn't your run-of-the-mill injury," Iblis explained. "Last time, you touched my transformed state—an ordinary wound. This time, you touched my true form, which counts as a genuine blasphemy. I didn't lift the ban in time, given my unconscious state..."

"So, no cure?" Seraphina's eyes widened, tears forgotten in her shock. Surely she wouldn't have to parade around with exposed bones forever? Her hands were vital—elegant, point-earning, and too pretty for such a fate.

"Not exactly," Iblis chuckled. "It just needs a little time. Two or three days, tops."

Seraphina let out a breath she didn't realize she was holding. "You nearly gave me a heart attack."

Iblis laughed softly. "Such a scaredy-cat. You were quite the hero back in the temple."

"I didn't have a choice. We'd have been stuck there otherwise."

"Let me stop the bleeding first." Iblis focused, channeling energy into the wound until a protective membrane formed over it.

The wind tousled Seraphina's golden hair, teasing it across Iblis's face, a reminder of their earlier shared breath. Iblis's gaze dropped to the wound, his lashes fluttering. "Why did you… kiss me again?"

Seraphina blinked, surprise mingling with the remnants of tears. "That wasn't a kiss."

"It wasn't?"

"Of course not," Seraphina insisted. "It was treatment, just like what you're doing now. Without my blood, you wouldn't have woken up."

Iblis eyed her, a smile ghosting his lips after a moment. "I see. That's comforting. I was worried for nothing."

"What were you worried about?" Seraphina asked, genuinely curious.

"I thought you might have taken advantage of me while I was out," he said, a lazy grin spreading across his face.

"Oh, please. I don't even like you. Ow!" Seraphina yelped as Iblis squeezed her hand, causing fresh blood to ooze out. "Sorry," he said, not sounding sorry at all, "I was so relieved to hear you don't like me, I lost control for a second."

Seraphina: "…"

The healing light faded. Seraphina inspected her hand. The wound still gaped, but at least it wasn't bleeding. A thin membrane covered it, though the ghastly view of bone and flesh remained.

Iblis conjured gauze, wrapping her hand with care. "After a couple of days, your hand will be as good as new, no scars."

"Thank goodness," Seraphina said, relief coloring her voice.

Iblis helped her to her feet. "We should head back. Don't you have classes tomorrow?"

"Yes," Seraphina replied. She had classes, a medicine run to Milos's, a meeting with Lily, and a trip north on her agenda.

The night embraced them as they made their way home. Amazingly, the maids hadn't noticed her absence.

Glancing at the clock, Seraphina noted it was already two in the morning. She'd been in the paper world for nine hours, yet it felt like an eternity.

Iblis yawned, casting a cleaning spell over her before occupying the bathroom. He transformed back into his mermaid form, finding solace in the bathtub's water.

Despite her exhaustion, Seraphina lay on her bed, determined to settle her account with Little N.

Little N reported, "We've got 45 favorability points, an SSR coin, and two days of life."

"Wait..." Seraphina frowned, confused. "I spent 20 points on that trash blind box. How do we still have so many points?"

"Yes," Little N confirmed. "We spent 20 points, but you gained another 20."

"Who gifted them?" Seraphina mused. She hadn't expected see god to be so generous.

"It was sea god Iblis," Little N announced with a flourish.

Ah, so it was him.

Seraphina blinked thoughtfully. Favorability points could mean many things. He was likely grateful for her last-minute rescue.

So now, she was sitting on a treasure trove of points and a collection of so-called "garbage" props.

But were they really garbage? The bad luck lollipop, for instance, could be a formidable weapon in the right hands—or rather, the wrong hands. Imagine gifting it to Princess Margaret. Talk about an unexpected turn of events!

With a hefty amount of points in her pocket, Seraphina felt content. As she relaxed, sleep came swiftly, wrapping her in its gentle embrace.

But soon, a fever crept in, making her restless. Half-conscious, she found herself back in her original world.

On a massive screen, a god in a dark blue robe stood tall and aloof, a figure of indifference. Although the sea country had land, the sea god was rarely seen ashore. He remained in Atlantis.

Seraphina's friends often gossiped about the sea god, for unlike other deities, Iblis seemed approachable. He entertained interviews and listened to his people. But the hot topic was always his rumored harem—spanning species from mermaids to plankton.

"If only I were a mermaid," her friends would sigh. "I heard he only fancies mermaids."

"No, he's into octopuses too," another would counter, citing dubious reports.

"Could gods really... with octopuses? Aren't they different species?"

"You'd have to ask him that," came the laughter.

"What do you think, Seraphina?"

"Seraphina?"

"Seraphina?"

Her name, repeated in a low voice, pulled her from the dream. She opened her eyes to find Iblis's youthful face mere inches away, concern etched in his features.

She shifted uncomfortably, noting the damp weight on her forehead. A wet cloth, perhaps? The shower's side effect had come to pass—a full 24 hours of cold-induced misery.

Iblis frowned, "Is it the blood loss or your hand? I'm not adept at light magic. You know, fish don't get fevers. I'm out of my depth here. If only that guy were around..."

Seraphina knew exactly who Iblis was talking about—the God of Light. But she wasn't about to risk a visit for treatment, lest he see straight through her like a window pane.

"It's fine," she croaked, her voice rough as gravel. "Just need a day to rest."

"Want some of your human medicine?" Iblis offered, looking concerned.

"Nope."

The medical knowledge of the time was practically prehistoric. Those little blue pills families kept around, claiming to cure everything from cholera to syphilis, were mostly laxatives with a side of mercury. Taking one was like playing Russian roulette—on a good day.

Seeing he had no other option, Iblis settled down beside her, ready to change her handkerchief as needed.

After a while, Iblis broke the silence. "You were talking in your sleep."

Seraphina tensed. "What did I say?"

"Something about the sea god and octopuses."

"Oh, did I really?"

"Yeah." Iblis nodded, a teasing glint in his eyes.

"Do you like them?"

"Sure." Iblis grinned.

Seraphina: "..."

"Out of all the seafood, octopus is my favorite," he said, lounging back on the pillow. "So firm and bouncy..."

"You eat them?" Seraphina choked out, stunned. "Not... you know, with them?"

Iblis's eyes nearly popped out of his head. "Who even started that rumor? Really?"

"No, I mean, mermaids can, you know, right?" Seraphina stumbled over her words, her mind a foggy mess.

Iblis crossed his arms, his patience clearly wearing thin. He looked like he was debating whether to laugh or just give up entirely.

On a normal day, Seraphina wouldn't have pressed the issue. But today, her head was spinning like a carousel, and reading his mood was as challenging as deciphering hieroglyphics. So she blurted out, "Can anyone be with a mermaid?"

Iblis raised a brow, a smirk tugging at the corners of his mouth. "Depends on what you mean by 'be with.' But if you're asking if it's possible, well, I suppose anything's possible."

Seraphina blinked, trying to process that through the fog of her fever. "Right, of course. Anything's possible. Try and see"

Iblis chuckled softly, shaking his head. "You're something else, you know that?"

Seraphina just nodded, the absurdity of their conversation somehow making perfect sense in her fever-addled state.

"But how? I don't have a mermaid around," Seraphina mumbled, still out of it. "Oh wait, there's one in the bathroom." She wobbled to her feet and staggered over, peeking inside.

"Where's that mermaid of mine gone?"

Iblis let out a soft chuckle, got up, and gently brought her back to bed.

A whisper of magic, and the bed dipped beneath her. Something cold and slippery brushed against her leg.

She turned, and there was Iblis, lounging beside her, upper body bare, lower half sporting a magnificent sea-blue tail.

From his sculpted shoulders to his tapered waist, he was the embodiment of youthful grace and danger, a walking (or rather, swimming) paradox of allure and taboo.

Iblis took her hand, pressing it to his chest. "Here."

Seraphina snapped back to reality. Her hand, encased in his warmth, lay on his chest, and she felt like the filling in a very strange sandwich.

Iblis guided her hand, trailing it down his torso, his eyes glinting with mischief, daring her.

His skin was smooth, warm, and firm beneath her touch. But at the juncture of waist and tail, Seraphina hesitated, pulling back.

"Don't be afraid," Iblis murmured, his voice a husky invitation. "Touch my tail. Let the scales get to know you, and they won't bite you again."

Tentatively, Seraphina placed her palm back. The scales were smooth and cool, not sticky like fish scales, but more like polished gemstones.

As her hand moved, Iblis's breathing hitched, and his tail flicked restlessly. When she brushed against something firmer, he quickly caught her hand.

His eyes, stormy blue, were clouded, his voice a ragged whisper. "Not there. Move on."

Seraphina's cheeks flushed with heat. "I'm done touching," she mumbled, hand retreating.

Iblis sighed, pulling her to rest against his chest, chin atop her head. "Got it."

"What?"

"You asked if anyone can be with a mermaid. The answer is yes."

Iblis's breath steadied, his demeanor cool and collected once more. "As a god, I can shift into many forms. If you're curious, I can turn into something else next time."

The same person who'd just been panicking was now nonchalantly boasting. It was almost endearing. If he weren't a legendary deity, she'd think she had him pegged all wrong.

"Sure," Seraphina grinned cheekily. "Why wait? Let's do it now. Human form sounds good."

Iblis widened his eyes, pinched her cheek playfully. "Your face must be as thick as Atlantis's walls! Do you do this with everyone?"

"Nope, just you." Seraphina's grin was pure mischief, words smooth as honey.

Iblis paused, then laughed, releasing her cheek. "You're quite the charmer. I almost believed you."

"Host, you've gained a point," Little N chimed in.

"Where's that point from?" Seraphina asked, puzzled.

"From touching a no-go zone," Little N snickered, clearly enjoying the moment far too much. "Didn't want to interrupt your... performance, so I kept mum until now."

Seraphina rolled her eyes, feeling her cheeks heat up. "Really, Little N? You're keeping score on that?"

"Absolutely," Little N replied with a mischievous tone. "I'm here for all the juicy details, you know."

"Well, aren't you just full of surprises," Seraphina muttered, half-amused, half-mortified, as she glanced at the still-swaying fish tail next to her.

In the grand scheme of things, it seemed even points had a sense of humor.

"I figured saying I'd only do that for him might score me some points," Seraphina mused, a wry smile playing on her lips. "But it seems our sea god's more interested in the physical than the sentimental."

Little N chimed in, "Well, at least you know where you stand. Or swim, in this case."

Seraphina chuckled, shaking her head. "Guess I'll have to work on my charm a bit more if I want to get through to that fishy heart of his."

"Good luck with that," Little N quipped. "Might need more than just sweet words to crack that shell."

"Tell me about it," Seraphina sighed, wondering what it might actually take to win over a god.

"So, what do you think, Host?" Little N asked, voice brimming with excitement.

"What do you mean?"

"You reached... the screenshot-worthy spot."

"Oh, that. I didn't actually touch it. Didn't you see him grab my hand?" Seraphina glanced at Iblis's tail, now smoothly swaying like a gentle fan. Those scales, capable of fierce defense, could hide anything. A truly fascinating species.

After all the fuss, Seraphina's head started to spin again. She snuggled under the covers, eyes closing as sleep claimed her once more.

When she awoke, daylight filled the room. Iblis was nowhere to be seen.

"Little N, where's sea god?"

"Not sure. He left a while ago."

Still groggy, Seraphina considered sleeping in. But at the mention of Iblis's absence, she jumped up, only to sway on her feet. The shower's side effects were lingering, and her legs felt like jelly. She clutched the wall for support.

"Where are you off to, Host? Get back to bed. You've got over ten hours before the side effects wear off."

"While the sea god is off doing whatever it is sea gods do, I've got to dash to meet Lily, snatch the potion from the God of Light, and then head north," Seraphina declared with determination.

"While sea god's off doing whatever sea gods do, I've got to dash to meet Lily, grab the potion from the God of Light, and then head north," Seraphina declared with determination.

"Wow, Host, you're so dedicated. I'm in awe!" Little N chimed in, adding with faux admiration, "And you didn't even lean on the wall this time."

Seraphina, too focused to entertain Little N's banter, slipped into a light purple dress and topped it off with a straw hat. She grabbed her trusty, albeit quirky, beaded handbag.

"A Bit of a Gorgeous Handbag: Can fit everything you need. Disposable item. After use, you won't be able to find openings of anything for an hour—no drawer handles, no door knobs, no shirt collars, not even your mouth when eating. Side effect lasts for one hour.]

It was one of those "gems" from the garbage blind box. Perfect for stashing her winter gear after meeting Lily. The side effect? Manageable, she thought optimistically.

"Speaking of side effects, why didn't sea god catch a cold from the shower?" Seraphina pondered aloud.

Little N replied, "Sea god didn't hold the shower. He was more of a water-dryer."

Seraphina frowned at her reflection in the mirror, cheeks flushed and eyes misty. She looked like a damsel ripe for distress. A powder puff helped mask the feverish blush, and she mustered a confident smile before heading out.

As she left, the maid informed her that Robus and Rose had conveniently skipped off to the academy. Good riddance, Seraphina thought, seizing the opportunity to skip class herself. She summoned the coachman and set off for the Oak Street Tavern.

Lily was waiting when Seraphina arrived. Without missing a beat, she handed over two teleportation arrays. "Should I head to your uncle's now?"

"Yes," Seraphina nodded, choosing her words carefully. "There's someone... a bit unusual. No one in the family can see him, except you."

"A ghost?" Lily asked, intrigued. "They're harmless, usually just hang around until you waste away. But divine magicians can keep them as servants or something."

Lily seemed to think Seraphina needed help dealing with the ghost. "Want me to tame it for you?"

"Oh, heavens no," Seraphina shook her head, horrified. "Just let him know who you are. Say I asked you to disguise me. Best to avoid any trouble."

Lily was puzzled but didn't pry. Curiosity was a taboo in their line of work. She transformed into Seraphina's likeness and headed for the carriage.

Once Lily was on her way, Seraphina summoned another carriage to whisk her to Milos's house.

***

Milos was in the garden, engrossed in a book, when the carriage arrived. Seraphina, in her light purple dress and wide-brimmed hat, practically bounced in, her cheeks rosy, albeit unnaturally so.

"Are you feeling alright?" Milos inquired, noting the blush.

"I'm fine," Seraphina lied smoothly, fanning herself with her hat. "Just a bit hot today."

"Is my medicine ready?" she asked, all business.

Milos produced a small crystal bottle filled with a brown liquid topped with bubbles. "Drink it all at once for the best effect," he advised, holding it out.

How could she let such a golden opportunity slip through her fingers? Just one tiny move, and Little N could waltz a step closer to Little R. It was practically destiny waiting to unfold!

With a flourish, she plopped her hat onto the chair and reached for the bottle. As her fingers brushed against the back of the other person's hand, it felt like a feather's caress—playful, with just a hint of mischief.

Milos, ever the enigmatic figure, fluttered his eyelashes with the grace of a butterfly, casting an indifferent glance her way.

The girl, with a smile as sweet as spun sugar, quipped, "Master Milos, you'd better hold on tight. Wouldn't want you to drop it and have it shatter into a thousand pieces."

"Host, add one point," chimed in a voice, as Seraphina, positively basking in her triumph, clutched the bottle. Yet, despite her efforts, it refused to budge. It was as stubborn as a mule on a Monday morning.

She glanced up, and there was Milos, still looking at her with that same, indifferent gaze.

"Oh, a thank-you gift, is it?" she mused, recalling the promise. With a dramatic sigh, Seraphina withdrew her hand, keeping her injured one hidden behind her back like a secret she couldn't quite bear to share.

From her pocket, she produced a sun-shaped gold brooch with her one good hand. It was a serendipitous find from the jewelry box. She felt a pang of regret for not having time to prepare a proper gift.

But surely, the God of Light would have a fondness for the sun, right? She could only hope her makeshift offering would shine in his favor.

Milos didn't reach for the brooch. Instead, he spun her around with a hand on her shoulder, exposing her bandaged hand.

"Been catching mermaids again?" he asked, eyeing the gauze.

"Of course not!" Seraphina scoffed. "Not every wound is from a mermaid. A maid left the iron on, and I accidentally touched it..."

"Let me see," Milos insisted, reaching for her hand.

Seraphina, fearing the gauze might vanish, pulled back, aggravating the wound. "No need," she said, feigning nonchalance. "I'm practicing healing magic myself."

Milos chuckled softly. "Alright, but if you can't manage, come back to me." He tucked the medicine bottle into her pocket.

"Thank you," Seraphina said, relieved. "I'll head home now."

"You forgot something," Milos said.

"What's that?"

"Proper goodbyes," he replied with a hint of amusement.

Oh, so he wants a kiss. Seraphina grinned, standing on tiptoe to plant a quick peck on his lips. "There."

"Host, one point." Little N's voice chimed in with the kind of cheerfulness that seemed to peel back the layers of Milos's stoic demeanor, revealing a hint of his inner musings.

Seraphina, with a light-hearted smile, picked up her straw hat. But as she turned, her gaze caught a figure lounging against the doorframe, and she froze as if caught in a spotlight.

There stood Iblis, inscrutable and silent, the length of his watchful presence unknown.

He clutched a bag of medicine, a veritable pharmacy acquired after scouring every corner of town. Not knowing what ailed Seraphina, he had bought a little of everything— diarrhea medicine, headache powder, dysentery relief, oriental plaster, and who knows what else. Enough to cure an ailment or two, or perhaps start his own apothecary.

But upon his return, he found the house vacant, prompting him to follow a trail of intrigue to this very spot. Only to be greeted by the sight of Seraphina in a rather intimate exchange with another man.

Iblis fixed Seraphina with a gaze that could melt glaciers at fifty paces, his eyes hooded yet sharp.

After a beat, he curled his lips into a smile that was anything but warm.

"Not bad," he drawled, voice smooth as silk and twice as cutting. "I forgot there was a pharmacist in the vicinity. Looks like my efforts were in vain."

With a dismissive flick, he let the bag tumble to the ground, its contents spilling out like secrets best kept hidden.